THE POLAR CHASE

Also by Cap Daniels

The Chase Fulton Novels Series
Book One: *The Opening Chase*
Book Two: *The Broken Chase*
Book Three: *The Stronger Chase*
Book Four: *The Unending Chase*
Book Five: *The Distant Chase*
Book Six: *The Entangled Chase*
Book Seven: *The Devil's Chase*
Book Eight: *The Angel's Chase*
Book Nine: *The Forgotten Chase*
Book Ten: *The Emerald Chase*
Book Eleven: *The Polar Chase*
Book Twelve: *The Burning Chase*
Book Thirteen: *The Poison Chase*
Book Fourteen: *The Bitter Chase*
Book Fifteen: *The Blind Chase*
Book Sixteen: *The Smuggler's Chase*

The Avenging Angel – Seven Deadly Sins Series
Book One: *The Russian's Pride*
Book Two: *The Russian's Greed*
Book Three: *The Russian's Gluttony*

Stand-alone Novels
We Were Brave

Novellas
The Chase Is On
I Am Gypsy

THE
POLAR CHASE

CHASE FULTON NOVEL #11

CAP DANIELS

ANCHOR WATCH
PUBLISHING
** USA **

The Polar Chase
Chase Fulton Novel #11
Cap Daniels

This is a work of fiction. Names, characters, places, historical events, and inci-dents are the product of the author's imagination or have been used ficti-tiously. Although many locations such as marinas, airports, hotels, restaurants, etc. used in this work actually exist, they are used fictitiously and may have been relocated, exaggerated, or otherwise modified by creative license for the purpose of this work. Although many characters are based on personalities, physical attributes, skills, or intellect of actual individuals, all of the characters in this work are products of the author's imagination.

Published by:

ANCHOR WATCH
PUBLISHING
** USA **

13 Digit ISBN: 978-1-951021-03-0
Library of Congress Control Number: 2020941802

Cover Design: German Creative

Printed in the United States of America

Dedication

This book is dedicated to...
My dear friend, teacher, advisor, and sometimes tormenter,
Frank Rush

I met Frank shortly after the publication of my second book, The Broken Chase. He discovered my work after reading a recommendation by the great novelist Wayne Stinnett. Frank and I exchanged a few emails and I instantly developed an overwhelming respect for his knowledge, experience, and candor. We arranged to spend ten or fifteen minutes together on a Wednesday afternoon in the spring of 2018 while he and his lovely wife, Lucy, were traveling through my area on their way to the Gulf Coast of Florida. Frank was, in fact, the first person I met who'd actually read my first two books who wasn't either a friend or relative. That ten-to-fifteen-minute first get-together turned into two and a half hours and spawned a friendship I'll treasure as long as I'm on this Earth. Since that day, Frank and I have shared days of our lives together and thousands of emails. He has come to mean more to me than I'm capable of putting into words. My respect for him grows exponentially with every conversation. He's quick with praise when I do things right, but he's even quicker to smack me back in line when I get off track. I find myself turning to him more and more as the days pass and my stack of novels grows ever higher. Frank is one of the first to read every word of fiction I create and never fails to find ways to make every story better. Having spent his professional life in sales and marketing, he carries an unfathomable wealth of wisdom based on experience in one of my greatest areas of weakness. I'm a terrible salesman and would much rather give my books away than spend time creating advertising campaigns. According to Frank, that's apparently a terrible business plan. His professional direction has changed my life financially, but his friendship has changed my life in ways that cannot be measured. Those are the things in life that truly have value. I only hope that I will, someday, find a way to repay the kindness and generosity he shows me every day.

During our first meeting, Frank patted me on the shoulder and said, "I can't wait to read your twelfth one when you hit that one-dozen milestone."

Although this is the eleventh book in the Chase Fulton Novels series, it is my twelfth as a professional novelist. As such, it is only right that this book be dedicated with my deepest respect, admiration, and appreciation, to my friend, the incomparable Frank Rush.

Special Thanks To:

My Remarkable Editor:
Sarah Flores — Write Down the Line, LLC
www.WriteDowntheLine.com

As always, I must thank Sarah for all she has come to mean in the creation of this series. She has embraced the characters and story lines as if they were her own. She's devoted countless hours to my education as a writer and to the development of this series into the amazing thing it has become. I treasure her friendship, professionalism, and tireless devotion to the Chase Fulton Novels series.

My Friends:
Trevor, Owner of Bigfoot Outfitters in Benton, TN.
Jerry, Operations Manager and Whitewater Guide Extraordinaire
Shawn "Animal" Malone, Extreme Whitewater Adventurer

I was fortunate to meet these three remarkable men earlier this year on a whitewater rafting trip down the Ocoee River in East Tennessee. Trevor and Jerry run the most professional guide service I've ever experienced. You'll meet them on the pages of this story, and my portrayals of their personalities are not an exaggeration. I recommend them and their operation, Bigfoot Outfitters, personally, for anyone who feels adventure calling.

Shawn "Animal" Malone is a personality too large to capture in fiction, but I've given it my best shot. He'll play a pivotal role in this story, and just like Trevor and Jerry, his personality is larger than my ability to capture. Animal is a whitewater legend and the best guide I've ever paddled with. I'd trust him to take me across Niagara Falls. I appreciate his friendship and willingness to play along in The Polar Chase.

The Polar Chase
CAP DANIELS

Chapter 1
Up Periscope

Every October, the town of Saint Marys, Georgia, hosts the Rock Shrimp Festival, an annual celebration of the local bounty of the sea that has contributed to the economy for decades. Vendors, restaurateurs, civic organizations, and a whole host of other folks set up tents and booths to peddle their wares and spread their message. The heart of the festival, though, is the shrimp—kettles, skillets, and platefuls of those amazing little crustaceans.

No matter where we went, my wife, Penny, was the belle of the ball. At six feet tall in her bare feet, and with hair that was impossible to control, she was the natural center of attention. Our attendance at the Rock Shrimp Festival was no exception. We'd lived in Saint Marys long enough for most of the locals to at least know our names, but we were careful to keep the reality of our lives out of public view.

I inherited Bonaventure Plantation on the banks of the North River from my great uncle, who'd inherited it from his father, and so on, for several generations before me. Bonaventure wasn't the most historic antebellum plantation home in the county, but it certainly qualified as being in the top five. I didn't love the spotlight of owning such a historic home, but I loved the history and the small-town feel of life at Bonaventure Plantation.

The place had been a commercial pecan operation in years past, but 2003 found the old property home and host to an entirely new industry. We didn't hang our shingle over the door, though. Nothing good could come of a few thousand locals knowing a team of tier-one covert operatives lived and operated on the edge of their quiet little town. The Rock Shrimp Festival was enough excitement for this waterfront chunk of Americana.

Penny precariously balanced a paper plate of boiled shrimp, grilled sausage, and corn on the cob as we strolled down Saint Marys Street and past the submarine museum and the Riverside Café, one of our favorite local restaurants. I may be able to sneak into the bedroom of a former Soviet Communist Party official and leave his brain strewn across the furniture with no one ever knowing I was there, but Penny Fulton could peel a boiled shrimp with one hand, and on that day, that was a far more valuable skill.

We polished off the plate of goodies and deposited the remains into one of the hundreds of trash barrels the city had placed all over the downtown area. Our walk continued past the last vendor until we found ourselves stepping across the low stone wall of Oak Grove Cemetery. As if we had some unspoken common destination, we walked hand in sticky hand through the forest of stone monuments, mausoleums, and headstones beneath canopies of Spanish moss dripping from aged oaks.

The name chiseled into the ornate, marble obelisk, Bernard Henry Huntsinger did little to define one of the greatest men I'd ever known. My great uncle and a pillar of the local community lived his life in service to the people of the small town, first as an attorney, then federal judge, and finally, as a symbolic patriarch to honesty, integrity, and godliness in the Old South.

Penny squeezed my hand. "He was a good man, Chase."

I stared down at the earth that still hadn't healed from having been opened to receive the man everyone called Judge. "Maybe one of the best," I said, then straightened a small American flag someone had stuck in the ground beside his monument.

My wife knelt beside me. "Is that one of Anya's flags?"

Anya Burinkova was a former Russian SVR officer who'd been sent to seduce me with the intention of infiltrating American covert operations under the guise of falling in love with me. She'd been nearly flawless in her execution. I'd melted like butter in her hands, and the drama that followed would be one of the most influential episodes of my life.

She was physically beautiful, intellectually brilliant, and tactically incomparable. The Russians had trained her from the age of five to become the perfect weapon of espionage for the Rodina, but fate or some other indefinable force had stepped in and put an impossibly complex set of events in motion that led Anya out of the former Soviet Union and into the shadow of Old Glory. She walked away from all she'd known and embraced the freedom and beauty of the nation she'd been trained to loathe, and defected to become an American citizen, and at least in some capacity, a member of my team of mercenaries. From the first time she held an American flag in her hand at a Fourth of July party at Bonaventure, I'd never known her to be without one of the tiny, novelty plastic flags in her pocket.

I brushed some leaves and twigs from the base of the obelisk. "I didn't sleep with her."

Penny ran her fingers through my hair. "I can't compete with her."

Kneeling on one knee in the soft soil, I turned to face her. "It's not a competition."

"Yes, it is," she said. "If I disappeared, she'd move into Bonaventure before the dust settled."

I reached up and took her hand. "You did disappear, and I chased you all over Texas to get you back."

"Yeah, I guess you did."

I stood and dusted off my knees. "I don't know what I'm going to have to do to make you believe I'm yours completely."

"That'll never be true, and you know it. Every time your phone rings, you instantly belong to the rest of the world."

Her hand felt cold in mine. "So, what's this about? Anya or my job? I've proven a thousand times that I've walked away from Anya, but if it's my job, this is a problem that's far bigger than we're going to solve here in the cemetery. You knew when you married me that I had responsibilities that outreached everything most people can understand."

She pulled her hand from mine. "It's about all of it, Chase . . . the combination of everything. When you leave, I never know if I'll ever see you again, and on top of that, you take her with you."

"She's a warrior, Penny, and a valuable member of the team. She can do things none of the rest of us can do."

She frowned and lowered her head. "Yeah, I'm sure she can."

"What do you want from me? Do you want me to quit? Just walk away from the team, my responsibilities, all of it? Is that what you want?"

She wiped a tear from her cheek. "Look what it's done to us, Chase. We can't have children because you got hurt in a gunfight on top of a mountain I've never heard of. I'm worried sick every second you're gone. And worst of all, I know I'm putting stress on you when you need to focus on . . . whatever it is you do when you go away."

"I can compartmentalize those things. I have to. When I'm working, I have to be completely focused, or I'll come home in a box. I've learned to separate the personal from the work."

She slowly shook her head. "That's exactly what I wanted to hear. You can forget all about me when you're gone, like I don't even exist. See the problem? Your work is always where you are. It's always what's most important to you, and I'm just an intermittent distraction."

"You're not a distraction, Penny. It's not like that."

The distinct sound of rifle fire crackled through the cool midmorning air. My eyes narrowed, and I listened intently. A second rifle sounded, and a pair of pistols answered.

I grabbed Penny's shoulders. "Call nine-one-one and report shots fired near Osborne Street downtown. Stay out of sight. I'll come back for you."

"But how can you know—"

"Just do it!" I ordered, and pulled my pistol from its holster as I sprinted toward the gunfight.

At a dead sprint, I can run for seven minutes and still have the breath to fight. Those seven minutes will put over a mile and a half behind me. The stopwatch in my head clocked eighty seconds, and I counted eighteen to twenty additional shots from at least four different guns in the quarter-mile sprint.

When I reached the corner of Bryant and Osborne, the gun battle continued amidst the screams of hundreds of terrified festivalgoers who were all running away from the fight while I continued deeper into the fray.

Moving against the terrified crowd, I turned south on Osborne and stayed tightly against the storefronts as I tried to identify the location of the shooters. Processing the scene as quickly as I could, the sound of lead striking flesh echoed in my ear, and the body of a uniformed Saint Marys police officer collapsed onto the grassy median in the middle of the street. He fell to the northeast and writhed in agony as the autumn grass turned from fading green to crimson beneath him. The bullet that tore through him had to have come from the southwest, but the mortified crowd made it all but impossible to piece together an accurate picture of what was happening.

The cop wasn't dead, but he would soon be leaving this world if I didn't get to him and slow the bleeding. I shouldered through the crowd as several more shots rang out. The look on the police officer's face when I loomed over him was the purest terror I'd ever witnessed.

"You've gotta help me," he mouthed.

I shot my hand inside the collar of his blue uniform shirt and grasped the shoulder strap of his ballistic vest. "This is going to hurt, but I've got to get you out of the street. I'm going to help you."

His face flushed pale, and he was on the verge of critical blood loss, so I dragged him across the street between a pair of buildings. I propped his legs up on the curb to keep as much blood as possible in his upper body and then tore away his bloody shirt. "It's a through-and-through in your shoulder. You're not going to die, but you have to do what I tell you, okay?"

He twisted to see his wound as I folded his shirt into a makeshift bandage. The exit wound at his back was the source of most of the blood, so I wedged the folded shirt between the wound and the street. "Lie back and stay that way. You've got to keep pressure on that wound. Give me your hand."

I yanked a pair of leather gloves from his belt and pressed them against the entry wound high on his chest. "Press your hand here, and don't let go! Got it?"

He nodded and blinked against the sunlight. "Who are you?"

"Did you see the shooter?"

He coughed, and in a pain-filled, breathy voice, he said, "I think there's two of them on top of the Riverview."

I shoved his radio mic into his free hand. "Call it in. Tell them where you are, and tell the ambulance to stay off Osborne."

He dropped the mic and grabbed my shirt. "Who *are* you?"

"I'm the guy who just saved your life. How many more cops are on the street?"

He closed his eyes as if he were dozing off, so I shook him. "How many more of you are there?"

"Ten," he breathed. "Ten of us, but they've got the high ground."

"Don't worry about that," I said. "I've got a plan. Just tell your buddies not to shoot me."

I shoved the mic back into his hand, sprinted down Stable Alley, and into the gravel lot behind the submarine museum. The back door to the museum was locked, so I encouraged it to open with the heel of my boot. Shoving my way through the back storage room of the museum, I continued toward the front until I found exactly what I was looking for.

My favorite part of the submarine museum is the working periscope situated near the front of the building, protruding through the roof, and well into the sky. It allows visitors to watch boats moving in and out of the Saint Marys Pass near Fort Clinch over five miles away, but that's not the view I needed. What I wanted to see was less than two hundred feet away.

I spun the periscope toward the roof of the Riverview Hotel and squinted to make out what I saw. The fifty-year-old optical device wouldn't focus on anything so close, but I didn't need details. I only needed a head count so I could turn it into a body count.

Chapter 2
Fire Support

Instinctually, I yanked my phone from my pocket and pressed the speed dial key for the one man I knew who could quiet the guns on top of the Riverview Hotel.

"Singer, it's Chase. Listen to me. There's an active shooter situation. I need you and your rifle on the upper gallery of the Spencer House."

His boots hit the floor before he spoke, and the sounds of one of the deadliest snipers who ever lived gathering his gear filled the earpiece. "I'm moving, Chase. How many targets?"

"Two," I said. "Both in dark clothes with rifles."

"Heavy rifles?" he asked as the door of his humble home closed behind him.

"It sounds like one thirty-caliber and one two-two-three. Definitely nothing heavier than that."

I ended the call and dialed the Spencer House. "This is Special Agent Chase Fulton with the U.S. Secret Service. I have a sniper moving to your location. I'm commandeering use of your upper gallery to resolve an active shooter situation downtown. Do not interfere with him, and clear your upper gallery now. Keep all of your guests in the rear of the house, and do not let anyone go outside. Understand?"

"Yes, sir," came the timid reply just as Singer came crashing through the ancient double doors of the bed-and-breakfast.

I didn't have to look down at my phone to dial the next number.

"Nine-one-one operator. What's your emergency?"

"This is Supervisory Special Agent Fulton with the Secret Service. I'm on scene of the active shooter in downtown Saint Marys. I have a sniper moving into position at the Spencer House, and I've located the shooters. I'll have the gunmen suppressed in less than sixty seconds. Did you get an officer-down call about four minutes ago?"

"Yes, sir, I did . . . at the corner of Osborne and Stable Alley."

"I pulled the officer from the street. He's critical and needs an ambulance immediately, but stay off Osborne Street. The shooters have a line of sight up the street. Got it?"

"The ambulance is en route now, and I'm notifying all officers on the scene of your presence. Where are you now?"

"I'm inside the sub museum using the periscope to provide fire support for my sniper. Tell your officers to expect two heavy rifle shots from the north. Do not return fire on the Spencer House. Do you understand?"

"Yes, sir. I've got it. Two shots from the north, and do not return fire."

I hung up and redialed Singer. "Are you in position?"

"I am. There's two shooters and a spotter on the roof. Can I engage the targets?"

"I can't see the spotter," I said. "The focus is no good at close range."

Singer said, "He's ducking in front of the air conditioner. You wouldn't be able to see him even if you could focus. Can I engage?"

I swallowed hard before giving the order to end three human lives. "Send it."

Singer's low baritone voice sounded just above a whisper. "Swing low, sweet chariot . . . coming for to carry me home . . ."

Before I heard the echoing report of the massive Barrett fifty-caliber rifle, I watched the blurred form of the northernmost shooter disintegrate, followed an instant later by the body of the second gunman torn apart. I waited for the billowing sound of the third round, but it never came.

"Chase? Are you there?"

I pressed the phone back to my ear. "Yeah, I'm here."

"The spotter is surrendering. He's on his face with his hands on his head. I'm not killing a surrendering man."

"Keep him pinned down. If he goes for a weapon, you've got to cut him down. I'll notify the police."

"Roger," he said.

I redialed the nine-one-one operator and got the same dispatcher as before. "Special Agent Fulton here. The two shooters are down, and a third man is pinned down on the roof and surrendering. Get a pair of officers up there to apprehend him. My sniper will keep him in place until your officers arrive."

Her voice crackled as she radioed the information to the officers in the field. "Four uniformed policemen are climbing the back stairs now, sir. They'll be on the roof in sixty seconds."

"Thank you, ma'am. How's the officer who was shot?"

"All I know is he's on the way to the hospital."

I folded the handles of the periscope and walked through the front doors of the museum. *What am I going to tell the cops when their inevitable questions come?*

I glanced up to see a pair of police officers leaning an extension ladder against the back of the Riverview Hotel, and I tried to imagine the scene on the old flat roof overhead. Two men, or what was left of two men who'd been cut down by a pair of enormous, fifty-caliber rounds from Singer's Barrett, were, no doubt, strewn about the scene. But the interesting part for me was the unarmed third—the only surviving member of the rooftop trio.

I would've loved to put him in front of Anya, our former SVR assassin and master interrogator, to see what she could drag out of his mouth. Although she denied having any skill as an interrogator, I'd watched her coax information out of men three times her size in a matter of minutes. Admittedly, she did so with threats, and in some cases, demonstrations of extreme violence, but her methods were effective, even if brutal. The detectives of the Saint Marys Police Department would be significantly less aggressive than Anya.

I'm amused by a great many things, but few things fascinate me more than watching people attempt something they've never done but believe they know how to accomplish. Watching two police officers attempt to descend a flimsy aluminum ladder with a handcuffed and shackled prisoner under control was the highlight of my day.

The man's ankles were shackled by a chain slightly shorter than the distance between the rungs of the ladder, but that was the least of the prisoner's problems. He was covered, head to toe, with the remains of at least one of his buddies who Singer had sent to meet his maker.

After the wrestling match successfully ended, leaving the bound, bloody man perched on the third rung from the top, he tried to hop down the ladder like a broken Slinky. It worked for the first five rungs, but on the sixth attempt, his feet slipped through the ladder, leaving him suspended by his armpits and dangling from the backside of the ladder like a worn-out ragdoll.

That's when the most physically imposing member of my team arrived. Marvin "Mongo" Malloy ambled across Saint Marys Street, casting a shadow unequaled by any man I'd ever known. At something over six feet seven inches and three hundred pounds, Mongo was impossible to ignore.

"You reckon they need some help up there, Chase?"

I pulled my cred pack from my pocket and flashed my Secret Service credentials to a plain-clothed officer who appeared to be in charge. "Chase Fulton, U.S. Secret Service. I've got a man who can solve your logistics issue up there if you'd like some help."

The officer turned, inspected my credentials, and then let his eyes climb Mongo's frame. The somber moment was broken by the slightest chuckle from the officer. "I'm Lieutenant Nichols, and we'd love your help."

Mongo climbed the metal stairs to the second story of the old hotel and hefted the ladder—prisoner and all—over his shoulder, and carried it to the ground. The ladder settled around the prisoner's feet, and Mongo planted an enormous hand on the man's arm. "Are you all right, sir?"

The terrified, blood-covered prisoner looked up at Mongo and nodded.

Lieutenant Nichols turned back to me. "We need to have a little chat. Do you want to ride with me or follow us back to the station?"

I glanced over my shoulder in the direction of Oak Grove Cemetery. "I'll meet you there, Lieutenant. I've got something to take care of first."

He shot a look at his watch. "Don't tarry, Special Agent Fulton. Something tells me this whole mess may be more in your jurisdiction than mine."

"I'll be there in fifteen minutes. I just have to make sure my wife is okay first."

He double-checked his watch. "Fifteen minutes. Bring your sniper . . . and your giant."

I headed back toward the cemetery. Penny was sitting on the low stone wall surrounding the old graveyard. The look on her face told me more than I wanted to know.

"So, did you save the world again?"

I sat beside her. "No, just a tiny corner of it that happens to be our home. There were two shooters and a spotter on top of the Riverview. Singer took out the shooters, and the Saint Marys PD arrested the spotter. I don't know if any civilians were hit, but at least one cop took a round in the shoulder."

"You couldn't leave it alone, could you? When the bullets started flying, you had to run straight into the fight."

I took a long breath and swallowed the bitterness that almost came from my lips. "Penny, it's what I do. It's who I am. If I hadn't gotten Singer on scene, God only knows how many people would be dead right now."

"That's what the police are for, Chase. Don't you get that? They're not all your fights. You ran off and left me alone during an active shooter situation. Alone! I'm your wife . . . or at least I'm supposed to be. I'm supposed to come first."

I'd never loved anyone or anything the way I loved Penny Thomas Fulton. She was the most amazing woman I'd ever met. Nothing I could say would bring her any measure of comfort. She was right. I had left her standing all alone in a cemetery while a pair of maniacs were shooting into the crowd a quarter mile away. My decision hadn't been conscious. It'd been instinctual, but I could never make her understand that. There were no words to explain the fire that burned inside me to save human lives and crush the skulls of those who would turn innocent people into victims.

"I have to go to the police department and give a statement. I'd like to walk you home before I go. Are you okay with that?"

She didn't look up. "No, I'm not okay with that. You go and give your statement. If I can survive by myself while some idiots are shooting up the town, surely I can walk home without an escort."

Chapter 3
Hide-and-Seek

The Saint Marys Police Department is bigger than the small-town departments depicted on prime-time television, but it certainly didn't qualify as One Police Plaza, either.

Lieutenant Nelson retrieved Mongo, Singer, and me from the front desk and led us down a short hallway to his office. The space would've accommodated four normal-sized humans comfortably, but Mongo made it look like we were meeting in a child's treehouse.

Nelson pointed with his chin. "Close the door, would you?"

I did as he asked and took a seat. His desk was neatly arranged with a single lamp, his nameplate, a stapler, and two stacks of files. The credenza behind him contained a printer and a framed photograph of his family.

The lieutenant pulled a yellow legal pad from his lap drawer and crossed his legs. "As you've noticed, this isn't a typical day for us, Special Agent Fulton. We're not accustomed to active shooter scenarios in our little town, especially when they involve three mysterious Secret Service agents."

He paused as if waiting for one of us to offer some explanation. We offered nothing.

He cleared his throat. "Well, then, I suppose that leaves me with asking direct questions. I've seen you around town, Special Agent Fulton, and from what I gathered, you bought the Bonaventure Plantation. I guess the first thing I want to know is why a Secret Service agent lives in Saint Marys, and what are you coincidently doing with a fifty-caliber sniper rifle on the day a couple of idiots decide to shoot up the town?"

The thing about the truth is that it's easy to remember . . . except when the truth is variable.

"Technically, Lieutenant Nelson, I am a Supervisory Special Agent with the Secret Service. However, I'm not the kind of agent who works on the Presidential Security Detail. I'm more of a freelance agent, you might say."

He clicked his pen closed, returned it to his shirt pocket, and tossed the legal pad onto the desk. "A freelance Secret Service agent, you say?"

I glanced at Singer and Mongo, but they were no help.

Nelson leaned back in his chair and propped his feet on the corner of his desk. "I think this might be a good time to tell me the whole truth, freelance agent Fulton. What are you really, not technically, doing in Saint Marys?"

I pursed my lips. "No offense, Lieutenant Nelson, but I'm not sure you have the clearance to know the whole truth. It would probably be a good idea to get the chief in here, and I need to make a call to my supervisor."

The lieutenant rubbed his forehead. "I knew it." He let his feet fall to the floor, and he pushed himself from his chair. "You boys sit tight, and I'll be right back."

"This is about to get ugly, isn't it?" Mongo whispered.

"Maybe," I said as I pulled my phone from my pocket.

Clark Johnson, former Green Beret and my current handler, answered on the second ring. "Hey, Chase. How are things up north?"

"Oh, just hunky-dory. Mongo, Singer, and I are hanging out at the police station after we took out a pair of shooters on the roof of the Riverview Hotel during the Rock Shrimp Festival. Now the local cops have a lot of questions I'm not particularly interested in answering."

"Sounds like a pretty routine day, then."

For almost six years, Clark had been my partner and primary training officer. He pulled my butt out of too many fires to count, but after a nasty gunfight on top of the Khyber Pass and a few surgeries that left over a quarter of his spine fused together, he'd been promoted out of the field and into management in Miami.

"Yeah, ops are pretty much normal here, but I'd appreciate you having a chat with the chief of police if you wouldn't mind."

Nelson stuck his head back into his office. "Follow me."

We rose, and I said, "We're being taken to see the chief now. Do you want to stay on the phone, or should I call you back?"

"Just hand the phone to the chief when you get in his office. I'll take care of you . . . just like I've always done."

I grinned. "You must mean like the time you pulled me off the Khyber Pass when I was too much of a wuss to hump it out of there. Oh, no, wait. That was me who pulled you off that mountain, so you can't be talking about that time."

"Okay, College Boy, I can run down the list of times I've saved your bacon if you'd like, but this is going to be a long phone call if I do."

"We'll save that one for cocktails and cigars. Here's the chief."

Nelson led us through a pair of double doors and into a modest conference room with a long table and perhaps a dozen chairs. The chief of police stood and motioned for us to have a seat.

We did, and I slid my phone across the table toward the fit, fifty-something, official-looking chief of police. "That's my supervisor."

The chief looked at the phone for a long moment and then pressed the red button, ending the call. "I already know who—and mostly what—you are, Mr. Fulton. Your Secret Service credentials were issued to you in a hotel room in New York City after you completed your initial training, but that training wasn't at any Secret Service facility. You're some kind of OGA, Other Government Agent. Am I getting warm?"

I carefully considered my reply. "Chief, I should've come to you when I inherited Bonaventure and let you in on who and what we are, but I thought we could—"

He cleared his throat. "You thought you could run a covert operations base out of my city and I wouldn't notice. Is that what you were going to say, Mr. Fulton?"

"Not exactly, Chief. Actually, I never thought we'd get involved in a gunfight on Osborne Street, so I didn't plan to cause you any trouble. I just wanted to live my quiet little life on the plantation and—"

He cut in. "Quiet little life? That's funny. A million-dollar piece of real estate, a five-million-dollar Mark V patrol boat, a three-million-dollar P-51 Mustang, a million-dollar Cessna Caravan on floats. Oh, and let's not forget *Aegis*, your two-million-dollar catamaran. There's nothing quiet or little about your life, Mr. Fulton. Around here, you stick out like Winnie the Pooh at a nudist colony. We may not be big-time crime-busters like the boys in D.C., but even simple, small-town cops like us tend to notice when a thirty-year-old multi-millionaire moves into our community."

"I'm not sure what you want me to say, Chief. I didn't really buy any of that stuff. I inherited Bonaventure Plantation from my great uncle . . ."

"Yes, I knew the Judge well. He was a pillar of the community, but we need to talk about you getting involved in a police action under the guise of being a Secret Service agent."

I shot glances at my two partners sitting silently by my side. "The situation was out of control, Chief. Someone had to do something to silence those guns. We saved a lot of lives today."

The chief stared down at his fingernails. "Maybe, but vigilante justice is not how things are done here in Saint Marys."

"We're not exactly vigilantes. We're tier-one operators in the business of saving lives."

"I'm not so sure about that. From what I've heard, and from what I've seen today, you're in the business of killing people. And you're pretty damned good at it from where I sit."

I narrowed my eyes. "Sometimes, Chief, killing a few people is exactly what's required to save a few thousand more."

He turned in his swiveling chair and stared out the window. "I suppose you'd know more about that than me, Mr. Fulton, but what I know is how to keep the peace in a small Southern town."

I looked out the window and wondered if he was staring at anything in particular.

The chief pressed his toes against the floor and spun back to the table. "And I know that having a bunch of vigilantes running amok in my town is not the way to keep the peace. I've got a mess on my hands." He pointed toward Singer. "You . . . you're the sniper, right? And aren't you the choir director at the Baptist church?"

Singer turned to face me, and the chief said, "Hey! Look at me. Don't look at him."

Singer didn't flinch. He kept his eyes solidly on me, and I nodded as if signing his permission slip.

He turned back to the chief. "We're all snipers, but I'm the one Chase called today. And, yeah, I lead the singing at church. You should come join us."

The chief looked around the room. "So, you're all snipers, huh?"

"We've all had the training," I said, "but none of us are as good as Singer."

"I see," the chief said. "Well, Mr. Singer, what's your first name?"

"Jimmy."

The chief wrote on his pad and turned to the giant. "How about you? What's your name?"

Mongo followed Singer's example and turned to me.

The chief slapped the table. "I'll say this. Your men are either the most loyal I've ever seen, or you've got the hell scared out of them."

I smiled. "My men aren't afraid of anything, especially not me. It's just that we've all been trained to resist interrogation, and this feels a lot like interrogation to us."

He leaned forward in his chair and rested his elbows on the table. "Take a look at my situation, here, Mr. Fulton. I've got two shot cops, three shot civilians, and blood in my streets and on my rooftops, all on the most important day of the year for this town. On top of all that, I've got you three smart-asses in here playing hide-and-seek with the truth. If my hunch is right —and it usually is—we're on the same side, but if I'm wrong— and that's rare—you're part of the bullshit that went on out there today, and it's my job to lock you up."

He slammed his pen down on the pad and leaned back. "If we're on the same team, start acting like it. If it's option two, you boys have the right to remain silent, and you can spend the next several nights of your life in my jail. Now, which is it?"

I pulled a business card from my Secret Service cred pack and slid it across the table. "Feel free to call that number, Chief. The person who answers will direct your call to the Attorney General of the United States, who will tell you that I'm a supervisory special agent in good standing with the federal government, and these two gentlemen are contractors working under my direction. Arrest us if you think it's a good plan, but don't expect to keep your job."

He pointed his finger toward my nose. "Now, you listen here . . ."

I pushed his finger away. "No, Chief, you listen. We saved a bunch of human lives today, and you get to take the credit. You get to do the six o'clock news interview and tell all about how your officers stopped a pair of mass shooters in record time. Nobody ever needs to know anything about the three of us. You save face. We remain anonymous. And two very bad men are dead. Everybody wins."

The chief drove the heels of his hands into his temples and squeezed his eyes closed. "Get out. Go home, and stay home. Don't shoot anybody else, no matter how many lives you think you're saving. But Mr. Fulton, don't leave town. You and I have a lot to discuss when this is over."

I slid his pad toward my side of the table and wrote my number on the bottom of the first page. "We're on the same team, Chief. I don't get to choose when I leave town. If a mission comes up, we go. It's what we do. But I'll answer the phone when you call, and you're welcome at Bonaventure anytime."

Chapter 4
Reasonable Men

Back at Bonaventure Plantation, the house was empty. I'd expected to find Penny in the reading nook on the second story overlooking the pasture, but her favorite chair was vacant. I loved the antebellum house, but the echoing emptiness made it feel like a cavernous void.

I've fought battles in the face of evil in almost every corner of the world, but the battles I waged inside my head have always been the most terrifying. Sliding my hand across the chair in which my wife spent countless hours, I let the two angels on my shoulders—one with horns and one with a halo—battle it out. Should I go in search of her, or should I sit in her chair and hope she comes to me?

The horned angel won, and I galloped down the stairs. Instead of being in her chair, I found Penny in mine. The gazebo by the river where the two-hundred-year-old cannon rested contained six Adirondack chairs and one of the most picturesque views in Camden County. My favorite of the chairs was the one situated directly behind the cannon. On its left arm were exactly eleven burn marks left by the stumps of Cuban cigars, and on the right was a permanent collection of ring stains left by my whiskey tumblers. Penny Thomas, the most beautiful woman I'd ever known—inside and out—sat with her feet curled beneath her and her fingertips tracing the lines on the arms of my chair.

I sat on the cannon's cradle. "Do you want to talk about it?"

She stared down at the planks of the gazebo's floor. "What is there to talk about?"

My mouth felt as dry as the Sahara. "Us."

She looked up at me. "What about us? We're who and what we are at our core, and that isn't going to change in either of us. I need to know you're coming home every night, and I need to know I'm the most important thing in your life."

She twisted in her chair and repositioned her feet on the gazebo's deck. "That's not the kind of man you are, though. There's something inside you that makes you prioritize people you'll never meet over the woman with your last name."

I picked at the metal of the ancient cannon. "That's not fair. What I do is important."

"Oh, I know," she said. "It's really important to get a rich guy back his oil rig."

My most recent mission had been the liberation of an enormous offshore oil rig and the rescue of three hundred human trafficking victims in the Gulf of Mexico.

I rubbed the cannon, imagining the lives it had taken and the ones it had saved in centuries past. "That mission paid very well. . . ."

She rolled her eyes. "Have you seen the bank statements? You've got ten million dollars in the bank and at least that much more in this property and your boats and airplanes. How much do you need? How much is enough?"

"I don't do it for the money."

She locked eyes with me. "Then why do you do it?"

"I do it to save lives and make the world a better place."

She scoffed. "What about *my* world, huh? Where does my world fall on that list of priorities of yours? When are you going to get around to making my world a better place?"

I frowned. "Look around yourself, Penny. You have everything anyone could want."

She stood from the chair. "Except a husband who puts his wife first. You sure went to a lot of trouble to get your girlfriend out of Russia and bring her back home so you could go play with her and save the world together, though, didn't you?"

It was my turn to lock eyes. "Do you remember the conversation you and I had in Alaska? You're the one who convinced me to bring her back to the States."

"Yeah, because you were going to let the Russians kill her, or worse, and even though I want to hate her, I can't just let horrible things happen to people . . . even the ones I hate. I'm not that cold."

"Then we're not as different as you want to believe, because that's exactly why my work is important. I can't just let horrible things happen to people. You had the ability to save Anya, and you did it. I have the ability to save thousands of lives. Why wouldn't I do that?"

"It doesn't have to be you," she said. "Do you really think nobody else would take the missions if you said no?"

A mini tornado of leaves and dust danced across the yard near the riverbank, and the air felt suddenly heavy.

"You're right. There are other operators, but what if they made the same decision? We can't all say somebody else will do it."

She planted her hands on her hips. "But they don't have me."

I stood from the cannon cradle and reached for her hand. "We can go away. We can sail anywhere you want and spend some time just for us."

She stared down at my waiting hand and finally laid hers in mine. "For how long?"

"As long as you want," I said, and immediately regretted my response.

For the first time that day, her eyes lit up. "Are you sure?"

I froze, unsure how to answer her question. Penny, no doubt, wanted to sail away forever, but I couldn't make that promise.

She yanked her hand from mine. "That's what I thought. I'm going to the Pacific to spend some time with my parents. I don't know when I'll be back."

"But you are coming back . . . right?"

Sometimes, the absence of an answer is more painful than the answer itself.

I watched her walk away, and it took every fiber of my being to let her go. Everything inside me wanted to chase her. I was faced with the most unthinkable decision of my life—a decision that should've been easy. Any reasonable man in my position would've unloaded his gun and spent the next fifty years exploring the world with that beautiful woman and spending the money he'd amassed, but reasonable men don't find themselves in my situation. Reasonable men become doctors, or plumbers, or small-town police chiefs. Reasonable men don't become spies.

* * *

I leaned against the cannon and stared out over the North River, where a pair of pelicans feasted on a school of fish on the outgoing tide.

What would my father have done?

Why did I insist on asking myself questions like that? Asking what my father would have done in my situation was like asking what George Washington would have done during the Cuban Missile Crisis. My father wasn't married to a civilian. My mother was an operative and knew the risks, rewards, and sacrifices inherent to the life I now led. My father wouldn't have done anything in my situation because he never would've put himself in the position I was in.

Choosing Penny over my responsibility to the world I'd vowed to protect was what I wanted to do more than anything else; however, some indefinable part of me made that decision impossible. Some force I would never be able to adequately define drew me into service to my country as powerfully as the pelicans were drawn to the baitfish.

My desire to turn from my responsibility and cling to Penny was powerful, but that draw, that irresistible need to protect what generations before me had fought and bled and died to preserve, anchored my life to a service and a destiny that had, perhaps, been preordained long before I drew my first breath, and would persevere long after I'd drawn my last.

As the October sun descended beneath the pecan trees and cast long shadows across the yard and the inky water of the river, the evening air cooled, but the sun's warmth remained in the iron of the cannon. The gun warmed my back as the breeze chilled my face. It was a study in contrasts as the heat of the past beckoned for me to stay while the chill of the coming night threatened to leave me cold and alone.

I clung to the ancient weapon of war and what it represented to me. Its steadfast indifference to its enemies shone in every pit and crack on its weathered skin. As long as men would keep loading it and pointing it toward the enemy, it would keep firing until there was no one left to light its fuse. The cannon was my brother, and I knew well the resolution at its core. That same emboldened, unafraid spirit burned in me, and I'd keep fighting as long as there were men who'd load me and point me toward my enemy. The difference lay in what the cannon could never have—the love of a passionate woman who wanted nothing more than to spend her life in my arms. The cannon's bore lay empty, never again to fire in anger, and as Penny packed her bags beneath falling tears, perhaps I, too, lay empty, alone, and still warm from the absent westward sun.

"You doing okay, Chase?"

I didn't look up. I didn't have to. The voice belonged to the only man on Earth who knew me well enough and possessed the wisdom to understand my answer.

"No, I'm not okay, and it feels like I'll never be okay again."

Jimmy "Singer" Grossmann stepped into my gazebo and settled into a chair.

I stared at my friend and de facto spiritual advisor. "How do you do it, Singer?"

"How do I do what?"

"Keep the faith when the whole world comes crashing down around you?"

He motioned out over the marsh and then back toward my house, where Penny was planning her escape from my chaotic world. "'Cause, Chase, all this is just temporary. What happens to me in the sixty or seventy years I'm here is just preparing me for something better. You don't have to believe everything I believe to live by that same philosophy. No matter what you believe, everything you can touch is temporary. Do you want to talk about it?"

I stared at the deck and studied a pair of ants carrying a piece of a leaf that neither could carry alone. "No, I don't want to talk about it, but I probably need to. Do you mind if I ask you a personal question?"

He cocked his head. "Sure, let's hear it."

"What did you do with your money?"

A month before I found myself sitting alone against a two-hundred-year-old cannon and wondering if I'd ever see my wife again, Singer had been one of seven members of my assault team who'd liberated an offshore oil rig from the hands of a Central American human trafficking cartel. We'd been paid thirty-five million dollars for the task, and I divided it equally among the team.

"Nothing yet," he said, "but the church needs a new roof, and the monks are raising money to buy the piece of property next to the monastery. I'll make up the difference in what they have and what they need to take care of those couple of things before I do anything else with the money."

For the first time in hours, I smiled. "Have you ever seen the movie *Rain Man*?"

"I don't watch many movies."

"It's about a guy who doesn't know the difference between the price of a candy bar and a compact car. Unless the monks want to buy ten thousand acres, you can build an entirely new church, roof and all, and buy the property for the monks, and you'd still have more than enough to live comfortably for the rest of your life."

He picked a pebble from the tread of his boot. "Yeah, well, I already live comfortably. I don't need much."

"I envy so much about your life, Singer, but what's the deal with you and those monks? You're not even Catholic, and I've never heard of a Baptist monk."

He closed his eyes and let his chin fall to his chest. The dichotomy of Singer's character was difficult to understand. He was a devout Christian with the voice of an angel and the kindest nature of anyone I'd ever met, inside the body of one of the deadliest snipers on Earth. Seeing him laboring to find the words to explain his affection for a monastery and an order of monks left me fascinated and even a little nervous to hear the answer.

When he opened his eyes, his face was set in resolution. "I've never told anyone this story. In fact, I've never considered telling anyone, but you deserve to know the truth."

Even more intrigued, I said, "You don't have to tell me anything you don't feel comfortable talking about. I didn't mean to—"

He held up his hand. "I grew up in a little town called Sumter, South Carolina. It's a military town built around Shaw Air Force Base. Other than the base, there's not much there. My father . . ." He bowed his head and again closed his eyes while I sat in silent support of my friend. After nearly a minute, he continued. "My father wasn't a good man. He was an alcoholic and an addict. My mother was a woman of enormous faith. I'm sure fear made her think about taking my brother and me and escaping the old man's abuse and the poverty we lived in, but something made her stay one day too many. Other kids played hide-and-seek, but my brother and I just played hide. I was nine and he was eleven when it happened. Momma was crying, and daddy was yelling. He was drunk or high on something. He'd hit her before, but never like that. It was different that night. He was in some sort of rage like I'd never seen."

He paused and took two long, slow breaths before continuing the agonizing story. "That's when Momma quit screaming. My brother and I both heard the blow that stopped her tears. We were scared, but in times like that, fear isn't enough to stop two boys from checking on their mother. We ran down the hallway of our trailer and saw Daddy standing over Momma's body. She looked dead to me, but he was too drunk or too high to stop beating her. My brother Billy ran into the living room and shoved him away from Momma. He stumbled and crashed into the bar separating the living room from the kitchen. When he came up, he had a knife from the sink, and he started for Billy. His old single-shot twenty gauge was propped in the corner by the worn-out recliner."

The tears trickling from the corners of his eyes seemed to burn his flesh, and he pawed at them as if they were acid. "I can't tell you what it was, Chase. I don't know. But something inside my little nine-year-old head made me pick up that shotgun. I remember thinking, I've got to stop him before he kills anybody else. I don't remember the sound or the kick, but I'll never forget the red spatter on the ceiling and the walls of that rundown, rotten trailer. Momma lived a few more days, but he'd caused an aneurism in her brain, and she never regained consciousness. I stopped him before he could physically hurt Billy, but physical injuries are the easy ones to overcome."

The man I turned to when I was falling apart had just turned the tables. He was pouring his heart out into my hands, and I was speechless.

He wiped his face again. "So, Billy didn't talk after that . . . at all. It was like he wasn't in there anymore. He just stared into space with a blank expression and didn't react to anything. He was like that for nearly a year. We didn't have any family, so a preacher and his wife took Billy and me in and treated us like we were their own children. They were good people, but they didn't know how to help my brother. In those days, there wasn't any help for a boy who'd been through what Billy had. We went to see a shrink for a few months. He did his best, and I learned to cope with what happened and what I'd done, but Billy never did. One day, the preacher put us in the cab of his truck and drove for what felt like hours. When we stopped, we were at the monastery. We left Billy there with the monks. He's still there, and now, all these years later, he's still never said a word."

When Singer stopped talking, he looked as if someone had lifted a thousand pounds from his chest. His smile returned. "Don't envy me, Chase. You don't want the burden I carry. I'm a sniper because I have the capacity to take human life when I believe doing so will protect the innocent. I'm a Christian because there's no other source of true peace on this Earth."

I wanted to say something, anything, but at a moment like that, words are weak and hollow, so I slid my boot against his as we sat there in my gazebo, reliving two of the most defining moments of our lives. His had been twenty-five years ago, and mine was unfolding with every tick of the clock.

He broke the silence. "I know you're hurting, but every relationship goes through hard times. It's the nature of things. I'm no marriage counselor, but I'm sure if you'll sit beside Penny and tell her how you truly feel and then let your actions mirror your words, all of this will eventually melt away, and both of you will remember why you fell in love in the first place."

I stared at my friend. "I don't think you understand."

He tapped my boot with his. "Maybe you're right. Perhaps I don't understand, but I care about both of you, and I don't want to see the two of you frozen in this moment forever."

He cocked his head. "Have you ever seen the big stained-glass window at the church? The one with the kids sitting at Jesus's feet?"

"Sure I have. Plenty of times. I've never been sure of what's happening in the scene, but it's a beautiful work of art."

He almost smiled. "Jesus is teaching those children something they need to know. That's what I *believe* is happening in that scene, but what I think doesn't matter. Regardless of what's going on in that stained-glass window, none of those people ever moved past that moment. They're frozen forever, exactly where they are. That's not what you want to be, is it?"

I felt the lines form on my forehead as I tried to apply Singer's wisdom to my situation. "If I could pick any moment in my life to freeze and never escape, it'd be the first time Penny told me she loved me."

Chapter 5
Indispensable

Not wanting to experience the awkwardness of being in the same house where my wife was packing to leave me—and perhaps never coming back—I stepped from the gazebo and headed for the water's edge. The Bonaventure dock jutted into the North River some hundred and twenty feet. At the end of the floating collection of ten hinged sections stood a pair of bollards jutting out of the water about ten feet at high tide. Those bollards, along with four shorter posts on the downstream side of the floating dock, were what kept the whole affair from washing out into the Atlantic. Part of me wanted my bollards, the posts anchoring me to reality, to give way and leave me tossed to the cold will of the sea.

On the downstream of the dock sat my eighty-five-foot Mark V patrol boat beneath a gray canvas cover designed to keep prying eyes from the decks of my most prized tactical asset. The boat was a bribe from the president of the United States to lure me into his debt. I needed a fast, dependable, tactical offshore boat, and he needed the plausible deniability of a warrior like me in his pocket. From my perspective, my debt to the president was paid in full, but I doubted if he shared my opinion.

On the upstream side of the dock rested what had been my home prior to inheriting Bonaventure Plantation. *Aegis* was my beloved fifty-foot, custom sailing catamaran. After Anya killed Dmitri Barkov on his yacht off the Florida Keys and sent his body to the bottom of the Straits of Florida, I traded the Russian oligarch's motor yacht for the catamaran. I'd never felt more at home than when I was aboard *Aegis*, under full sail, without a speck of land in sight.

As badly as I wanted to stop Penny from leaving, there was nothing I could do or say that would keep her from getting on the plane to the South Pacific, so I climbed aboard my sailboat. She felt like an old welcoming friend as I strolled the deck and inspected the rigging. Everything was shipshape. With a push of the button, the chart plotter came to life, showing the status of each satellite as the antenna gathered the data from the flock of orbiting feats of engineering marvel. My GPS position finally appeared on the screen, and I quickly zoomed out to the plotter's limits. The island continent of Australia loomed large on the bottom left of the screen while the peninsula of Florida dominated the upper right.

Ten thousand miles, I thought to myself. That's almost as far away as it's possible to be from another human and still be on the planet. The idea of Penny being on the opposite side of the world, both emotionally and physically, sickened me. As I stood, staring down at the long, arching, magenta line connecting Saint Marys, Georgia, to the island nation of Vanuatu, the most difficult—and simplest—decision of my life unfolded before my eyes.

Both diesels hummed to life at the touch of the starters and began warming up to operating temperature as I leapt back to the dock. I have no memory of crossing the two hundred feet of yard between the river's edge and the back gallery of the house. Likewise, I don't remember ascending the wide, arching staircase to the second story. What I'll never forget was the look on Penny's face when I stepped through the bedroom door.

She was sitting cross-legged beside the bed, holding our two-hundred-fifty-year-old Huntsinger family Bible in her arms. The Bible had been our wedding gift from the Judge, and it contained two and a half centuries of marriages, births, and deaths in my mother's family. Penny's beautiful eyes were red and her cheeks were tearstained.

I knelt in front of her and laid my hands on her knees. "Have you bought your ticket yet?"

She pressed her lips into a thin, horizontal line and shook her head.

I tightened my grip. "Good. Don't. I'll take you."

She frowned. "You'll take me to buy my airline ticket?"

I tucked a long strand of hair behind her ear. "No, I'll take you to Vanuatu to see your parents."

She sighed. "We don't have an airplane that can make that trip."

I smiled. "No, but we've got a boat."

She cocked her head. "*Aegis?*"

I stood, took her hand, and helped her to her feet. "Yes, *Aegis*. It's about seventeen hundred miles to Panama and then just eight thousand across the Pacific when we get through the canal."

She laid the Bible beside her and took my hands in hers. "Chase, that's . . ."

I smiled. "That's two or three months we can spend together without worrying about anything or anyone else in the world. Besides, I still owe you a honeymoon."

The first signs of a smile formed at the corners of her eyes. "Are you serious?"

I nodded toward the river. "*Aegis* is warming up. Her tanks are full, and she's in perfect shape. We can be headed for Panama before the moon comes up."

"That's crazy," she said. "We can't just take off on a ten-thousand-mile trip at the drop of a hat."

"Why not? What's stopping us?"

"It's just crazy. I mean, who does that? And what if a mission comes up?"

I held her face in my hands. "I'll tell them no. Besides, Hunter, Singer, and Mongo can do anything I can do. The world will be just fine without me for a couple of months."

She ran her hand through my hair. "What about after that? What happens after a couple of months when a mission comes up?"

I kissed her forehead. "It's just as far back to Saint Marys as it is to Vanuatu, so that's at least five or six months. When we get back in the spring, maybe everything will have changed, and we'll figure out a way to keep what's most important most important."

"Six months? Chase Fulton, since I met you, you've never gone six months without a mission. What makes you think—"

I pulled her against me and kissed her as if my life depended on that single kiss. Perhaps it did. When we parted, I whispered, "So, are you coming with me, or are you going to make me sail across the Pacific by myself?"

She wrapped her arms around me. "Okay, let's do it, but . . ."

"No buts," I said.

She pressed her finger to my lips. "Yes, one but. We sleep in our bed one last time tonight and leave in the morning."

I surrendered. "Okay, I can deal with that but. I'll go shut down the diesels."

I kissed her again and made my way back to the boat. On the walk, I dialed Hunter's number.

Stone W. Hunter was my partner, dear friend, and in many ways, the most capable member of the team. Having attended every elite military school imaginable on his way to becoming an

Air Force combat controller, he was proficient in every aspect of tactical operations, and few men understood the overall battle-field mentality as well as him. He could fly, run boats, shoot, fight, think on his feet, and survive when most people around him would not. He was the epitome of the modern warrior and my most trusted ally when the bullets started flying. He had not merely stepped into Clark's shoes; he'd leapt into them with a knife in his teeth and a grenade in each hand.

"Hey, Chase. What's up? I heard about the shootout down-town this morning."

"Evening, Hunter. Good news travels fast, I guess. Singer took out the two shooters, and the cops arrested their spotter. The chief wasn't exactly happy about us jumping into the middle of his circus, but I think he secretly appreciated the help."

"Yeah, subtlety isn't exactly Singer's M.O."

I laughed. "No, it's not, but that's not why I'm calling. Listen, I'm going away for a few months. . . ."

"A few months?" he said. "Where are you going for a few months?"

"I'm taking Penny to see her folks."

"In Vanuatu?"

"Yeah. We're taking *Aegis*. That's why I'm calling. I need someone to watch the house. Singer will look after the horses, but it would be nice to have somebody in the house while we're gone. Could I talk you into camping out over here from time to time? You know, I need someone to call a plumber if a pipe breaks. That sort of thing."

"Yeah, sure. I don't mind. When are you leaving?"

"Tomorrow morning."

"Are you serious? That's pretty short notice."

"Well, I wanted to leave tonight, but Penny talked me into sleeping in our bed one more night."

He chuckled. "No problem. I'll keep an eye on the place. But what if we get a tasking?"

"That's the other thing I wanted to talk about with you. I'm taking a break . . . a little hiatus. Penny and I need the time."

"You got it, boss. Does that leave me in command if a job comes down?"

I let out a long, slow breath. "It does. Singer and Mongo are all yours if you need them. Clark won't send you anything you can't handle. In the meantime, it goes without saying that Tina is welcome here as well."

Tina Ramirez had been a parole officer in Lubbock, Texas, before she let her tender heart lead her into making some decisions on behalf of a parolee who just happened to be Penny's mother. The job as a parole officer ended, and a relationship with Hunter began. They were practically inseparable.

"Thanks, Chase. I'll take you up on that. She's not moving here yet, but if I have my way, she will be soon."

I made similar calls to Mongo and Singer. They were supportive of my decision, and neither made any effort to talk me out of it.

Singer said, "I'm proud of you, Chase. Some temporary things are more important than others. Don't you worry about a thing. Mongo will be in Athens following Anya around like a puppy, and I'll be right here. Have you told Hunter yet?"

"I just hung up with him before calling you," I said. "He'll be the team lead while I'm gone. If you need anything, just let him know. I'll have my satellite phone, but I don't want it to ring unless the world is burning down."

The call I dreaded most lay ahead. My father had a saying about procrastination: "If you have to eat a frog, don't look at him too long. Just eat him. And if you have to eat two frogs, eat the big one first."

I saved the big frog for last.

My former partner, Clark Johnson, answered before I heard the ring. "Hola, College Boy. What's shakin'? I figured you'd have been in jail after the fiasco this morning. I assume it was the police chief who hung up on me, huh?"

"You assume correctly," I said. "He already knew more about me than you could've told him. I can't say we parted as friends, but he didn't arrest me."

"Something tells me that's not why you're calling."

I laughed. "There's that intuition of yours again. No, that's not why I'm calling. As you know, things haven't been great with Penny and me since the mission in the Gulf, so I'm going to take a little time off and work on us."

"How long?"

"At least six months," I said, a little nervous at the thought of his reaction.

"Fine. If anything comes down, I'll call Hunter."

"That's it?" I said. "You're letting me get away with 'fine'?"

"What else am I going to say? It's not like we're the White House. We don't order. We ask. If you say yes, you get the briefing and a pat on the ass. If you say no, we move on to another team. You're good, Chase, but you're not indispensable."

Chapter 6
Downriver

As expected, merciful sleep didn't take me that night. I lay awake listening to Penny's breathing and painting scenes of how the rest of my life might look. Some of the scenes terrified me, while others, mostly the ones of Penny and me under tropical sunsets, left me tugging against the spirit inside my chest—the spirit that drew me to the battlefield.

Aegis seemed to know what lay ahead and sprang from the dock with an energy I'd rarely seen from her. Penny overpacked, but it didn't matter. We had plenty of room, and she didn't pack everything she owned. That gave me hope that she hadn't spent her last night at Bonaventure Plantation.

We motored through the Saint Marys inlet and unfurled full sail once the North Atlantic welcomed us. The wind was not in our favor. Blowing from the southwest, it made a direct course to our first stop impossible. *Aegis* is a remarkable vessel, but like all sailboats, she has her limits. No boat can sail directly into the wind, but some can sail closer to the breeze than others. Sleek, racing monohulls can sometimes sail less than thirty degrees off the wind. *Aegis* could not. She was fast, but her catamaran design limited her upwind performance to forty-five degrees off the wind. This left us sailing southeast, well offshore, and leaving the coast of Florida ever farther off our starboard beam.

As we settled into our stride, Penny looked up at the Windex on top of the mast. "This wind is great if we want to land in Puerto Rico, but it's going to take a long time to get to Saint Augustine."

I studied the chart plotter. "I know, but I'd really like to have Earl give the boat a once-over before we set out across the Pacific."

I could see the mental calculations behind her eyes. "Yeah, you're right. And we can have dinner at the Columbia and maybe even go salsa dancing. It's been a while since we've had a date night."

"You're the captain," I said. "I'm just the deckhand."

She reached for me. "You're a little more than a deckhand."

We held each other as the brisk morning breeze blew through our hair. We were the only pleasure craft in sight, but a few freighters and commercial fishermen passed as the east coast grew smaller in the distance.

I scanned the horizon. "It's easy to believe the world is at peace out here."

She peered up at me with a long, thoughtful look. "Thank you for doing this for me. I know it's tough for you, and it really means a lot to me."

"I wish I could explain it," I said, "but as simple as it is in my head, I can't put it into words."

"I'm sorry for the things I said last night," she whispered. "I was upset, and I know you're not sleeping with Anya. At least you better not be. Mongo would kill you."

I stifled a laugh. "Yeah, I don't want that guy after me."

She smiled. "Seriously, though, this means the world to me that you'd walk away from all of that for six months or whatever, and just be with me."

I kissed her forehead and listened to the bows cutting through the building waves. The sound could've been hypnotic in its regular intervals of swooshes and slaps, but my mind was tormented with a million repercussions to a thousand questions.

Focusing on the wind and weather gave my brain something to do other than think about all the bad guys on Earth who wouldn't have to deal with me for the coming months. A big low-pressure weather system was moving slowly through the Tennessee Valley, so as it continued its push to the northeast, the wind off the coast of Florida would gradually turn to the west. That would allow us to sail parallel to the coastline and stay out of The Bahamas in the coming days. Subtropical wind forecasts were relatively reliable in October, so once we were south of Miami, the trip to Panama looked spectacular.

Penny broke my concentration. "Do you want to motor in or sail far enough south to tack our way in?"

I checked our course. "We settled this already. You're the captain."

She leaned against my chest. "Yeah, but you're the big, strong man."

"That doesn't make me the smart one. I'm in no hurry, so my vote would be to have a little fun with the wind and pretend like we don't have engines."

"I like the sound of that."

"What, having no engines?"

She grinned. "No, the part about you not being in a hurry."

The sixty-mile trip that should've taken five hours took almost eight, and Penny sailed our twenty-ton boat through the Saint Augustine Inlet as if it were a twelve-foot dinghy. I loved watching her at work. Her skill at the helm was just one of the thousands of things I loved about her.

I picked up the radio mic as we headed south on the Matanzas River. "Bridge of Lions, this is the sailing vessel *Aegis* requesting you open the bridge for southbound traffic."

"Is that you, Chase?" came the bridgetender's response.

"Hey, Charlie. It's good to hear your voice."

I'd befriended the bridgetender while I was a resident of the municipal marina several years before.

"It sure is good to have you home, Chase. The bridge is coming up. How long are you staying this time?"

I keyed the mic. "Just a day or two. I need to have Earl take a look at the boat before we head for the Pacific."

The horn sounded, and the drawbridge started its slow ascent into the sky as a long silence befell the radio. I keyed up. "You still there, Charlie?"

In a cautious voice, he said, "Uh, yeah, I'm still here, Chase. I guess you haven't heard about what happened to Earl."

I crushed the mic button. "No! What happened?"

"Why don't you give me a call? Do you still have my number?"

Instead of replying, I dialed my phone. "Charlie, it's Chase. What happened to Earl?"

"Somebody sank her boat. They beat her up pretty bad and left her for dead, then cut a hose in the bilge."

"Is Earl—"

"She's still alive," Charlie said, "but she lost the boat. They cut the dock lines on an incoming tide. The boat washed away from the marina and sank about half a mile downriver. She got out by some miracle, but she's in bad shape."

"Did they catch the guys who did it?"

"I haven't heard, but as far as I know, she's still in the hospital at Flagler."

"Thanks, Charlie. I'll check on her."

"You do that and let me know what you find out, will you?"

"I will. If they've got room for us, we'll be at the municipal marina."

"They've got plenty of room."

I signed off with Charlie and called the marina. He was right. They offered my choice of slips, and I chose number seven. Penny laid *Aegis* into the slip as I deployed the fenders and tied the lines.

I handed the shore power cables up to her. "Nice job, Captain. I'm going to run up to the office and check in."

She took the cables and made the connections. "Ask them about Earl while you're up there."

I returned to the boat to find Penny climbing the stairs into the main salon with her hair still wet. "Wow, that was quick. I didn't expect you back so soon."

I couldn't look away. "Yeah, I was the only one in there. The guy at the desk confirmed that Earl is in the hospital, but he didn't seem to know anything else."

She ran her fingers through her wet hair. "Boy, folks around here don't know much about what's going on, do they?"

"It's weird," I said. "Most of the time, marina people know everything that's happening."

She checked the clock on the console. "Are you going to shower before we go to the hospital?"

I gave a little self-analyzing sniff. "I think so. I'll be ready in ten minutes."

We hailed a cab on Avenida Menendez and arrived at Flagler Hospital fifteen minutes later. The lady at the information desk greeted us in an unexpectedly friendly manner. "Hey there. How are you guys this afternoon? What can I do for you?"

I smiled back. "We're fine. Thanks for asking. We'd like to see Earline . . ."

I froze, and the information lady leaned in. "Earline who?"

I turned to Penny. "Do you know Earline's last name?"

She stared at the ceiling. "I . . . I don't think I've ever heard her last name."

"Can you just look up Earline? I can't imagine there being more than one in this hospital."

The lady pecked at her keyboard with two fingers. "It's Buck. Earline Pendergrass Buck and she's in room four twelve. You can take those elevators right behind you."

I snapped my fingers. "Yep, that's it. Good ole Pendergrass Buck. Thank you, ma'am. Have a great evening."

We made it into the elevator without laughing out loud, but when the doors closed, we couldn't contain it any longer.

"Pendergrass?" Penny choked out. "I can't wait to hear that story."

I took her by the shoulders. "You've got to stop laughing. This is serious."

"Me? What about you? You're laughing just as much as I am."

"Yeah, but I'm laughing because you are."

The muted bell clanged, and the doors opened into an environment I loathe. In my life, nothing good has ever happened in a hospital. I spent days, or perhaps weeks—I choose not to re-member—in a hospital recovering from the psychological trauma of losing my parents to murderers in Panama. I'd believed Anya had died in a VA hospital in Miami. Snake was murdered in an Air Force hospital in Germany. And I'd watched my partner and closest friend Clark Johnson's career spiral down the drain at Emory Hospital in Atlanta.

The sight of the nurses' station and long corridors flanked by rooms full of patients expecting their world to improve sickened me, and instantly, my laughter ceased. The knowing look on Penny's face reminded me how much she knew about what hap-pens inside my skull.

She took my arm. "Come on. We're here to see Earl."

I let her lead me down the hall to room 412, and I tapped on the heavy oak door. No one answered, so I turned the handle and pushed inward. The door gave way without a sound, and ten feet away, I saw Earl at the End, the best diesel mechanic I'd ever met, lying helplessly amid a bevy of IV poles and machines I couldn't identify. An oxygen cannula rested beneath her nose, and she lay propped up on a mountain of pillows, mouth agape.

We crept into the room, and I reached for her hand. She was bruised and swollen almost beyond recognition. The vibrant, sassy woman I'd known for years was lost behind the wounds and implements of modern medicine.

As I slid my hand beneath hers, she wrapped her fingers around mine ever so lightly and forced one of her eyes open. Her voice came in hoarse, breathy bursts. "Is that you, Stud Muffin?"

I fought back the tears of anger and pain. "Yeah, sexy momma. It's me. I came by to see if you'd change the oil in my diesels."

The bruised flesh around her mouth quivered at her effort to smile. "I wish you would've called." She coughed and caught her breath. "I would've fixed my hair."

The crazy old woman I loved was still in there, and I sat on the edge of her bed. She rolled her head toward Penny. "Which one is that? Is it the crazy Russian or the pretty one I like?"

"It's the pretty one you like, Earl."

"Good," she breathed. "That other one would've probably tried to finish me off."

Her voice was growing clearer, and both eyes were open. "They've got me on a lot of painkillers. I'm sorry."

I squeezed her hand. "Don't be sorry, Old Girl. You look as beautiful as ever."

"Ah, that don't mean nothin' comin' from you, Baby Boy. You're blinded by your love for me, but that's understandable."

I chuckled. "Who did this to you, Earl?"

She closed her eyes, and her hand fell limp in mine.

I leaned in close to her. "Earl, tell me who did this. Did the cops catch them yet?"

She made a gurgling sound like a sink unclogging, and then wiped at her mouth with the edge of a bedsheet. "You gotta keep your nose outta this one, and the cops aren't going to find the guys."

"What are you talking about? Tell me what happened."

She cast her gaze on Penny. "Honey, would you mind shuttin' that door?"

Penny closed the door and returned to her chair without a word. Earl cleared her throat. "Get me some water, will you?"

I poured a cup of water from the Styrofoam pitcher and handed it to her. She drank the water in tiny sips as if each drop burned like acid. I was aching for her to tell me what happened, but I tried everything in my power to wait patiently.

She handed the cup back to me and pressed the button on the bedrail to raise her head. I scooted back to give her plenty of room, but she clasped my hand, not letting me move. "It was some boys who used to be like you."

"What are you talking about?" I asked, still trying to be patient.

She patted my hand. "Just listen."

I placed the cup back on the bedside table and turned to face her.

She said, "You know my husband Boomer was an Air America pilot."

"Yeah, I know he was an Agency man."

Her voice was still raspy, but she was easier to understand with every sentence. "I always hated it when they called the CIA 'The Agency.'"

"Go on," I said.

"Anyway, there's been this rumor for a lotta years that Boomer, another pilot, and a flight engineer was runnin' guns for money off the books."

She reached for the cup, and I put it in her hand. After swallowing the last of it, she said, "I want you to know it weren't true."

"I believe you," I said, "but where's this going?"

"Keep your shirt on, Baby Boy . . . or on second thought, take it off. It might do an old woman plenty good to get a look at you without it."

"Finish the story, and I'll give you a lap dance."

She laughed until it became an agonizing fit of coughs and gasps. "Thanks, Baby Boy. I needed that. Anyway, there's still a lot of folks who think maybe Boomer left a bunch of money somewhere, and I might know where it is. If there was any money, I wouldn't be livin' on that piece of crap boat, and I sure as hell wouldn't be workin' on motors at my age."

I furrowed my brow. "Are you saying some Agency guys did this to you to get at some twenty-five-year-old money your dead husband might've had? I'm not buying it."

Someone knocked sharply on the door, and a nurse stuck her head into the room. "Visiting hours are over in fifteen minutes."

Penny stood from her chair and pushed the door closed. The nurse pulled her head away just in time.

Earl said, "It don't matter if you buy it or not. That's what happened."

"Describe the guys," I said.

"One of 'em was tall and skinny with a shaved head. He looked like he just come from hookworm treatment. And the other one had a big scar runnin' through his eyebrow. It must've been two or three inches long. I put a bullet in his leg, but the skinny bald one grabbed my gun before I could get off another shot."

"When did this happen?"

"It was Friday night, about midnight. What day is it today?"

"It's Monday evening."

She screwed up her face. "Monday? How'd it get to be Monday so fast?"

"You've been through a lot," I said. "You get some rest. We'll be back to see you in the morning."

She squeezed my hand with the grip of a lifelong mechanic. "I mean it, Baby Boy. Stay out of this. If you go to pokin' your nose around where it don't belong, you're liable to get it blowed off . . . or worse."

I pulled my hand from hers. "We'll be back in the morning. Where's your son?"

"He's workin' on a cargo boat somewhere in the South China Sea or somewhere over there."

"How about Cotton?" I asked.

She looked toward the door. "He was here before you came in, but he had to get back home. His wife is having some complications from her diabetes. I guess he'll be back sometime."

"I've got his number. I'll call him. You get some rest, momma, and we'll see you in the morning."

She looked at me with pain in her deep-set eyes. "You ain't gonna leave it alone, are you?"

"You know the kind of man I am, Earl. And you knew exactly what you were doing when you gave me the description of the men who did this to you."

Chapter 7
The Good Guys

The cab ride back to the marina was an exercise in psychological isolation. I needed someplace for my mind to go without distractions. The scenario Earl had laid out was only one of the possible options for what had actually happened to her. The greatest mistake an operator can make is rushing into a fight on false pretenses. I needed more information.

"What are you going to do? Chase! What are you going to do about Earl?"

Penny's voice penetrated the veil I'd hung around me, and I shook myself from my stupor. "Huh?"

She leaned toward me. "I said, what are you going to do about Earl?"

"I don't know yet. I was just thinking about that. You said you didn't want me to work anymore, but this is Earl."

She laid her hand on my thigh. "No, that's not what I meant at all. You have to help Earl."

A degree in psychology is not a decoder ring for the mind of a woman. Penny was on the verge of leaving me because I didn't put her first ahead of everything else in my life, but now she was insistent I delay our passage to the South Pacific to help Earl.

She was right. I had no choice. Something had to be done about the men who attacked Earl and sank her boat, regardless of who or what they were.

"I'm going to make some calls first," I said. "There's too much I don't know. If these guys are spooks, or former spooks, they're not going to be easy to find. And even if I do find them, there's a huge problem."

She looked up as if she were hanging on my every word. "What's the problem?"

"I don't have any tricks they don't know. If these guys were part of Air America, they're some real cowboys, and I'm not sure I want to get tangled up with them . . . especially alone."

Penny frowned. "Okay, slow down. First, what's Air America?"

It was easy to forget Penny lived on the fringes of my world rather than down in the trenches with the rest of us. "Air America was an organization run by the CIA during the Vietnam War. They flew mostly out of Laos, and they flew the kinds of missions the Air Force and Navy couldn't afford to get caught doing. On paper, they were wholly funded by the black ops budget, but the guys who flew for them knew the truth."

She focused on me as if I were spilling the secret of life. "Yeah, so that truth. What is it?"

I stared out the window of the cab and tried to keep my voice down. "The truth *was*, they were hauling a lot more than military assets. It's likely they flew tons of heroin and other drugs all over Southeast Asia."

"Drugs? Why would the government be trafficking drugs in Southeast Asia?"

I checked the driver in the mirror. If he was listening to our conversation, there was no evidence of it. "Don't be naïve. It takes a lot of money to run an air operation of any kind, and there's not a lot of money in picking up downed pilots and hauling refugees. To keep gas in the planes and parts for the mechanics, like Earl . . . to keep them up and running took truckloads of money. Well, planeloads, actually."

Her frown persisted. "Are you saying Earl worked for the CIA?"

"I think so," I said. "Her husband, Boomer, was an Air America pilot, and she was a mechanic. I think that's where they met."

It was time for Penny to get a little nervous, and she checked the driver. "Why don't we talk about this back on the boat?"

"That's a good idea."

I looked up at our driver. "Were you working the night the boat at the marina drifted off and sank?"

He ignored me . . . or pretended to.

"Hey, driver."

He shot a look into the mirror and pulled a pair of earphones from his ears. "Yeah, I'm sorry. I was listening to a book."

"A book?" I said.

"Yeah, you know . . . an audiobook. I love to read, but this job makes it a little tough, so I listen to books now."

"Okay. Were you driving last Friday night?"

"Yeah, sure. Friday and Saturday nights are when we make our money."

"You weren't near the municipal marina around midnight by any chance, were you?"

He locked eyes with me in the mirror. "Are you talking about that thing with the lady on the boat?"

Penny squeezed my thigh, and I covered her hand. "What thing with what lady?"

"Yeah, man, it was messed up. Some guys attacked this lady on an old beat-up boat. It don't make no sense, though, man. There was like two dozen big nice boats . . . you know, the kind people with money have. Anyway, some dudes hit this chick on a POS boat and cut it loose. I heard it sank like a mile or something down the river. It was pretty messed up, man."

"No kidding?" I said. "Were you around when it happened?"

"No, man. I had a weird fare Friday night. This dude and a chick wanted me to take them to Pensacola, at first, and then they changed their mind and wanted to go to some messed-up place in Alabama. It was weird, man, but they paid me, and I did it."

He was taking us down a rabbit hole, and I had to do something to steer the conversation back to the marina. "Do you know anybody who was around when it happened?"

"No, it was just me and the couple."

I chuckled. "No, I meant, do you know anybody who was around the marina when the guys attacked that woman?"

A look of suspicion came over his face. "What, are you writing a book or something?"

Penny patted my leg. "Actually, *I'm* writing it. I'm a screenwriter, and that sort of thing makes for great TV. I'm down here doing some research."

"For real?" he said. "That's pretty cool. So, yeah, like my boy . . . he was down here Friday night when it was all going down."

"Your boy?" Penny questioned.

"Yeah, man, my boy. You know, my friend. He drives independent, and he was picking up some girls from a bachelorette party or something down here when all that shit was going down."

Penny squeezed my leg even tighter. "That's awesome, man. You think he'd talk to me about what he saw?"

The driver abandoned his use of the mirror and turned to face my wife. "Are you for real? 'Cause this is some pretty far-out stuff you're throwin' down."

Penny smiled. "Yeah, I'm for real. I'm really a screenwriter, and I'd really like to talk to your boy. And if he's got a story to tell, there's a nice little finder's fee in it for you."

She suddenly had his attention. "No shit? Like how much?"

She glanced up at me, and I stuck out one finger as if I were calling for a fastball from behind home plate.

She smiled and accepted the pitch call. "I don't know. Maybe like a grand if his story's any good."

I grunted when my wife turned my one-hundred-dollar suggestion into a thousand-dollar offer.

The driver's eyes lit up. "No, I meant the finder's fee for me."

"Yeah, I know," she said. "If your boy's story pans out, there could be a grand in it for you."

He let out a low whistle and snatched his phone from the cupholder. The next two minutes were spent in rapid-fire Spanish, which I pretended not to understand.

He ended the conversation with three words in English that even Penny recognized as the best news we'd heard all day. "Cool, man. Peace."

The driver shot a look over his shoulder. "He says he'll rap with you, but he ain't goin' on the record, and you ain't using his real name or nothing. You cool with that?"

"Oh, yeah. I don't want to drag your boy into anything. I'm just looking for a little background and some insight into what happened that night."

He pulled the cab to a stop in front of the Saint Augustine Municipal Marina and stuck a card toward us. "Here's my numbers. Hit me up anytime for a ride or whatever. I'm on twenty-four, so you don't need no other driver while you're here. Cool?"

Penny reached for the card. "Yeah, it's very cool. How about your boy's number?"

He motioned toward the card with his chin. "It's on there. He's looking for your call. And hey, don't forget about me after you talk to him."

Penny shook his hand. "Oh, we won't forget about you"—she glanced down at his card—"Jesus."

"Oh, yeah, it's fifteen eighty for the fare."

I slipped a fifty into his hand. "Thanks for everything, Jesus. We'll be in touch now that we have our own private driver."

He folded the bill into his palm. "Hey, man. Jesus loves you. Know what I'm sayin'?"

We stepped from Jesus's cab, and I entered the code into the cipher lock securing the marina.

Penny pressed her hand against the chain-link gate. "How do you suppose those guys got past this Friday night?"

I lifted a medium-sized rock from the landscaping, applied a little tension to the latch, and dropped the rock over the top. It fell on the other side and struck the exit handle, momentarily depressing it. The gate swung open into my hand.

"That's how I'd do it," I said, "but I doubt they came in this way. If I were going to hit a boat in a marina like this in the middle of the night, I'd swim in and out, or come and go by boat."

Penny laughed. "You never cease to amaze me, Chase Fulton."

Back aboard *Aegis*, Penny dialed the number inked on the back of Jesus's card, and his friend answered quickly. "Ride in style with Ricky. Where can I take you?"

"Hey, Ricky. It's Penny. Your boy Jesus gave me your number and said you might be willing to talk to me about some stuff that went down on Friday night."

"Oh, yeah, hey. Say, you ain't like no cop or nothin' like that, right?"

"No, Ricky. I ain't no cop. I'm a writer, and I'm just looking for some information about what you saw."

"Okay, cool. So, Jesus said, like, you pay for information like that, and if I take time off from driving to talk to you, I won't be getting paid, and I gotta get paid. You know?"

Penny smiled. "Everybody's gotta get paid, Ricky. Your time is valuable, and I'll take care of you. How about tomorrow morning?"

"Yeah, okay. Tomorrow morning's cool. Where and what time? I could pick you up, and we can talk while I'm driving if you've got some place to be."

She pressed the mute button and glanced up at me.

I shook my head. "Tell him to meet us at our hangar at the airport at ten."

Penny touched the mute button again. "How about this, Ricky? Meet us at the Saint Augustine Airport tomorrow morning at ten. We'll be in hangar T-eight."

"All right, cool. I'll be there. You know, man, it's the law. If I ask you face-to-face if you're a cop, you gotta tell the truth, right?"

"Cops don't pay for interviews, Ricky. They hook you up and stick you in a room and read you your rights."

"Cool, then. Tomorrow at ten."

He hung up before Penny could say goodbye.

"What do you think?" she said.

"I don't know," I admitted. "Maybe he saw something. Maybe he didn't. We'll find out."

She cocked her head. "Why didn't you want to talk to him in his cab?"

"I like to get people out of their element when I question them. He feels too much at home and in control in his cab. I want him a little bit on edge. That'll make it easier to tell if he's lying."

"Okay, whatever you say. You're the spy. I'm just the screenwriter. So, tell me more about this Air America business."

I wanted to protest and say I'm not a spy, but I let her get away with it.

"Okay, so, officially, Air America broke up in seventy-five, but there's a lot of rumors that it only shut down on paper. Air assets are valuable all over the world, especially where large quantities of anything need to be moved without attracting a lot of attention. Who's better at covertly moving things than the people who've been doing it with the government's blessing for fifteen years?"

"Good point," she said. "So, what do these rumors say about what happened after Air America was *officially* shut down?"

"A lot of people say they went to work in Central and South America moving drugs and guns and whatever else needed to be somewhere it wasn't. A lot of the guys who flew in the jungles in Southeast Asia would've been right at home in Central America. A jungle is a jungle, after all."

The look on Penny's face said she was making copious mental notes. "Was Earl's husband involved in that?"

"I don't know, and she's not going to come out and tell us. Even if it wasn't the same operation that had been Air America, it was likely a lot of the same people and airplanes. If you change the name but don't change the players, does anything really change?"

She raised her eyebrows. "I suppose not, but if Boomer and Earl were running guns and drugs in Central and South America, aren't we getting in bed with the bad guys by helping them?"

"Not everybody who runs guns is a bad guy. Do you remember Lieutenant Colonel Oliver North and the whole Iran-Contra thing and the rebels in Nicaragua?"

She smirked. "I was too young to understand anything about all that, but I remember hearing stuff about it on the news."

"Sometimes it gets pretty hard to keep track of who the good guys are. I'll put it this way. Just because Boomer and Earl were flying in Central America doesn't mean they weren't doing what they thought was right. It's really not my place to judge. Earl is my friend, and people don't get to beat the crap out of my friends, sink their boats, and leave them for dead without me squaring the score."

Chapter 8
Down We Dive

Like hundreds of mornings before, the next morning I watched the sun breach the eastern horizon as I held a cup of coffee in my hand and a thousand questions in my head. As much as I wanted to handle this one alone, I was likely already in over my head, and it was time to call in some reinforcements—if only in a support role . . . for now.

Maebelle, my second cousin—I think—answered Clark Johnson's cell phone. "Good morning, Chase. Sleeping Beauty is still snoring away. Do you want me to wake him?"

"Hey, Maebelle. I'm sorry to call so early, but I've stumbled into a bit of a mess up here in Saint Augustine, and I could use a little fatherly advice. What time do you think your narcoleptic boyfriend will come to life?"

She giggled. "Hang on a minute, and I'll get him. Heaven knows he'll go right back to sleep after you hang up."

"No, that's not nec—"

But she'd already begun the waking ceremony. Her muffled tone trickled through the phone. "Hey, sweetie, wake up. Chase is on the phone, and he's in trouble."

Less than a second passed before my former partner and current handler stuck the phone to his ear. "Chase, where are you, and what do you need?"

"Maebelle may have overstated the situation just a little. I'm not in trouble, yet, but I do need a little direction."

He cleared his throat. "Okay, so where are you, and what's up?"

"I'm in Saint Augustine, and Earl is the one who's in trouble."

"Earl? What kind of trouble could Earl be in?"

"Do you remember what she told us about her husband flying for Air America when she was with us in Saint Marys?"

I could hear him pulling on his shirt. "Yeah, sure, but I didn't think anything of it. We've all got a past. What could Air America have to do with Earl thirty years later?"

"I'm not sure yet, but a couple of guys hit her Friday night on her boat. She got off one shot and stung one of them in the leg, but she lost the fight. She thinks they were there looking for some money they think her dead husband hid from some hinky stuff after the war."

"Is she all right?"

"She will be," I said. "They did a number on her, and they sank her boat somewhere between half a mile and a mile south of the marina. She's still in the hospital, but she says there's no money. And I believe her. Why would she be living on a floating disaster area if she had any real money stashed away?"

Clark was silent for a long, uncomfortable moment. I pulled the phone away from my ear to make sure we'd not been cut off. "Clark? Are you still there?"

"Yeah, I'm here. I'm just thinking. If these guys came looking for some thirty-year-old cash, they must've had some reason to believe it was there."

"That's exactly what I was thinking, but Earl swears there's none."

He sighed. "Is it possible she just doesn't know about the money?"

The beams of the morning sun danced across the ripples of the Matanzas River as I considered Clark's question. "I hadn't thought about that, but maybe."

"You said the boat sank, right?"

I slid my sunglasses onto my face. "Yeah, it's on the bottom, as far as I know. I've not seen it yet."

He clicked his tongue against his teeth, a tell-tale sign of his brain going to work. "So, there won't be any fingerprints or blood left from the leg wound."

"No way. If it's on the bottom, there won't be any forensics."

Sounds of him brushing his teeth roared through the phone. Clark Johnson's brain works best when his body is in motion, so I didn't interrupt. A rinse and spit came next, followed by the sound of a towel leaving the bar. "Okay, I'm back. Is it safe to say it's a foregone conclusion that you're going to help her?"

"It is."

"I thought so," he said. "All of that Air America stuff was before my time, but I'll get my dad's take on it and get back with you."

"That's what I hoped you'd do. Let me know as soon as you talk to him."

His tone turned stern. "Listen to me, Chase. If these guys are former Air America, they're likely the kind who aren't accustomed to living by the rules, so stand down until we know more. Got it?"

"I'm not good at standing down, but I won't go chasing them just yet. We're talking to a cabbie later this morning who was in the area at the time of the hit. Then, I plan to go back to the hospital. I may take the RHIB down the river and try to find Earl's boat. I'd like to dive it and see what I can find."

"All of that is fine, but don't start shaking too many trees until we know what's likely to fall out."

"Okay, boss. I'll be a good little boy until you tell me I can misbehave."

"I'm serious, Chase. You don't want to mess around with these guys. There's no such thing as a former bad-ass. If they're alive, they're still dangerous. I can't sanction this mission, but it's my job to keep you alive."

"I know," I said. "But it's Earl."

"Yeah, I know, College Boy. Keep your head on straight, and we'll get some answers before lunchtime. I'll call you as soon as I talk to my dad. I'm out."

He was gone before I could tell him goodbye, but I was confident he was already dialing Dominic Fontana, his father and my former handler. Dominic was a Cold War survivor and one of the sharpest intel minds on the planet. If he didn't have the answer to what I should do next, no one would.

* * *

Penny joined me on the upper deck with a mug of coffee and her hair dancing above her head even more wildly than usual. She leaned down and kissed my cheek before settling in beside me on the settee. "Good morning. How was the sunrise?"

I took her hand in mine. "Almost as beautiful as you."

She pretended to gag. "Wow, that was cheesy, even for you."

"Hey, a guy can try, can't he?"

She rolled her eyes. "Let me guess. You've talked to Clark and Dominic already, and they're hard at work trying to figure out who the two guys could've been."

I smiled. "You're half right. I talked with Clark, and he's calling Dominic. Hopefully, we'll have some answers by lunchtime."

She sipped her coffee, and I said, "I'd like to run downriver in the RHIB and see if we can find Earl's boat."

There are a thousand reasons I love Penny Thomas Fulton, but her sense of adventure was near the top of the list. Somewhere close by on that list was her ability to be ready to go anywhere in less than ten minutes.

We lowered the Rigid Hulled Inflatable Boat into the water at *Aegis*'s stern and climbed aboard. The engine fired at the touch of the key, and we were soon headed south on the Matanzas River with the bottom machine in wide-angle scan mode.

Penny checked her watch. "Don't forget, we've got to be at the airport at ten."

"We'll make it, but I'd love to find Earl's boat first. We can always keep searching later in the day, but it'd be nice to find and mark the coordinates before we go."

Just over half a mile south of the marina, the sonar painted the perfect outline of a thirty-six-foot cruiser resting on its side in twenty-eight feet of water. I held the two buttons on the GPS that would tell the computer to calculate and mark the coordinates of the sunken vessel. From the surface, there was no way to know if it was Earl's boat, but ten minutes and a set of scuba gear would remedy that little problem.

"Take the helm. I'm going in the water."

Penny slid into the seat behind the wheel. "I have the controls."

"You have the controls," I returned.

Two minutes later, I was descending through the black water and waiting for my fins to hit the hull of Earl's former home. I missed the mark and felt the mucky bottom instead of the hard fiberglass hull of the cruiser. My torch illuminated the water a few feet in front of me, but the particulates suspended in the murky water reflected most of the light, making it appear as though I was driving in a blizzard.

After taking a compass bearing, I finned in the direction I thought I'd find Earl's boat. My guess—and that's all it was—turned out to be a lucky one. My outstretched hand struck the boat before my head, and I swam over the portside gunwale and toward the companionway below. The murky water rendered my eyes useless orbs behind my mask, and my torch did little to change that. The eerie silence between breaths made the world inside Earl's former home a lifeless void. I'd been aboard her boat when it was afloat only twice, and never below the main deck. The vessel was, I guessed, thirty-four feet in length and perhaps twelve feet in beam. Lying on the muddy bottom of the Matanzas River, it felt like a coffin.

I'll never know what I was searching for when I rolled over the side of my RHIB, but ten minutes into my tactile search, I found it behind a hinged panel that would've been invisible before the boat had warped and buckled as she sank and came to rest on the bottom. The stress on the hull flexed the molding just enough for my fingertips to feel the crease and pry the panel from its seat. With my mask only inches from my fingertips, I squinted and strained in an effort to reconcile what my fingers felt with what little my eyes could piece together. My eyes told me it was the face of an old alarm clock, but my fingers said it was the dial of a safe.

Cracking a safe in a silent room with excellent light and a stethoscope is challenging for all but the best safecrackers, but accomplishing the task in the dark, on the bottom of a river, while wearing scuba gear was something even Houdini couldn't pull off. I either needed a wrecking bar, saw, and lift bag to get the safe to the surface, or I needed the combination.

Before the water stopped dripping from my face, Penny's barrage of questions filled the air. "Did you find the boat? Is it in one piece? Can it be saved? Did you go inside? What did you find? You didn't get hurt, did you?"

"Penny, relax. I'm fine, and yes, I found it."

She rolled her eyes. "I don't know why I do that. I'm sorry. I just get excited and can't control myself. I wanted to be down there with you so badly."

I shrugged off my BCD and tank and pulled my feet from the fins. "It's cold and dark. That's how it is. Trust me. You don't want to be down there. I couldn't see six inches in front of my face, but I did find something interesting."

"What? Tell me! What did you find?"

I pulled a towel across my shoulders and patted my face dry. "I found a safe that was hidden behind a molded hatch that would've been invisible before the wreck. I only found it because the hull warped pretty badly when it hit the bottom."

Her eyes turned to saucers. "A safe? Did you open it?"

It was my turn to roll my eyes. "Really? Do you think I could crack a safe, especially down there?"

She pulled the towel from my hands and dried my hair. "I believe you can do anything, Chase."

I watched the ripples of the current dance past the hull of my boat. "I wish that were true."

"It *is* true to me. Now, you need a shower, and we have to get to the airport. I've got a date with a cabbie who thinks I'm a cop."

Chapter 9
The Interview

The muck of the Matanzas River ran off my skin like lava down the steep slope of a volcano, but I kept my shower brief so we wouldn't be late for Penny's meeting with Ricky. Jesus was waiting beside his cab with the rear door held open when we walked through the marina gate onto Avenida Menendez.

Penny slid onto the rear seat. "I guess you really are our private driver now."

"Yes, ma'am. You know it. Jesus loves you."

I followed her inside the cab and pulled my foot in just before Jesus closed the door. Seconds later, he was behind the wheel and headed north, away from the Bridge of Lions.

We arrived at the hangar just in time to see Ricky pulling up, and Jesus shot a look over his shoulder. "If you don't mind, let me holler at my boy for a minute."

"Sure," I said. "We need to check on the hangar anyway. Take your time. We'll be inside when he's ready."

I pressed the code into the cipher lock on the walk-through door and flipped on the lights. Our voices echoed through the cavernous interior of the hangar.

Penny kicked a set of hard rubber wheel chocks across the concrete floor and watched them bounce into the corner. "What are you going to do with this place?"

I stared at the overhead lights slowly coming to life and remembered the day I met Cliff Fowler and bought the hangar and his One-Eighty-Two. "I don't know. Maybe I'll give it to Skipper. Now that she has a little money, she'll probably want an airplane of her own, and this wouldn't be a bad place for it to live."

She laughed. "Yeah, I'm not sure I see Skipper moving here."

"You're probably right. I guess I'll get somebody to move all this stuff up to Bonaventure and sell the hangar."

Before she could respond, Ricky came through the door behind us. "Hey, man, I'm Ricky. Jesus says you guys are cool, but this is like, kinda weird, meeting in a hangar and all."

Penny stuck out her hand. "Hey, Ricky. I'm Penny, and this is Chase."

He shook her hand but couldn't stop looking up at me. I had been Ricky's size at some point in my adolescence, but not for long.

I offered my hand, and he shook it with reluctance still in his eyes. "Come on upstairs," I said. "We've got an office up there where it's more comfortable."

His eyes followed the wooden stairs to the elevated office. "Yeah, okay . . . whatever."

We settled in, and Penny pulled a notepad from the desk. "Okay, Ricky. I know you're a busy man, so we won't waste your time. I'm writing a collection of stories about screwed-up stuff that happens all the time that most people never hear about."

He furrowed his brow. "Really? Is that something people buy?"

She smiled. "Yeah, you might say that. People love reading about true crime. It gives them an escape from their boring lives, but I bet there's nothing boring about your life, is there?"

He glanced briefly at me and then back to the wild-haired beauty with the notepad. "Yeah, you know. I see some shit and hear a lot, too. You know how it is. Cabbies are invisible, like bartenders."

She smiled, pushed her notepad aside, and leaned in. "I like that, Ricky. That must be like being a fly on the wall. I'd kill for that kind of access into people's lives."

Penny shot her eyes toward me and then to the door in a motion so fast it would've been impossible for Ricky to notice.

I stood from my chair. "Well, I've got some stuff to do in the hangar, and none of this means anything to me, so I'll leave you guys to it."

Penny made no effort to acknowledge my departure from the room and focused instead on Ricky. I closed the door behind me and slipped into the storage closet beside the office. The wall vent between the office and closet allowed not only the closet to keep from getting musty, but it also allowed me to just make them out and listen to every word . . . almost as if I were a cabbie like Ricky.

"So," Penny continued, "how long have you been driving?"

"Ah, I don't know, man. Maybe like three years."

Although I couldn't see her, the squeaking of her chair said she was leaning in farther with every sentence that came out of his mouth. "That's cool. I'm sure you've got some great stories, but I really want to hear about last Friday night—the night the lady's boat drifted away from the marina."

He fidgeted in his chair. "Okay, yeah, sure. I was down there. I was, you know, I've been talking to this chick, Maria. She drives one of them horse-drawn carriages. I hate them things, you know, but hey, man, whatever. Anyway, I've been talking to her, and I was chillin' and messin' with her, you know. So, this couple walks up, and they want a carriage ride, and Maria took off." Ricky patted his jeans pocket. "Hey, do you mind if I smoke in here?"

"Oh, man, I wish," she said. "I'd love to have one with you, but he gets freaked out if anybody smokes in his hangar."

"No, no, it's cool. I understand."

Penny may have been a better psychologist than me. She was saying everything Ricky wanted to hear, and he was eating out of her hand.

"What happened after Maria pulled away with the couple?"

Ricky sighed. "You're sure you're not a cop? 'Cause I don't need to get into the middle of no shit with the cops. Know what I'm sayin'?"

"Yeah, Ricky, I'm no cop. I'm a writer. That's all. Like you said on the phone, if you ask me directly, I've got to tell you the truth, so I'm telling you the truth. I don't even know your last name. I just want to hear your story about what you saw. That's all. After that, you'll never hear from me again . . . unless you call me with another good story."

"Okay, yeah, I guess I believe you, then. So, here's what went down. I was sittin' on the hood of my ride, you know, just havin' a cigarette before I hit the road again. It was about time for shit to start gettin' lit down there. I make a lot of money takin' drunks back to their hotels from the old town, you know?"

"I'm sure you do. Jesus said you're an independent driver. Does that mean you drive your own car?"

"Yeah, it's my car. I worked for Mikey for a while, but he got a cut, you know, and I didn't like that. I figured, hey, I've got a nice ride. I don't need him, so I'm on my own now."

"I like that," she said. "That entrepreneurial spirit is how you get rich."

"Yeah, that's right. You know how it is. Say, how does that writing thing pay? You sell a lot of books or whatever?"

"I write for TV and movies," she said, "but I'm thinking your stories might make a good book."

"Yeah? You're thinking that?"

She leaned back in her chair. "Yeah, I'm thinking exactly that."

"Okay . . . okay. I like the sound of that. So, anyway, back to Friday night. Like I said, I was just smokin' and waitin' to get back on the road, and these two dudes . . . one of 'em was a Lurch-looking dude, like from *The Munsters* or some shit. He was like real tall like your man, but bald."

Penny slid her notepad back across the desk and put her pen to work on the page. "Don't stop now, Ricky. What did the other guy look like?"

"The other dude was normal size, you know, but he had this messed-up scar on his face, man. It was like right here, running through his eyebrow. Like somebody tried to cut his head off with a can opener or something. It was freaky looking, man."

Penny was writing almost as fast as Ricky was talking. "What did these guys do?"

Ricky cleared his throat. "That's the part that made me look at 'em. They didn't look like the guys who come and go out of the marina, you know? They had on cargo pants and long-sleeved shirts. It wasn't even cold or nothin'. It was like seventy degrees or whatever, and they were wearing hiking boots. I know, 'cause I'm big-time into kicks. Check out these Timberlands." Ricky's boot landed on the corner of the desk.

Penny said, "Nice. You gotta look good, right?"

"That's right. You know what it's like. So, the other thing that made me look was that these guys didn't push no code into the lock. They just walked through it like they was all 'open sesame' or some shit. I know that gate was locked 'cause it's always locked. It closes like *bam!* every time somebody comes out of it, and them boat people are all like, 'Damn, I gotta put that code in again.'"

"And these two guys just walked through it like it was nothing? Is that what you're saying?"

"Yeah, like they had a magic key or whatever. Then maybe three or four minutes later, I heard a gunshot. I know what a gunshot sounds like. This was like a thirty-eight, maybe. It wasn't nothin' big like a forty-five or nothin' like that. The horses heard it, too, man, 'cause they jumped. But nobody did nothin'. It was like loud and stuff with the bands playing and people partying, but it was loud enough for me and the horses to hear."

"What did you do then? Why didn't you call the cops?"

"Hey, man. I ain't no snitch. I ain't callin' no cops for nothin'. It ain't none of my business, but I was curious, you know."

"Of course you were curious. You've been on the street long enough to know when something isn't right."

"Yeah, that's right," he said. "I knew there was something going down, but I couldn't really see out on the docks. There's a lot of boats out there. That's when these three chicks hit me up for a ride and I had to go. They wanted me to take them to the B and B. It was just like eight or nine blocks down, but hey, they were fine, so I said, 'Get in, ladies.'"

"Is that all you saw, Ricky? I was really hoping for more than that."

"Woah. Hang on, lady. My story ain't over. I took them girls down the street and dropped them off at the B and B. That's when I seen a boat drifting down the river with no lights or nothin'. I headed back up Menendez, and them two same dudes came out of the marina, but they wasn't comin' out of the gate. They was crawling around the end of the fence up on the bank, and the Lurch-looking dude was hangin' on to the other dude's belt like he was helping him walk, or like draggin' him. They got in this jeep that was parked off the street, like up behind the sidewalk, like they was some kind of police or something, but these guys weren't no cops. I don't know how they didn't get towed. Man, they tow everybody down there for parking like a jackass."

Penny was still writing furiously. "Ricky, you didn't get a tag number, did you?"

"No, man. That's the weird part. There weren't no tag on the jeep, but it was like dark blue or black, maybe. It was late, but there was some light on the street. It had these big four-by-four tires on it."

"What else did you see?"

"That was it, man. They turned out on King Street, and they was gone, man."

"Who do you think they were?"

He scoffed. "How should I know? Just some freaky-looking white dudes is all I know. They were messin' with the wrong dude, though, whoever they were. The way that tall dude was draggin' that little one, I figure he got shot in the leg or something. Whatever it was, I figure it was taken care of, and I didn't think nothin' else of it 'til my boy Jesus called."

Penny laid the pen on the desk. "That's a great start, Ricky. Thanks a lot."

"Hey, man, you said I'd get paid. I got bills, and I had to take time out of driving to come all the way up here."

"Relax, Ricky. You're getting paid."

Penny slid an envelope across the desk. "There you go. A thousand bucks, just like I promised."

"I guess you ain't no cop after all. Pleasure doin' business with you, lady. I'll call you when something else happens that you might like . . . if you got more cash."

"I'm not from here, but you can call anyway if you've got something good. It'll have to be better than this, though. You've given me a place to start, but not much else."

He shook the envelope. "Hey, I gave you a thousand dollars' worth. You got any more of these envelopes back there?"

That was my cue. I opened the office door just in time to see Ricky pushing himself out of the chair.

I said, "I'm sorry to interrupt, but I just found a snake downstairs. I'm going to put a bullet in his head, and I didn't want to scare you. You know how much I love putting bullets in snakes' heads."

Ricky froze, and Penny grinned. "No, we just finished up, and Ricky was leaving. Thanks for letting me know, though. It would've scared me to death if you'd have shot the snake without telling me. Is it poisonous?"

I stepped into the office and put my hand on Ricky's shoulder. "No, I don't think it's poisonous. I think it's harmless but wanted me to think it was dangerous. It probably would've tried to scare you, too. The snakes who try to scare my wife are my favorite kind to kill."

Ricky slithered away, and Penny barely contained her laughter long enough for him to get down the stairs.

Chapter 10
Don't I Know It

Jesus deposited us at Flagler Hospital ten minutes later, and we left him another nice tip to keep him at our beck and call.

We found Earl out of bed and standing at the window. Seeing her in a hospital gown instead of greasy shorts and flip-flops felt strange. "Hey, Old Girl. It looks like you're feeling better."

She turned from the window, revealing the fact that she'd put her gown on backward and failed to tie it. Modesty had never been one of Earl's qualities, but the gaping gown was more than either of us wanted to see.

I looked away, trying not to laugh. "You're going to have to do something with that gown, Earl."

She glanced down and gathered the thin cotton fabric around herself. "Aww, come on, Stud Muffin. You know you like it, and little Miss Whistle Britches there is just jealous."

Penny couldn't stop laughing. "You've got me, Earl. I'll never be able to compete."

"As good as it looks, you're wearing the gown backwards," I said, still diverting my eyes.

Earl huffed. "I know, but when I wear it the other way, I can't reach around to get it tied. This way, I can flash you and go to the pot without throwing out my shoulder trying to reach the ties."

We pushed the door closed behind us and settled into a pair of vinyl-covered chairs by the window. "We found your boat."

Earl's eyes lit up. "You did?"

"Yeah, we did, but I'm afraid that's the end of the good news. She's on her starboard side in about thirty feet of water. I marked the coordinates, but I didn't float a buoy. It's deep enough to not be a hazard to navigation, but it's going to have to come up."

She swallowed hard. "It's not just a boat, you know. It's my home. It's all I've got. Or I guess, now, it's all I *had*."

I didn't like myself for what I was about to do, but it had to be done. "What's in the safe, Earl?"

To my surprise, she never changed expressions. "What safe?"

"The safe on your boat," I said.

"There ain't no safe on my boat."

I slid forward in my chair and leaned in close to my old friend. "I found the safe, Earl. I want to help you, but I have to know the truth."

"I ain't never lied to you, and I ain't never owned no safe."

Nothing about her expression said she was hiding anything. She showed none of the tell-tale signs—no fidgeting, pupil dilation, sweating, or refusal to make eye contact. Earl was telling the truth.

"When I dived on your boat this morning, I swam down the companionway and ran my hand along the molding to keep from getting disoriented. When the boat hit the bottom, I think she hit on the starboard stern, and she must've hit pretty hard. She's twisted and badly warped."

She cast her eyes to the floor. "So, even if we get her back up, she's a loss."

I lifted the edge of her gown and re-covered her leg. "Yes, the boat's a loss, but that's not where I'm going with this."

"Then stop telling about the flight and land the plane."

I tried not to laugh. "Fine. When your boat hit the bottom, she hit hard enough to tear the molding down and warp the woodwork. I found a panel and pried it open. Behind it was the dial of a safe."

She wrinkled her forehead. "You must be mistaken. I've got a strongbox with a padlock on it with Sonny's birth certificate and some papers in it, but I've never had a safe. Are you sure it was my boat?"

"Yeah, I'm sure," I said. "I need to know if you and Boomer owned that boat before he died."

"Well, yeah, Boomer had it built in Cartagena about a year before he died."

Penny's eyes had been darting back and forth between Earl and me as if she were watching a tennis match. "Are safes water-proof?"

Before I could answer, Earl said, "Some of 'em are, but mostly no."

Penny licked her lips. "Chase, we've got to get that safe out of the water."

I turned back to Earl. "When are you getting out of here?"

She shrugged. "I don't know, but I ain't got nowhere to go when I do get out. My house is busted up on the bottom of the river . . . in case you forgot."

I winked at Penny. "I think we'll get Jesus to take you home."

Earl's eyes became giant orbs. "Woah! Hey! You're getting ahead of yourself. I'm all for prayin' and Heaven and stuff, but I'm a long way from the pearly gates."

I laughed. "Relax. Jesus is sort of our personal driver. We'll get him to take you to Bonaventure while we sort all of this out. I'm starting to think there's a lot more to this whole thing than we know."

"Chase, I can't let you do that. I'll find a place."

"You've got a place," I said. "You'll be safe and comfortable at Bonaventure. If these guys figure out you're not dead, they'll try again, and I'm not willing to let that happen."

"I can go to Cotton's place down in New Smyrna Beach," she argued.

Penny stood. "That'll just put your brother in danger, and you don't want that, do you?"

Back to the floor went Earl's eyes. "I guess you're right. I don't know what I'd do without you two. I'm so glad you didn't marry that Russian one. She's trouble."

My wife threw her arms around my old friend. "Don't I know it?"

* * *

As soon as Penny and I were back aboard Aegis, my phone chirped. "This is Chase."

"Chase, it's Dominic. Clark says you've gotten yourself wrapped up with some old Air America guys."

I pulled the door closed and settled onto a settee. "I don't know for sure yet, but it looks that way. Two guys hit Earl's boat last Friday night. She got off a shot and hit one of them in the leg. We've corroborated the story with an eyewitness."

"What did the hitters want?" he asked.

"Apparently, they think Earl's husband, Boomer, had some cash stashed from when he was flying in South America after the war."

Dominic made a grunting sound I didn't like.

"What does that noise mean?"

"Uh, Chase, I'm going to read you in on some old intel, and you may want to take some notes."

I pulled a pad and pen from the chart table. "Let's hear it."

He cleared his throat. "Earl's husband was with Air America, and so was she. She was one of the first female Marine crew chiefs on the Sikorsky H-thirty-four Seahorse. She got booted out of the Corps for beating the hell out of a twenty-one-year-old second lieutenant for crashing *her* helicopter. The poor guy survived the crash, only to have a female corporal break his jaw. Needless to say, the Corps decided they didn't need Earl in the jungles of Southeast Asia anymore."

"Earl was a Marine?"

"Come on, Chase. You know there's no such thing as a *former* Marine. Earl is a Marine. Anyway, when they sent her packing, she ended up in Laos, turning wrenches for Air America. That's where she met Boomer."

I stood from the settee. "Hang on a minute, Dominic. This is all a little too much for me. I'm going to need a drink."

"You might want to make it a double. We've not even gotten to the good part yet."

I poured a cocktail, covered the mouthpiece of my phone with my palm, and whispered to Penny, "Earl was a Marine in Vietnam."

Her reaction was nearly identical to mine.

"Okay, Dominic. I'm back."

"Where were we?"

I said, "Kicked out of the Corps, went to work for Air America, met Boomer."

"Oh, yeah. So, Boomer was an Air Force bomber pilot in Korea, and he never really found his way when the war was over. He got in some trouble, and when Vietnam kicked off, he didn't qualify to put the flight suit back on with 'Air Force' written across the patch. Those were exactly the guys Air America wanted. They were wildcards, completely fearless, and most of them didn't care if they lived or died."

I'd given up trying to take notes. "Okay, so Earl met Boomer in Laos, and they stayed together after the war. Is that right?"

"Keep your pants on, kid. I'm getting there. When Air America was officially shut down, most of the aircrews I knew headed for another jungle, but this time, it was in the western hemisphere. They ran everything from guns to drugs to boxed lunches for school kids."

I cut in. "This is pretty interesting stuff, but I'd like to get to the part about why two guys would be trying to kill Earl twenty-five years after Boomer died."

"I told you, I'm getting there. Just listen. A lot of those guys were skimming and building their own little nest eggs. Ten grand here, six grand there, and pretty soon, it starts to add up. The rumor was that Boomer had been doing the nesting for a few guys. He apparently had some scheme to get the cash back to the States, and three or four other pilots were giving him a cut of their stash for him to get their pesos back to the north side of the equator."

"So, that's what this is about," I said.

"Slow down," he said. "It's not that simple. The story goes that he was holding over a million bucks—and that was a lot of money in seventy-eight. He was supposed to be on a milk run—some kind of a humanitarian thing into Costa Rica in a Curtiss C-Forty-Six—when he took off and never came back. They never found the plane, the crew, nothing. He just vanished."

"How could he just disappear in a plane that big?"

"That's a big jungle down there. It happens all the time."

"So, you're saying the other pilots thought he made off with their cash, and poof, he was just gone?"

"Yeah, something like that."

I scratched my head. "But why would they wait a quarter of a century to come after Earl and try to get their money back?"

"Beats me, but you need to know what you're up against. These guys have probably been in the mercenary game for that quarter century, and they've probably learned some nasty tricks. They're not spring chickens anymore, but they're dangerous, Chase. Remember what Richter told you. Old guys get old by being smarter than everybody around them."

"So, what am I supposed to do now?"

"Hell, I don't know. I'm just a retiree who your handler recruited to give you a history lesson. You'll have to take that one up with your boss."

"And my boss just happens to be your son, right?"

"How should I know? I'm just an old man."

The line went dead, and I turned to Penny.

She raised her eyebrows. "Well? What did he say?"

"You wouldn't believe me if I told you, but it's time to call in the cavalry."

Before I could push the button to call Clark, he called me. "Hey, College Boy, sounds like you're gonna need some help. We can't sanction it, so you're footing the bill, but tell me what you need, and I'll help you put it together."

"Lawyers, guns, and money might be a good start."

He chuckled. "Well, guns we can do, and you've got plenty of money, so, two out of three ain't bad."

My next call was to the one person I knew who could get that safe out of Earl's boat, even if he had to tear it out with his bare hands. "Hey, Mongo. It's Chase. I need your help, but don't bring Anya."

As badly as I needed some muscle on the job, I definitely didn't need the drama of Anya Burinkova after what happened in Panama City.

My third call was answered on the first ring. "Hunter here."

My partner, Stone Hunter, former Air Force combat controller and the most fearless man I knew, would wade through

Hell with me and never ask why. Other than Clark Johnson, prior to his injuries, there wasn't a man on the planet I trusted as much as Hunter.

I said, "I know you won't believe this, but I've gotten myself into a little trouble, and I could use a hand in Saint Augustine."

"Five-five-six trouble or seven-six-two trouble?"

Weighing my situation on the scale of combat rifle ammo, Hunter left little doubt he was already packing his gear.

"I'm afraid this may be fifty-caliber trouble."

He said, "I'll be there in an hour."

Chapter 11
Nothing More Important

Hunter arrived well within the promised hour, and although he never needed approval, he stood beside *Aegis* on the floating dock and yelled, "Permission to come aboard?"

Penny stuck her head through the door to the cockpit. "You know better than that. Get up here."

Hunter slipped off his boots and stepped aboard. "Chase said there was trouble, and I don't step aboard boats without permission when the owners may be on edge. I've seen him shoot, and I don't want to be on the receiving end of anything he sends downrange."

He and Penny came into the main salon, and I handed out cocktails. "Thanks for coming. I've got a lot to tell you."

He took the tumbler from my hand. "Clark briefed me on the ride down, but I do have a few questions."

"I should've known," I said. "Let's hear the questions."

He stared into the tumbler. "What is this? It's really good."

"It's Jack Daniels and sweet tea, believe it or not."

He scoffed. "How about that? I'm digging it. Anyway, Clark said there's a safe. Have you got it open yet?"

I motioned downstream with my chin. "It's still on the bottom in Earl's boat, half a mile south of here. I don't have the tools to cut it out of the boat, but Mongo's on his way."

Hunter chuckled. "Who needs tools when you've got Mongo?"

"My thought, exactly. I assume he can dive, but I've never thought to ask."

Hunter took another sip. "This is *really* good. If he can't dive, you can teach him, but I don't know where we'll find gear big enough to fit him."

"We'll figure it out," I said. "What's the next question?"

"Are you sure these guys are former Air America pilots? And if so, what have they been doing since that well dried up?"

I took a sip and had to agree with my partner. Penny's Jack and tea was quickly becoming my new favorite. "No, I'm not certain of anything except that somebody tried to kill Earl. The few things I do know lead me to believe these guys are former flying mercenaries, but I don't have names or anything yet."

He raised his glass. "If they've ever been on Uncle Sam's payroll, I'll bet Skipper can figure out who they are."

Instead of responding, I pulled out my phone. Skipper was way ahead of me. "Hey, Chase. I thought you'd be calling soon. Clark already has me on the task, but it's not like we're searching for former IRS agents or meter maids. This one's going to take a while."

"What's a while?" I asked.

"Maybe twenty-four hours, but hopefully sooner. I talked to Ginger, and she gave me some places to start. She'll be here in an hour or so, and two analysts are better than one."

Ginger was a former CIA intelligence analyst turned freelancer. The agency I worked for kept her busy most of the time, but her greatest gift to me had been the year she spent teaching my little sister almost everything she knew about running the analysis side of operations.

Skipper had learned well and quickly. As hard-hitting and deadly as my band of operators was, none of us doubted that Skipper was the most valuable member of the team. Shooters are a dime a dozen, but great analysts are worth their weight in gold. Skipper, at just over a hundred twenty pounds, was worth Mongo's weight in gold.

"Thanks, Skipper. Keep me posted."

"I'll call as soon as we have anything worth sharing. If you learn anything you don't think I know, send it up the chain. Oh, and how's Earl?"

"She's going to be okay," I said. "They'll most likely let her out of the hospital today or tomorrow. I'm sending her up to Bonaventure until we sort this whole thing out."

"Do I need to go down and stay with her?"

I considered her question. "That might not be a bad idea. I'd like to have somebody there to make sure she's okay. I'll let you know."

"All right. I've got to get back to work now. See ya."

She hung up before I could say another word, and Penny looked up. "What might be a good idea?"

I enjoyed another sip. "Skipper asked if she should come down to Bonaventure to stay with Earl, and I'm thinking that might be a good plan. I don't like Earl being there alone."

"Singer will be around," she said.

"Yeah, but there's no way to know when he'll disappear to the monastery, and it's possible we'll need him down here."

"You don't need me," she said.

"Of course I need you."

"No, I don't mean in general. I mean, you don't need me here while all of this is going on. I can take Earl back to Saint Marys and stay with her until you get this whole mess cleaned up."

I glanced at my partner, and he shrugged. "It's not a bad idea, boss. If this thing gets as ugly as you and Clark expect, I don't think you'll want Penny anywhere near it."

Penny met my gaze. "I don't bring anything to the equation except liability, Chase. I'll take Earl back to Bonaventure when they release her from the hospital. Jesus can drive us."

She and Hunter were right. I didn't want my wife anywhere near the train wreck that was about to happen in St. Augustine.

I stared at the deck. "Okay. I think that's best for now."

Hunter broke the uncomfortable moment. "So, what do you think is in the safe?"

I drained my glass. "If Boomer was skimming and stashing, I'd say there's likely a million bucks or more in there."

Hunter let his gaze drift outside. "How long has the boat been down?"

"Five days."

He pursed his lips. "Hmm. A million bucks in cash takes up a lot of space, even if it's in hundreds, and five days underwater in a safe that surely isn't watertight is going to do a lot of damage to paper money."

"We've got to get that safe back to the surface," I said.

Hunter nodded. "Yeah, and we've got to do it before those two dudes beat us to it."

I let my head fall backward. "I didn't even consider that, but you're right. If they think the stash is still on the boat, they'll definitely be back."

Penny spoke up. "But why would they sink the boat if they think the cash is still there? That doesn't make sense."

"Desperate people rarely do what makes sense," I said. "We have to go back in the water as soon as Mongo gets here."

"I didn't mean to butt in," Penny said, "and I know that isn't my thing, but it sounds like you're not sure who or what you're up against. This morning you were concerned about these guys being some bad-ass mercenaries, and now you think they're desperate."

She was right, but that didn't mean I was wrong.

"It's possible, and even likely, that they're both. Mercenaries run out of money and job prospects and get desperate. I can't think of any other reason why they'd come looking for the money all these years later."

Penny wrinkled her forehead. "But wouldn't they get paid like you guys? I mean, a million bucks is a lot of money, but we're doing okay. And in forty years, I don't think you'll be attacking old women and sinking boats over a million bucks."

I set my tumbler aside. "Actually, we're the exception. Most people who do what we do never make the kind of money we've made. We've been incredibly lucky to have stumbled into good work that's paid exceptionally well. Most shooters make a few hundred bucks a day when they're working, and nothing when they're not."

"Chase is right," Hunter said. "You paid me more for the oil rig job than I figured I'd make in my whole life."

Penny bit her lip. "So, you're saying you're up against at least two guys who have ten times your experience, and they're desperate?"

I looked at Hunter, and he looked away. "Yeah, that's what I'm saying."

"Are you scared?" she said, barely above a whisper.

I didn't hesitate. "No, it isn't fear. They hurt Earl and destroyed her home. They have to pay for that."

"Is that what you're doing? Making them pay?"

"No, not just making them pay. I'm protecting Earl. If we let those guys, whoever they are, get away with this, they'll try again. And I can't let that happen."

She frowned. "You know what they say about the man who sets off on a mission of revenge. . . ."

I sighed. "Yes, he's supposed to dig two graves. And that's exactly how many we'll need if the two guys who attacked Earl put up a fight."

Without another word, Penny disappeared down the stairs to our cabin.

Hunter watched her go. "Is she okay?"

"I don't think so. She's in over her head, and I don't know how to keep her afloat."

My partner leaned toward me. "I know it's too late now, but what we do isn't exactly what you'd call a marriage-friendly profession."

I glanced down the stairs. "You're right about that, but what am I supposed to do about it now?"

He threw up his hands. "Hey, I'm not your priest. That's Singer's job. I'm just here to keep you alive."

"What about the money?"

"What about it?" he asked.

"Doesn't it make you want to quit?"

He gave a long pause. "I believed it would at first, but the more I think about it, the more it makes me want to do the things we do for people who need our help but could never pay for it. I know that sounds corny and all A-Team, but the money takes the pressure off to some degree. Does that make sense?"

I leaned back against the cushions of the settee. "It makes perfect sense, and I feel the same way. But when I was recruited into this crazy game, they sold me the whole bit about preserving freedom and democracy, and I bought it. I still buy it. Our country does some stupid stuff sometimes, but it's the best system there is, and it's worth fighting for. Like you said, it sounds corny, but I believe it's what I—what *we*—do. I'm with you about helping people who need us and can't pay, but there are going to be times when Uncle Sam dials my number, and I can't see myself ever sending that call to voicemail."

He smiled. "I guess that makes us a couple of Yankee-Doodle dandies, huh?"

"It's funny you say that. The old guys who recruited me called me a Yankee-Doodle bad-ass, just like my father. And to be honest, I think that may have been the line that made me bite."

"Hook, line, and sinker. That's how I took the bait. I wanted to be a pilot, but when the Air Force dangled pararescue in front of me and told me I'd be pulling pilots out of the crap they got themselves into, and that nobody was more important to the mission than the guys brave enough—and maybe stupid enough —to jump into hell to bring downed pilots home, that's all it took. I couldn't wait to save the world, one downed pilot at a time, but it didn't quite work out like I'd planned. It turned out that eighteen-year-old Stone Hunter couldn't stand the sight of blood and guts, so I ended up being a combat controller. Instead of bringing pilots home, I called them into battlefields all over the world and learned I was a lot better at making other people bleed than patching up Americans with holes in them."

I gave my partner's boot a kick. "The roads that brought us here aren't even on the same planet, but I'm glad they ultimately ran together."

"Me, too, partner. Now, what's the plan?"

"The plan is to put Mongo in the water the second he hits the dock. Right now, there's nothing more important than getting a look inside that safe."

He shot a look over his shoulder and down the stairs. "Are you sure about that?"

Chapter 12
Nothing to It

The courtesy and caution Hunter had shown by asking permission to come aboard was not repeated by Clark and Mongo. I don't know how much Mongo weighed, primarily because scales for men his size only exist at the stockyard, but his heft was enough to feel *Aegis* sway ever so slightly when he stepped aboard.

I assumed the responsibility of greeter and stuck my head through the doorway. "Permission granted. Come aboard."

"Oh, yeah. I always forget that part," Clark said.

"How was the trip?" I asked.

"The departure sucked," Mongo said, "but the trip wasn't bad. I caught a charter on a Pilatus, so it was a nice ride."

I frowned. "What was wrong with the departure?"

Ducking through the doorway that easily accommodated my six-foot-four-inch frame, he said, "I live with a former Russian spy who thrives on any opportunity to put her impressive skill set to work. Convincing her to stay home isn't the easiest task on Earth."

I glanced down the stairs to where Penny had yet to emerge. "This would not have been the best time for Anya to be on-scene."

He shrugged his mountain-sized shoulders, and Clark broke the tension. "I know you have a plan, so let's hear it."

"I have the makings of a plan," I admitted. "Step one is getting that safe out of Earl's boat."

Mongo grinned. "Let me guess. That's where I come in."

"Imagine that. You showing up just in time to break something."

"There's just one little chink in my armor," he said. "I'm not a diver. I took a Discover Scuba Diving class fifteen years ago but never got certified. I can get the safe out of the boat, but you guys are either going to have to bring the boat to me"—he pointed toward the surface of the river—"or teach me how to stay alive down there."

Clark sized up our resident one-man wrecking crew. "This is shaping up to be a case of taking Mohammed to the mountain, except our Mohammed is a Mongo, and he *is* the mountain. You got any gear that'll fit him?"

Penny finally emerged from below and hugged the new arrivals. "Hey, guys. It's great to see you. Chase is sending me back to Bonaventure, so I won't be in your way. Where's Anya?"

Mongo shot a look at me. "You're never in the way, and Anya isn't coming."

Penny gave me the first semi-approving look of the afternoon.

I nodded. "We're going to do a little dive refresher for Mongo up by the beach at the bridge. You're welcome to come. If you wouldn't mind, I could also really use your help on the RHIB when we retrieve the safe."

She actually allowed a smile to form. "Sure, I'd like that."

We pulled every piece of dive gear from the locker and cobbled a buoyancy compensator together with a couple of strap extensions that almost fit Mongo.

Penny ran us upriver until we'd reached the beach just south of the Usina Bridge.

I dropped the anchor in ten feet of water just off the shore. "This looks like the perfect spot. There's no current, and the visibility is great."

Clark sat opposite Mongo on the starboard tube of the RHIB and demonstrated how to set up the dive gear. "Remember, if the air is on your right, you're all right. Always bring the regulators across your right shoulder. Make sure the tank valve is clear and that the O-ring is in place."

Mongo followed his instruction and never missed a step as Clark continued the class. "Hold the pressure gauge away from your face in case it blows up when you pressurize it. I've never seen one blow up, but that doesn't mean it can't happen. Now, slowly open the valve and check the pressure."

Mongo turned the console over in his hand, making the gauges look like a child's toy. "Three thousand pounds."

Clark checked his. "Good. Me, too." He then slung the BC onto his back and looked up at me. "If you want to continue with the entry procedure, mask, and regulator skills, I'll check the area."

Before I could answer, Clark stuck a regulator in his mouth and rolled over the side.

I tossed a mask to Mongo and showed him how to adjust the strap. "You want it snug, but not tight. Believe it or not, the tighter it is, the more likely it is to leak. I wear mine just tight enough to keep from floating off. Once we're underwater, the surrounding pressure will hold your mask in place."

Mongo adjusted the strap and found the fit he liked.

I held up my regulator. "As you remember from the DSD class, you just stick this in your mouth and breathe normally. Take nice, slow, relaxed breaths. Go ahead. Give it a try."

He stuck the reg in his mouth. "Nothing to it," he grunted through the regulator.

At least I think that's what he said.

"Okay, it's time to get in the water. We won't roll in like Clark this time. We'll slide in over the side with our BCs fully inflated, masks on, and regulators in. When you get in the water, continue to breathe normally, and hold on to the line on the RHIB. Got it?"

He pulled the reg from his mouth. "Got it. Let's go."

I kicked a pair of fins toward him and slipped mine onto my booties. "The water's a little chilly, but I don't have a wetsuit big enough for you. If you get too cold, let me know."

He slid over the side. I followed him into the water and flashed him the okay signal. He returned the sign, and we swam on our backs toward the beach until we reached water shallow enough to stand.

"Here's where the rubber meets the road. I want you to keep your regulator in your mouth and lean forward until your face is completely underwater. Continue to breathe normally. I'm going to kneel on the bottom in front of you and watch you breathe, okay?"

He flashed the okay signal again, and I descended to my knees. Reaching the sandy bottom, I looked up to see him doing exactly as I'd instructed.

A minute later, I returned to the surface. "How did that feel?"

He spat out the regulator. "Fine."

"Good. Now we're going to clear our masks. Do you remember how to do that?"

"Yeah. Breathe in through my mouth, look up, exhale through my nose."

"That's it," I said. "We'll flood the mask by breaking the seal at the top with our finger and letting a little water in. I'll demo it first if you want."

As we floated in the shallow water, the man who I believed feared nothing, turned pale and narrowed his eyes.

"Is everything okay?"

He licked his lips and looked past me. "Yeah, I'm okay, but this is the part that freaked me out a little. To be honest, this is why I didn't get certified years ago."

It's difficult to imagine someone of Mongo's size, strength, and fortitude being uncomfortable flooding a dive mask. "I understand. It's a little unnerving to have your eyes and nose flooded with water, but it happens when we dive. Masks get kicked by other divers, and water comes rushing in, and most masks leak for various reasons. That's why it's critical to master this skill here in the controlled environment of the shallows. Once we get you through it, you'll be amazed at how simple the task is. It's just a matter of learning the mechanical skill and overcoming the psychology of a flooded mask."

The look on his face said my pep talk didn't ease his trepidation, so I said, "A flooded mask is uncomfortable at first, but it's far from an emergency. We can breathe perfectly fine with our mask completely full of water. Watch."

I stuck my regulator in my mouth, descended below the surface, and intentionally filled my mask with water. Returning to the surface, I demonstrated breathing normally through the regulator with my eyes and nose completely engulfed with brackish water. I continued the demonstration for well over sixty seconds before pulling my mask from my face and allowing the water to drain. "See? Breathing with a mask full of water is no big deal. You simply have to remember to only inhale through your regulator and not your nose. We're going to turn you into a mouth breather."

He let out a nervous chuckle. "Whatever you say. Let's give it a try. I'll watch you clear your mask, and then I'll give it a shot."

We descended to the bottom, and I once again gave the hand signal asking if he was okay. He flashed his in return to let me know he was doing fine.

While kneeling only feet in front of him, I broke the top seal and allowed an inch of water to flow into my mask. I continued to breathe normally with the small amount of water covering my nose. Finally, after I believed I'd adequately demonstrated the technique of breathing with water in my mask, I looked up, took a full breath from my regulator, pressed the top of my mask to my forehead, and exhaled through my nose. The result was as predicted. The exhaled air from my nose filled the dive mask, forcing out the water. Mongo watched as if his life depended on the technique.

I demonstrated the skill again, but the second time I allowed my mask to flood completely. Although I couldn't see the details of his expression through my diminished vision behind the wall of water, it was clear he didn't like what I was about to ask him to do. Once I'd cleared the mask, I motioned upward, and we ascended back to the surface.

"See, there's nothing to it. Just don't panic, and don't stop breathing. As long as the regulator is in your mouth, you have plenty of air strapped to your back. I'll never be more than two feet away. If it goes south, I'll bring you to the top immediately."

He nodded, with an edge of hesitancy still on his face. "Okay. Let's go."

We descended back to the bottom with the surface of the water less than three feet above our heads. I demonstrated the flood-and-clear technique one more time, and then motioned for him to try. I leaned forward and took his inflator in my hand in case the next few seconds turned into a race for the surface.

He pressed his hot dog–sized index finger against the skirt at the top of his mask, and water slowly trickled into the space behind the plastic lens. His breathing rate doubled, and his eyes widened, so I nodded in an attempt to reassure him. When the water rose above the tip of his nose, flooding his nostrils, the giant lunged for the surface, shoving the mask onto the top of his head as he went.

Seeing Mongo panic in response to a cup of water in his nose sent a pair of diametrically opposed thoughts rushing through my head. First, I found the tiniest bit of humor in the situation because of his typical fearless personality. Second, if I couldn't teach him to clear his mask, I'd be left with Hunter and a pair of crowbars to retrieve the safe from Earl's sunken boat.

"I'm sorry. I didn't mean to freak out." The big man sputtered and snorted water from his nose. "But that's not easy."

"It's okay. You're not alone. A lot of people struggle with clearing their masks. We'll keep at it until you get it."

He glanced over his shoulder at the sun, which was well beyond its zenith and headed for the horizon. "We're running out of daylight."

I helped him pull his mask back into place. "Don't worry. You'll get it."

We wrestled through three more panicked explosions for the surface before he was finally able to tolerate a tablespoon of water in his nose and successfully clear a partially flooded mask.

Back on the surface, I said, "You're doing great, but now we have to completely flood the mask and clear it. The task is identical to the partial clear, except it requires more air. If you have to take a second breath through your regulator to get enough air in your lungs to clear the mask, that's fine. But remember . . . never stop breathing."

It was getting easier, but Mongo never looked like a seasoned diver. He could awkwardly clear his mask without panicking, but he was still a long way from becoming a combat diver.

The remainder of the essential underwater skills came easily for him. He recovered, replaced, and cleared a lost regulator as if it were child's play, and even mastered finning in minutes. To see three hundred pounds moving gracefully underwater was quite an unexpected surprise.

Clark rejoined us as I was teaching the importance of ascending slowly to avoid the bends.

My former partner grabbed my BC and gave me a shake. "Yeah, Mongo, you should've seen this poor sap down in Panama. He got the worst case of the bends I've ever seen and ended up in the recompression chamber. If you get bent, you're screwed. There's not a chamber on Earth big enough to fit your enormous butt. Don't stay down too long, and don't come up too fast, and you'll be just fine."

Satisfied our giant could safely get to the wreck, break the safe free of the crippled boat, and return to the surface, I declared our training session over.

Penny motored us back to *Aegis*, where we refilled our tanks from the onboard compressor and ran through the function of the gear one last time with Mongo.

He said, "I feel good about everything except clearing the mask. I can do it, but I don't like it."

"It'll be muscle memory before you know it, and you won't realize you're doing it."

"Here's the bad news," I said. "It's dark, cramped, and claustrophobic down there on Earl's boat. There was barely room for me to turn around. For you, it's going to be even tighter."

"I'm not afraid of the dark," Mongo said, "and I'm definitely not claustrophobic. How long can we stay down on a tank of air?"

"Under relaxed conditions, we could stay down over an hour on one tank, but working in the dark, in a confined space, we'll have less than half that amount of time. And you'll use a lot more air than me because your body requires more fuel. I'd like to be back on the surface twenty minutes after we splash in."

"Okay. Are the tanks full yet? I'd like to get this done before I forget that I'm not nervous."

With each of the four tanks I had aboard *Aegis* topped off at three thousand psi, we loaded the RHIB and headed for the wreck of Earl's former home.

Chapter 13
Plan the Dive . . . Dive the Plan

Penny motored us just north of the wreck, and I lowered the anchor to the muddy bottom. The hook found purchase, and we swung downstream on the incoming tide.

I drew the wreck on a small piece of paper. "Since neither of you has been down there yet, I have to prepare you. It's a mess. She's lying somewhat upright, but listing to starboard and badly twisted. She's likely unstable, and I honestly don't know what'll happen when you start pulling the safe out of the hull. I don't know how it's connected to the boat, and I don't know exactly how big it is."

Mongo and Hunter leaned in while Penny peered over their shoulders.

I continued. "I'll go in first with Mongo on my heels. We'll penetrate the companionway and pull ourselves into the salon. Don't fin. You'll just stir up the silt and make the visibility even worse than it already is. We'll pull our way in and feel for the safe as we go. Everyone has two lights, but they're not going to be much use. The water is so full of particulates that it's like high-beam headlights in fog."

Mongo studied my sketch. "When I get the safe out of the boat, what are we going to do if it's too heavy to carry to the surface?"

I pulled a pair of deflated fenders from the foredeck of the RHIB. "That's what these are for. Normally, we'd use lift bags, but these are just as good. I have an inflator on my low-pressure hose. We'll tie the safe to the fenders, I'll inflate them, and she'll float to the top. It may be another Mongo-show getting it into the RHIB, but if all else fails, we can tow it to the shallows and carry it out onto the bank."

Mongo cocked his head in a thoughtful gaze. "If you think those two fenders will float it, you must not think it weighs much. Physics wasn't my strongest subject, but I seem to remember Archimedes' principle saying something like an object is buoyed upward by a force equal to the weight of the liquid it displaces. Those fenders are probably a little less than two cubic feet each for a total of maybe three and a half cubic feet. If fresh water weighs sixty-two point four pounds per cubic foot and salt water weighs sixty-four, that would make this brackish water around sixty-three and a quarter pounds, so those things should generate around two hundred twenty pounds of lift. That's not much of a safe if it only weighs two hundred pounds."

We stared up in disbelief at the man whose brain had just proven to be as big as the rest of him.

Penny said, "If physics wasn't your strong suit, what was?"

Mongo winked at my wife. "I was pretty good at home economics if you need any sewing done."

I tried to stifle a chuckle. "I wish Clark had been here for that little lesson. He and I have both been through the Instructor Development Course, and I'm sure neither of us could've done that math so easily."

"It's just math," Mongo said. "It's not like it's anything complex."

I studied my deflated fenders and tried to remember how the safe felt beneath my hands. "If your numbers are close and that safe weighs much more than two hundred pounds, we're going to need *Aegis*'s winch to haul it up."

Penny plucked her phone from the console. "I'm on it."

Three minutes later, Clark was motoring *Aegis* from her slip at the marina and heading downriver to join the recovery effort.

Hunter said, "I thought you wanted to keep Clark in the marina to avoid drawing attention to the scene here at the wreck."

"I did, but I'll have him lay off a thousand feet or so until we need him. There's too much that can go wrong. Now that we know my fender-floating idea may not be adequate, I don't want to risk things falling apart without Clark and *Aegis* nearby."

Penny offered a brief smile. "I like that you're being careful."

"I'm always careful," I said, trying not to laugh.

She rolled her eyes. "Yeah, right."

By the time Clark anchored *Aegis* a thousand feet upstream, Hunter, Mongo, and I were suited up and ready to splash.

I checked my watch. "It's three twenty-five. We're back on the surface no later than three fifty. Any one of us can call the mission. To call for an abort, find your partner's arm, squeeze once, and tap three times. That means we're coming to the surface no matter what else is happening. We'll have no verbal coms, so everything is hand signals. If the visibility is anything like it was yesterday morning, it'll be near zero, so stay close, and do not deviate from the plan. Any questions?"

Hunter and Mongo shook their heads in unison.

I turned to Penny. "If we're not back by fifty, get Clark in the water."

"I will," she said. "Please be careful."

I offered an abbreviated salute and rolled over the side. We descended side by side, and the visibility was dramatically better than the day before. I could see the tips of my fins and both of my dive partners. Things were starting nicely.

Earl's twisted boat came into unfocused view like a ghostly apparition in the haze. Her outline resembled the boat she'd been only a few days before, but her back was clearly broken, and she lay helpless and defeated, twisted amidships with her bow wrenched at a thirty-degree angle to the stern.

We held our noses and exhaled against our eardrums, equalizing the pressure inside our sinuses with the surrounding water pressure. Mongo looked relaxed and competent. My concern over his mask anxiety was waning as we descended toward the wreck.

Landing on the portside gunwale, we inflated our BCs with just enough air to hover neutrally buoyant a few inches above the deck. I flashed the okay sign, and both divers returned the signal. Exactly as we'd briefed, none of us kicked; instead, we pulled ourselves through the vessel with gloved hands. A time check showed 3:29. We had twenty-one minutes to work.

The companionway came into view, and I motioned for Hunter and Mongo to wait outside while I did a brief recon of the interior. My partners froze in place, and I pulled myself through the opening. My torch cast its beam into the space, revealing absolute chaos. Nothing was in its place, and the wood and fiberglass of the vessel were torn and splintered in every direction. The forces the boat endured on her way to the bottom and the collision with the mud must have been enormous.

Unlike the day before, I could see the opening in the woodwork, revealing the dial of the safe. I gave the remaining wood around the safe a pull and felt the elasticity of the woodwork, but I couldn't pull it free. My hand and arm slid easily into the space around the safe, and I found the back edge of its upper surface. I pulled on the metallic box, but unlike the woodwork, it made no offer to move.

Still confident Mongo could muscle the safe from its confines, I pulled myself back through the companionway. Two pairs of eyes awaited me, and I motioned through the opening and to the right.

A thousand thoughts poured through my head, but the one I couldn't ignore was the fact that Earl's toolbox would be in the aft compartment on the main deck, so I broke the cardinal rule and changed the plan.

I pointed to Mongo and Hunter and motioned for them to move into the salon and start working on the safe. Mongo moved immediately, but Hunter glared at me with a knowing look as if to say, "Plan the dive and dive the plan."

I flashed the okay signal and motioned for him to stay with Mongo. The disappointment in his eyes was clear, but he followed my instructions as I swam toward the stern.

Before I reached the aft compartment, I heard fiberglass and wood being torn to shreds, and I imagined Mongo's enormous hands doing their work.

The deck hatch gave way, revealing tools strewn about the compartment. I retrieved a pry bar, a huge chisel, and a small sledgehammer. The additional weight of the tools required extra air in my BC to keep me neutrally buoyant and off the deck.

Back at the companionway, my watch revealed 3:34 . . . sixteen minutes to go. My submersible pressure gauge read 2,600 pounds of air remaining in my tank.

I pulled myself through the opening and toward my partners. The visibility in the salon had diminished by half thanks to Mongo's demolition project, so I didn't see either of them until I was within four feet of Mongo's right shoulder. I reached out and nudged the mountain-sized diver and held up the tools I'd retrieved. As he turned toward me, a remnant of shredded woodwork caught the edge of his mask, breaking the seal and allowing water to pour in. I froze in place. There was nothing I could do to clear and reseal his mask. The moment of truth had arrived, and I was a helpless spectator.

I'd taught Mongo the most basic rule of scuba diving—never hold your breath—but following the rule was up to him.

To my horror, he stopped making bubbles and started thrashing about, causing the already diminished visibility to decrease even more. I dropped my tools and held his shoulder with one hand while pressing rhythmically against his two-acre chest. I couldn't breathe for him, so the next best thing was to remind him to breathe for himself.

My effort and encouragement worked. His breaths came, first, as jerking, spasmatic, terror-filled gasps, but quickly turned to deep inhalations, followed by long, bubble-filled blows. The initial panic that tried to overtake his mind lost its battle with the warrior, and he calmed himself enough to reposition the mask where it belonged. His chin rose, and a cascade of bubbles poured from beneath his nose, forcing the water from his mask.

My heart rate returned to normal as Mongo raised his thumb and forefinger in the okay signal I'd been praying to see. Although a smile from behind a regulator is often invisible, I'm confident Mongo saw mine.

I descended to the deck below to recover the tools I'd dropped, and again showed them to Mongo. He reached for the pry bar. I surrendered the tool and descended, reaching beneath him to check his pressure gauge: 1,700 pounds. The moment of panic, coupled with the physical labor, had burned through nearly half of his air. My gauge read 2,150, and Hunter flashed 2,300. Hunter and I were in good shape, but Mongo was using a lot of air. My watch showed 3:41. Nine minutes to go.

As if nothing had gone wrong, Mongo was back at work, this time with the pry bar. Hunter moved debris as quickly as Mongo created it, and soon, the safe was completely exposed. As the beam from my torch cut through the suspended particles, the safe revealed itself to be the size of four full-sized briefcases stacked together. To guess its weight would be impossible, but there was no guesswork required to know exactly why it wasn't moving. It was fiber-glassed into the hull of the boat, clearly from the time the boat was built in Cartagena while Boomer was building his fortune flying low over the Central American jungle.

Mongo extended the pry bar toward Hunter and reached for the hammer and chisel. As he took the tools from my hands, I checked his gauge to find just under 1,200 pounds of air remaining for the human wrecking ball.

He sank the blade of the chisel into the fiberglass an inch with every blow of the hammer. Even underwater, his strength was unmatched, and soon, the glass seam looked as though it'd been sliced with a chainsaw. All that remained was to pull the safe from the remnants of the shelf and get it close enough to the companionway for *Aegis's* winch to haul it to the surface.

Mongo wedged a ham-sized hand behind the safe and gave a tug, but it didn't budge. Hunter and I added our claws to the effort, and the metal behemoth inched forward ever so slightly. Mongo held up a finger, indicating for us to wait as he repositioned himself. The fins precariously perched on his island-sized feet caught on every nook and cranny as he tried to find purchase.

Finally, he drained the air from his BC, sank to the cabin sole, and yanked the fins from his feet. His heels were firmly anchored against the angle where the gunwale met the deck. With both of his hands behind the safe and his footing secure, he gave a nod. The three of us pulled with every fiber of our bodies, and the remaining structure securing the safe to the hull surrendered with a thundering report. The box, clearly heavier than two hundred pounds, separated from the boat as if fired from a cannon, and with it came debris of every shape and size. The world around us

vanished in a veil of fiberglass, thirty years of grime, and uniden-
tifiable junk.

Sound travels almost four times as quickly underwater as it
does through the air. The barrage of sound bombarding our
hearing, coupled with the near blindness of the environment,
overwhelmed the three of us and sent us sprawling through the
salon like drunken idiots. When our bodies came to rest, the catastrophic result of our efforts slowly unfolded before my eyes.
Hunter landed facedown with Mongo diagonally across his body.
The safe landed firmly on Mongo's chest with my arm pinned
between the heft of the iron box and the giant.

Don't panic. Assess, evaluate, plan, execute.

Hunter was hopelessly trapped, but prior to the catastrophe,
he had more air than anyone else. If he were alive and still capable of breathing, he would be able to remain alive longer than
Mongo or me. Mongo was pinned beneath the safe that likely
outweighed even him. I had no feeling in my right arm, and I
couldn't tell if my fingers were moving when my brain told them
to do so. My pressure gauge read 1,800 pounds. Hunter likely
had at least that much, and probably more. Mongo's pressure
gauge was buried somewhere between him and Hunter, making
it impossible for me to find. He had to be below 1,000 pounds,
but he was also dazed and barely conscious. If he could keep his
regulator in his mouth, he wouldn't drown anytime soon, and he
wouldn't use much air. My watch showed 3:49. Our situation
was serious, but not hopeless.

Panic: controlled.

Assessment: at least two out of three still alive.

Evaluation: situation dire.

It was time to plan. If I could reach Hunter's inflator, I could
blow air into his BC and possibly roll Mongo and me off his
body. Mongo had drained the air from his BC, making himself
negatively buoyant, but not one hundred percent. His heft was

still being buoyed upward by Archimedes' principle. The concern was the weight of the safe. I wasn't adding to the weight Hunter was bearing, but I wasn't sure how badly my arm was broken and if I was bleeding. My torch landed just beyond my arm's reach, but it was shining toward Hunter. As the visibility improved, I could see both him and Mongo producing exhalation bubbles at slow, regular intervals. Inflating Hunter's vest was my only plan.

Planning: done.

I stretched to the limit of my muscles, bones, and flesh, but Hunter's inflator remained less than an inch from my fingertips. My feet weren't bound, and my legs appeared uninjured, so I slid off my left fin and forced the bootie from my foot. The inflator lay within easy reach of my foot if I could muster the dexterity to press and hold the button with my toes.

My watch read 3:50. Clark would be arriving soon, but it would take several minutes for him to decipher the scene. Regardless of the cavalry coming, I had to keep working.

My toes found the button, but the angle made it impossible for me to grip the inflator and see it simultaneously, so I was left working entirely by feel . . . foot feel.

I wrapped my toes around the inflator and squeezed with all my might. My foot cramped and sent lightning bolts up my leg. I ignored the pain and curled my toes even tighter until I felt the inflator buck and come to life.

Air from the tank was pouring through the first-stage regulator, down the low-pressure hose, and through the plastic inflator. In less than a second, the air would flood into the bladder of Hunter's BC and turn it into a balloon. If the god who hears the prayers of an assassin was smiling down on me, the safe would roll one direction, and Mongo would roll the other. If they both rolled toward me, I would never see the surface of the Matanzas River again.

Chapter 14
Angels from Above

My plan—if it qualified as a plan—was, at least, based in solid science. Air and water don't occupy the same space, so inflating Hunter's BC would displace not only water, but hopefully, also Mongo, me, and the safe.

The harder I curled my toes into the inflator, the more punishing the cramps became. The lightning bolts of electric pain piercing my foot, calf, and thigh left me gasping and strengthened my resolve.

Finally, the spring and friction in the inflator succumbed to my assault and opened the tiny valve in the inflator. Air poured through the hoses, fittings, and valves, and into the empty bladder of the buoyancy compensator. I waited patiently for the rise to come. It would be subtle, but everything would change—hopefully for the better.

The rise never came; instead, a column of golf ball–sized orbs rose through the water above Hunter's head. The air that should've been forcing Mongo and the safe off my partner was pouring through the BC that had been torn during the chaos. I relaxed my tortured foot, and the bubbles stopped coming. With them, my plan melted into dark water.

The movement I'd prayed for didn't come, but as Hunter regained his faculties, the reality of his predicament obviously became clear to him. What little light there was came from my torch a few feet from his face and a second torch somewhere in the haze beyond the pile of bodies, steel, and debris.

He was pinned to the cabin sole, but he was alive, awake, and thinking. He twisted his neck in a wasted attempt to see what was crushing him. There was no way he could see Mongo, but I slid my bare foot toward him until I could nudge his forearm. Wrenching his arm, he forced his hand to meet my foot and squeezed twice. I returned the primal communication with pressure from my heel.

Most people would panic if they found themselves facedown at the bottom of a thousand-pound pile of bodies thirty feet underwater, but not Stone Hunter. He initiated the same checklist I'd been through.

Don't panic. Assess, evaluate, plan, execute.

His hand felt for anything he could use to work the problem, and it landed on his inflator. His efforts didn't require the removal of a fin and boot. He squeezed the button, and the plume of bubbles—wasted air—rose above his head.

His next attempt was, perhaps, based in desperation, but our situation justified any effort toward a resolution. He flattened his palm against the cabin sole and pressed as if he were on the verge of knocking out a few hundred push-ups. I'd seen him do exactly that on more occasions than I could count.

Stories of superhuman strength are the things of urban legends: mothers lifting cars off of their babies, and soldiers running miles with their wounded brothers-at-arms across their shoulders, gave all of us the false hope that we could do the same if lives depended on it. Ours likely did.

No human possessed the strength to heft Mongo, me, and a four-hundred-pound safe, but perhaps two humans in a combined effort could pull it off. I dug my heel into the deck and joined my partner in his press. I could move most of my weight, but the safe remained fixed as if it were glued to my arm and Mongo's chest.

Lifting until muscle failure was something Hunter and I had done in the gym hundreds of times, but we'd never done it when our lives were on the line. Less than a minute later, we each reached the limit of our ability to continue pushing. An exasperated sigh left my partner's regulator in the form of a long stream of bubbles.

I reached for my pressure gauge and pulled it toward my face. The human need to watch the sand fall through the hourglass is, somehow, ingrained in our psyche, but before the gauge came into focus, I let it fall from my hand. The air remaining in my tank was irrelevant. My time left on Earth meant nothing if I was destined to drown on the bottom of the Matanzas River. Nothing remained except refusal to surrender. I started over.

Don't panic. Assess, evaluate, plan, execute.

There was no panic. Our situation hadn't changed. Our environment hadn't changed. But I had an incomplete evaluation of our environment. I knew who and what was beneath me, and I knew the safe had my right arm locked against Mongo's chest; however, I didn't know what was above the safe.

I contorted my body until I could see over my shoulder. The light from behind Mongo reflected against a smooth, dark surface, but I couldn't piece together what I was seeing. Pancakes of shape-shifting objects danced against the surface like liquid mercury poured on a hard, horizontal surface. My mind couldn't piece it together, and I grew mesmerized by the oscillating reflections until I couldn't look away.

As I stared into the mysterious forms, a face slowly appeared impossibly deep inside the vision. It was the face of an angel with skin like amber and flowing hair dancing on the wind. As quickly as the angel, or mermaid, or perhaps the harvester of souls had appeared, she vanished, but the softness of the liquid light remained.

Hallucinations are not uncommon at the moment of a man's death, but the face I saw was no figment of my tortured imagination, for it appeared again, this time, only inches away, and she was reaching for my alternate air source. My angelic mermaid stuck my second regulator in her mouth and took a breath. I'd never been so happy to see Penny Thomas Fulton in my life.

As my focus returned, it became clear that she'd dived on the wreck with no scuba gear and on a single breath. Her bright yellow mask and fins were unmistakable, but without a tank on her back, she was one additional pair of lungs in need of the limited air supply we had left. The panic I expected to see in her eyes never came; instead, determination shone on her face. She moved about the cramped space with the grace of a dolphin and the efficiency of a predator.

She found Mongo's pressure gauge and showed me four fingers. Four hundred pounds of air wouldn't last long in lungs the size of Mongo's, but as long as he was semi-conscious and not burning energy, it was enough to keep him alive long enough to work through our drama now that help had arrived.

Penny returned and drew another breath from my regulator, then picked up the hammer from the deck beside Hunter. Her knee landed on my shoulder, and she drove the head of the steel hammer against the reflections above my head. When the tinted hatch finally cracked and crumbled away, the dancing reflections that had been the trapped bubbles we'd been exhaling escaped and raced for the surface some thirty feet above.

Penny took one more breath from my reg and slithered through the hatch. Seconds later, she was back with a line in one hand and the fourth scuba tank in the other. She drew another breath and began working the line beneath the safe until she'd tied a cradle around the steel box.

Another breath. . . .

Four powerful yanks of the line. . . .

A force from above brought the line taut, and the safe slowly lost its grasp of my arm. There was no blood, and my arm moved as it should've when I commanded it to, but there was no feeling.

The safe rose until it met the limits of the hatch less than half its size. Mongo raised his head as if waking from a long winter's nap. He cleared his flooded mask with robotic precision and scanned the environment. Hunter felt the relief of having the heft of the safe lifted and pressed against the deck again, sending the biggest man either of us knew rolling onto his side.

My wife snatched Hunter's alternate air source from his BC and shoved it toward Mongo. He stared at the regulator, unsure what he was supposed to do, so she plucked the reg from his lips and stuck Hunter's alternate into Mongo's mouth. He cleared the regulator and continued breathing, but he was obviously still confused. Penny shut off the valve on Mongo's tank and exchanged the nearly empty cylinder for the fresh bottle she'd brought from above. With 3,000 pounds of air, Mongo had a new lease on life.

We exchanged a hearty round of okay signals, and Penny led Hunter through what remained of the companionway. There was no chance I would make it through the hole Hunter had fit through, and for Mongo, it would've been like swimming through a pinhole. He and I weren't the only things stuck on the shipwreck. The safe wasn't going through the overhead hatch, either.

There was no question that Penny or Clark would arrive with a plan to get us out of the wreck, but waiting to be rescued didn't sit well with either of us. Mongo found the chisel and hammer and went to work on the frame of the overhead hatch. In minutes, he had chiseled away two feet of fiberglass and aluminum.

With the framework weakened, he elbowed and shouldered his way through the opening until it was big enough to drive a dump truck through. With a dramatic courteous bow, he motioned through the hole as if to say, "After you, sir."

With one hand on the line Penny had delivered, I ascended from the bowels of the wreck with Mongo close behind. My single fin felt awkward as I swam toward the dim light of the surface. About halfway to the top, we met Penny coming back down the line in her glowing yellow mask and fins with Hunter's BC loosely hanging around her body. She wore the beautiful look of relief on her face as she turned and rose back toward the sun with the two of us behind her.

As our heads broke the surface, Mongo spat out his regulator and pulled his mask beneath his chin. "I think I need a new scuba instructor. I thought this was supposed to be fun and relaxing."

Aegis lay alongside the RHIB with the line rigged to the dinghy davits and winch. Clark sat on the stern with blood pouring from his chin.

I stuck a finger in the air and sent it twirling in a circle—the signal for winch-up. "What the heck happened to you?"

Penny sat on the starboard tube of the RHIB and bellylaughed. "Some people will do anything to avoid freediving. Your friend, the Green Beret, took a nasty spill and hurt his little chin."

I joined Penny in laughter. "Well, Glass Jaw Johnson, get on the winch and haul that safe up here if you've got enough blood left in your body to push the button."

Two minutes later, the black box potentially holding Boomer's darkest secret saw the light of day for the first time in a quarter century.

Chapter 15
Crackers

Mongo hefted the safe from the dinghy davit and duckwalked to the cockpit with the ungainly weight cradled in his arms. Hunter helped him place it as gently as possible on the deck. Five pairs of eyes stared down at the black behemoth. If the others were sharing my thoughts, we each hoped someone else had safe-cracking in his bag of tricks.

I massaged my arm as the feeling slowly returned. "I can open it with a cutting torch, but there's no way to predict how much damage that might do to whatever's inside."

Hunter said, "Unless it's waterproof, I don't think fire is going to hurt the contents."

Clark pressed the corner of the safe with his boot. "I didn't see any water run out of it when it came out of the river, so it may be watertight."

Mongo rubbed his sore ribs. "I may be able to pry it open if you have a way to hold it still."

Penny cleared her throat. "Uh, I'm sorry to be a buzzkill, guys, but technically, that safe and its contents belong to Earl, and I think it'd be wise to get her permission before you go torching or prying on it."

All eyes turned to me, and I checked my watch. "You've got a point. Visiting hours will be over soon, so you call Jesus, and I'll get out of these wet clothes."

* * *

Penny and I found Earl dressed and sitting on the edge of her hospital bed while a nurse shuffled through paperwork. Instead of barging in, we hovered near the door to her room and did a little eavesdropping.

"Do you have any questions about the medication the doctor prescribed?"

Earl grumbled. "Yeah. Do I really need to take all of them?"

The nurse took the resistance in stride. "You only need to take them if you want to get better. If you're happy the way you are, then, by all means, feel free to ignore the doctors."

"Fine. I'll take the damned pills."

"Good. Now listen closely. You are to rest. No lifting anything heavier than a gallon of milk for at least three weeks. Walk every day, but don't overexert yourself. And Doctor Gandy would like to see you again in three weeks."

Earl rolled her eyes. "Okay, whatever."

The nurse slid the stack of papers across the elevated table. "Sign the bottom of these four pages. Do you have someone to stay with you for a few days until your full mobility returns?"

Earl looked up at the nurse as if she'd asked for directions to the moon, and Penny made her entrance. "Yes, she does. I'll be with her as long as necessary."

Earl turned and smiled. "It looks like I do. This is the girl who married my Stud Muffin. She'll look after me."

The nurse tried in vain to avoid laughing, and then glanced at me. "So, that must make you Stud Muffin."

I bowed. "At your service."

The nurse motioned toward Earl. "You've got your hands full with this one."

"Don't I know it?" Penny said. "But we'll take good care of her."

"In that case, she's all yours."

Earl hastily signed the forms and slid them back toward the nurse. In her trademark waddling walk, she gingerly made her way toward the door and handed out a pair of genuine Earl-from-the-End hugs. "Thanks for coming to get me, you two. I ain't got no idea where to go, but I'm glad to have you two in my corner."

Penny returned her hug. "I'm going to take you back to Saint Marys with me while Chase and the boys get to the bottom of whatever you've gotten yourself into down here."

Jesus was waiting for us by the exit doors and helped Earl into the back seat. He slid behind the wheel. "Where to, boss?"

"Back to the marina, first," I said. "Then, I need you to take these two up to Saint Marys. Can you manage that?"

"Anything for you, boss. You know that. But it's a long way up there, and it'll cost me a couple of hours of fares if you know what I'm sayin'."

I met his stare. "Have I ever let you lose out on any fares, Jesus?"

He grinned. "No, boss, you ain't, and Jesus loves you for it, you know."

We pulled up to the curb at the municipal marina and climbed out of the car. As we descended the ramp toward the slips, Earl stopped and stared out over the river.

I took her arm. "Are you okay?"

She looked away and rubbed her eyes. "Yeah, Baby Boy, I'm okay. I just ain't never looked out over them slips and not seen my old boat. It just feels weird, you know."

"I'm sure it does, but the world is full of boats. We'll find you another one if that's what you want, but that's not something we have to worry about right now. Come on. We've got something to show you."

Penny and I matched Earl's pace. The pain in every step reminded me of Clark after his back surgery. Earl wasn't going to win any foot races, but just like an old tortoise, she kept moving forward.

It took a little effort to get Earl aboard *Aegis*, but once on deck, she seemed to feel right at home. "You ain't been lettin' nobody mess with them motors, have you?"

"I wouldn't dream of it, Earl. Yours are the only hands that fondle my diesels."

"I intend to keep it that way," she said. "But it may be a few days before I can crawl back into them engine rooms."

We made our way into the main salon where the heavy metal safe rested on the deck.

Earl stared down at the box. "Is that it?"

"That's it," I said. "It took some work to get it out, but we did it."

She stared in silence at the safe until finally saying, "I can't believe that thing's been in my boat for all these years, and I never knew it."

"There's no way you could've known unless you'd torn out the interior. It was as well-hidden as anything I've ever seen."

"How did you manage to get it out of the water?"

Before I answered, I felt and heard the rest of the team descending the ladder from the upper deck.

"You remember Mongo, right?"

The giant ducked through the doorway to the main salon, and Earl handed out more hugs. "Of course I remember all these guys. Especially that yummy Clark. Come here, you hunk of man."

Clark accepted the compliment and the hug but quickly got down to business. "Do you know what the combination might be?"

Earl shuffled onto the settee and focused on the safe's dial. "I can try a few dates, but this is the first time I've ever seen that thing."

As she turned the dial, it emitted scratchy, coarse sounds as if it hadn't been turned in over twenty years. Every time she stopped and tried to turn the handle, nothing moved.

Finally, she sat back. "I'm out of ideas. Can't one of you superspies crack it?"

"We're not spies," came the cacophony of replies.

She waved a dismissive hand. "I think we're beyond that point, boys. You ain't foolin' old Earl, so do whatever you have to do to get that thing open. I'm dying to see what's inside. Come to think of it, I almost died because somebody else wanted to see what was inside."

The somberness of the moment returned.

I said, "Yeah, well, we're going to make sure that doesn't happen again. I'm going to find out who—and what—those guys are, and we'll put an end to whatever this is."

Earl looked up at me. "It ain't worth gettin' hurt over, Stud Muffin. Maybe they're gone, and maybe they figure I'm dead."

"If they're former spooks, they're not in the game of making assumptions and giving up."

"I just don't want any of you gettin' hurt on account of me."

Hunter weighed in. "Earl, after what you did with the patrol boat, you're the same as family to me, and I'm pretty sure the rest of the guys feel the same. We've got your back . . . and your front."

If I didn't know the hard-as-nails diesel mechanic so well, I would've sworn she almost teared up, but Earl would never actually shed a tear.

I slapped the top of the safe. "Are you sure you want us to open this thing up? None of us can crack it, but I've got the tools to cut it open down in the workroom."

Earl laid her foot beside the safe and gave it a push. "If you can get that safe—and me—down them steps, I'll cut it open."

Without a word, Mongo hefted the safe into his arms and headed down the steps into the portside hull, where my workshop took up the aft section.

Hunter and I descended the stairs behind him and stopped on the second step.

"Come on, Earl," I said. "We won't let you fall."

She carefully eased herself down the stairs, clinging to the bulkhead as she went. It took a couple of minutes to get her into the aft section of the hull, but she came alive in the environment where she felt most comfortable.

She studied the safe. "I'm gonna need an angle grinder and some glasses."

I opened the locker of power tools and pulled out the grinder, then snatched a face shield from the bin above the workbench.

In short order, sparks were flying from the top right corner of the safe as Earl guided the grinder with her expert hand. The thick steel of the safe put up a good fight, and Earl made slow, consistent progress until the cutting wheel was worn down beyond usable size and we had to replace the wheel five times.

Earl pushed up the face shield. "I'm gonna need to sit down. This is kicking my tail."

I took the grinder from her hand and helped her to a stool built into the bulkhead of the shop.

She wiped sweat from her brow. "Give me a minute and let me catch my breath. I'll finish it."

I handed her a clean rag and a bottle of water. "No, you just sit there and rest. I'll finish."

As I leaned into the project and watched the snail's-pace progress, I wondered if I had enough spare cutting wheels to finish the job. I was tempted by the torch in its bracket to my left, but I continued the trek with the grinder.

After demolishing three more cutting wheels and only two-thirds of the safe, Penny's voice echoed through the boat. "Chase! Get up here, now!"

My wife was the least-demanding person I'd ever met, so when Penny Fulton ordered me to get up there now, I was smart enough to heed her call.

The grinder whined to a stop, and I took the stairs in one leap. I expected to see Penny in a state of near panic, but to my surprise, Ricky, the cab driver, stood in *Aegis*'s main salon.

I lowered my chin and narrowed my eyes. "The well is dry, Ricky. You're not getting any more money from us."

He shot a glance back through the open door toward the old town of Saint Augustine. "No, man, it ain't that. I just thought you'd want to know that those two dudes—the ones I seen the night that lady's boat sank—they're up on the deck at O.C. White's Restaurant right now. They're looking this way, man."

Chapter 16
Tradecraft

I yanked my money clip from my right front pocket and shoved a hundred dollar bill into Ricky's hand. "Thank you. Now, get out of here. If you're lying, I'll cut that hundred out of your thigh."

Ricky vanished like the wind just as Hunter topped the stairs behind me. "What's going on?"

I turned on my heel. "Do you have your pistol?"

He wrinkled his brow. "I'm alive, so . . . yeah."

"The two guys who hit Earl are across the street at O.C. White's. Let's go have a little chat with them."

He turned and yelled down the stairs. "Hey, Mongo. Let's go! It's time to do some cage rattling."

There were few things Mongo loved more than leaning on uncooperative souls who needed a little encouragement to make their confessions. Suddenly, he reminded me of Beater, the old brawler who helped recruit me into the life that had become my world. Those two were definitely cut from the same cloth.

Our not-so-gentle giant leapt up the stairs as if he were a man of half his heft. "One dose of cage rattling coming up."

I grabbed my pistol from the chart table, and Penny grabbed my arm. "Chase, please be careful. You said it yourself. . . . These guys are dangerous."

I slid the holster inside my waistband and took her hands. "From now on, we can consider 'being careful' my default position. I've got two of the best operators on the planet backing me up, and it's all happening in public. It'll be fine. Stay here with Earl and Clark, and we'll be back before you know it."

She pressed her lips together and exhaled through her nose. That particular action meant *something* in Penny-speak, but I didn't have time to interpret.

Hunter, Mongo, and I jogged up the ramp and across Avenida Menendez. The hostess at O.C. White's stepped in front of us at the top of the wooden staircase. "I'm sorry, gentlemen, but you'll have to wait downstairs. There are no more tables available up here."

I sidestepped the girl who was, after all, just doing her job. "We're meeting a couple of friends, and we'll only be a few minutes."

Mongo posted up near the top of the stairs, and Hunter moved to my eight o'clock position, one stride behind me. The two men Earl and Ricky had described sat at the rail overlooking the marina and Avenida Menendez. The tall, bald man had his back to us, but the smaller one with the long, definitive scar through his eyebrow locked eyes with me before we were ten feet from their table. The man appeared to be in his early sixties and well beyond his operational prime. His right hand disappeared beneath the table, and he whispered something to his partner, who, from my perspective, looked a lot like Lurch from *The Addams Family.*

I leaned toward my partner. "He's going for a gun."

Hunter flashed a finger gun to Mongo and whispered, "Yeah, I've got him. The bald guy has an ankle rig and one on his left hip."

"If it goes down," I said, "I've got Scarface, and you've got Lurch."

"Roger."

My partner landed a foot behind the leg of Lurch's chair and pinned the long, lanky man against the table. Scarface went to raise his right hand, and I laid my switchblade against his collarbone. "Gentlemen, we need to talk."

Scarface gritted his teeth. "I could put two in your gut before you scratch me with that toy knife of yours. Then I can drop Goliath over there with one to the forehead. Now, back up, boy."

I let a smile cross my lips. "Oh, look. Isn't that cute? He called me *boy*."

Hunter drew his pistol and slid it behind Lurch's shoulder, hidden from the other patrons of the restaurant by his body.

That's when everything went wrong. Lurch was the first to move. He hopped upward and forward about four inches in a lunge so efficient it was barely noticeable. The right rear leg of his chair landed solidly on top of Hunter's foot, and the man pressed his back against the cane chair, pinning my partner's pistol harmlessly against the seatback.

Scarface shot his left hand into the pocket of my pants and yanked me toward him, leaving me leaning back and pointing my toes in a wasted effort to regain my balance. Before I saw his right hand move, he crushed three of my fingers against his collarbone and twisted the knife from my hand. With blinding speed, he slashed downward with my knife, severing my belt and one belt loop without so much as a scratch to my skin. In an instant, he stuck the knife into the table, snatched my Walther from its holster, and cycled the slide eight times, emptying the rounds from the magazine and chamber onto his plate.

Hunter sent a crushing elbow shot to the back of Lurch's head, sending the man crashing forward. While I was watching my pistol eject its ammo, Hunter withdrew his Sig from behind the man's bald head and pressed it against his throat. Baldy continued his motion forward and sent his sinewy claw into Hunter's crotch, clamping down like a vise. My partner's eyes rolled back in his head, and his knees turned to pudding. Lurch stripped the Sig with his left hand and pinned my partner's free hand to the table with the muzzle.

Lurch spoke in soft, measured cadence. "You boys are in over your head and way out of your league. Take your grizzly bear from the stairs and walk away. If you do as I say, the cute little girl with the wild hair on your boat gets to keep her pretty long legs. If you want to continue this fight you can't win, you boys won't live to see the sunrise, and I'll feed your girl's gams to the sharks."

Every instinct inside me screamed to fight. I wanted to pummel those guys into the dirt, but we'd been outplayed by a couple of old pros, and we had no choice but to tuck our tails between our legs and retreat.

I yanked my empty gun from Scarface's hand and shoved it into my pocket. Lurch expertly stripped Hunter's Sig of its slide and tossed the barrel over the railing and into the landscaping below. He yanked Hunter's belt away from his abdomen and dropped the remaining pieces of the weapon down the front of his pants.

Scarface folded my switchblade and studied the handle. "I think I'll be keeping this as a little souvenir."

Surprised Mongo hadn't waded through the sea of tables and torn the two men in half, I scanned the top of the stairs where we'd left him. To my horror, he was on one knee, rubbing his face as if he'd been maced.

Hunter and I retreated in temporary defeat and tried to get Mongo to his feet. "What happened to you?"

He kept pawing at his eyes like a man possessed. "Some bastard blew pepper in my eyes. I can't see a thing."

We finally got him upright and moving, but he was completely dependent on us for his sight. Navigating the stairs with a blind giant wasn't easy, but we made it back to the street, where Hunter dived into the bushes and quickly returned with his chrome barrel in his grip. The three of us crossed the street and rounded the corner of the marina office.

I tugged Mongo toward the wall. "Here's a water fountain. Wash out your eyes."

He felt for the fountain and let the cold water flush the pepper from his eyes. By the time he was finished and regaining his sight, Hunter had his pistol reassembled, and he was glaring around the corner and back toward the restaurant.

"Are they gone?" I asked.

"No. They're having dessert like nothing happened."

I let the sound of exasperation escape my lungs and then headed for my boat.

"What happened? Did you find them? Are they the guys? Are you okay?"

Penny's rapid-fire questions had stopped surprising me, but after the defeat I'd suffered, I was in no mood to field her machine-gun queries.

"They handed us our asses on a silver platter. That's what happened. They got the jump on all three of us. Whoever they are, they're good. I definitely underestimated them."

The look on Clark's face was disappointment of the highest order, but Penny wore the look of concern. She went first. "Are you okay? Are you hurt?"

Hunter spoke up. "Nothing but our pride is hurt, but that's only because they chose not to kill us in public. They had the drop on us, no doubt. As Chase said, they're good."

Penny's hands landed on her hips. "I thought *careful* was the default condition now. Isn't that what you said?"

I looked down at my wife. "I'm still alive and unhurt. That qualifies as careful."

"You're going to be the death of me, Chase Fulton."

I threw up my hands. "Hey, I was headed to the South Pacific. You're the one who said we have to help Earl."

She lowered her chin and gave me the look.

I tried to ignore her as I pulled a fork from my pocket. "They may be good, but I got a fingerprint."

Clark's disappointment morphed into pride as he cautiously took the fork from my fingertips. "Leave it to the great Chase Fulton to get his ass kicked and still come away with forensics."

"What are we going to do with a fingerprint?" Penny asked.

"We'll find out if Scarface is in any databases, and maybe we'll be able to put a dossier together on who at least one of these guys is."

I motioned for Penny to have a seat, and I joined her. "Listen to me. Whoever these guys are, they've seen you, and they made a threat. I have to get you out of here, and I don't think Bonaventure is far enough."

"What are you talking about? What kind of threat?"

I swallowed hard. "I told you I'd never lie to you, and omission is the worst lie. They threatened to feed your legs to the sharks if I didn't back off."

She huffed. "They obviously don't know how much my man loves my legs. Since when are you one to back off?"

I pulled her against my chest and kissed her forehead. "I'm putting you on an airplane tonight, and you and Earl are going somewhere nobody can find you. Have you ever heard of Red Feather Lakes, Colorado?"

She leaned back and smiled. "Yeah, I think I have. I seem to remember my dad having a place up there."

"That's the one," I said.

Turning to Mongo, I asked, "Do you have the number to the charter service you used to get down here?"

His eyes were still weeping, and the skin of his face was as red as fire. "Yeah, I do, and I've got them on retainer. The plane is still at the airport, and the pilots are waiting for me to call."

Two phone calls later, my wife and the best diesel mechanic on Earth were heading for the mountains of Colorado, while I was left trying to figure out how I was going to outfox a pair of old-school spooks who were still a long way from the assisted living facility.

Hunter, Clark, Mongo, and I sat on the upper deck, watching the moon rise over the trees.

I surveyed my team. "You guys have any ideas?"

"Yeah, I've got one," Mongo said. "How about we call Singer down here and get him to put a couple of rounds in their heads from a mile away? After what those guys did to us, I think that's our best choice."

"As tempting as that sounds, I'm going to hold off on the death-from-a-distance plan for now. We really need to know who these guys are, and we need to figure out a way to turn the tables."

Clark swallowed the last sip of whatever was in his glass. "I think you hit the nail on the head, Chase. We probably don't know any tricks these guys haven't seen a thousand times. If their tradecraft is as good as you say, we'll have to think outside the box on this one."

Hunter laughed. "There's a box?"

"If we're not careful," I said, "that box is going to become our coffin."

Chapter 17
Judging Covers

The chirping from my phone woke me the next morning.

"Hello. Chase here."

"Hey there, sleepyhead. You sound like I woke you up. You're usually on your third cup by now."

I rubbed my eyes and checked my watch. "I guess I overslept. Did you make it to Red Feather Lakes okay?"

She yawned. "Yes, we made it about two a.m. eastern time. I guess that's midnight here. I couldn't sleep."

I climbed the stairs from the starboard hull into the galley and started the coffee maker. "So, you've been waiting up all night to call?"

She hesitated. "Yeah, I guess so."

"Penny, you should've called when you landed."

"No, you needed your rest. You've got a lot on your shoulders right now, and I didn't want to add to that."

I sighed. "Please, Penny. You're never a burden. You know that. You're important to me."

"I know, but. . . ."

"But what?"

"Nothing, Chase. Just focus on your work. And I know you

said I should consider it the default position, but please be careful. I don't want to lose you."

I watched the black liquid drip from the filter and slowly fill the pot. How much darkness can one vessel accept before it's stained forever, too unsightly to ever be seen as clean again? How much darkness could I allow to filter into my soul and still be human and clean enough for the ones I loved to still call me their own? How far can any man descend into the depths of depravity ruled by the demons living lives of the unhuman and inhumane? When would the blade cut deeper than my belt, and would the plunging blade come first, or would it be my devolution from clarity to opacity that would be the killing blow?

"Chase? Are you still there?"

I shook myself from my stupor. "Yeah, sweetheart, I'm here. I was just. . . ."

She whispered, "Yeah, me too."

I took a breath and stilled myself. "You get settled in and try to get some rest. I'll call you tonight, okay?"

"Chase?"

"Yeah?"

"I love you."

I swallowed the lump in my throat. "I know, and I love you, too."

The line went dead, and I stared into the phone as if it held the answers to every question I didn't have the strength to ask. Perhaps all of those answers were high in the Rockies at Red Feather Lakes.

I climbed the ladder to find Clark, Mongo, and Hunter huddled around the small, fiberglass table on the upper deck.

* * *

136 · CAP DANIELS

"What is that?"

My team looked up as one.

Clark said, "Well, if it isn't Rip Van Winkle. Good of you to join us at midday."

I shrugged off his jab. "Yeah, yeah, whatever. My body needed the rest. Now, what are you studying so closely?"

"While you were catching up on your beauty sleep—it didn't work by the way, since you're still as ugly as a bowling shoe—we were chipping away at the rest of the safe."

He suddenly had my attention. "And? What was inside?"

"Don't get too excited, College Boy. Turns out, the safe was watertight, but the bad news is that it was also airtight. Every piece of paper inside the thing is as brittle as ash. Professor Mongo, here—I'm starting to think he's smarter than you—rigged up a contraption with a teakettle and a cutting board to rehydrate the dried-out remnants. We're trying to decipher the first one now. Take a look."

Hunter slid his chair to the side, and I took a knee beside the table. The document pinned to my cutting board looked like something from the Dead Sea Scrolls.

I examined the scraps of curled paper until my eyes crossed, then I looked up in surrender. "What's this supposed to be?"

Clark shrugged. "We don't know, either, but every piece of paper in the safe looks just like this one."

I turned to Mongo. "Is this the best you can do to bring these back to life?"

His plateau-sized shoulders dropped. "I did an internship at the Smithsonian a long time ago. That's where I learned about rehydration with steam. Maybe in a lab somewhere I might be able to do a little better, but this is the best I can do with what I have here."

I glanced toward the marina office and remembered an old friend. "Give me just a minute. I may know where we can find you a lab."

I scrolled through the contacts in my phone until I found the number I wanted.

A few seconds later, a pleasant voice answered. "Good morning. Saint Francis School. Sister Mary Flannigan."

"Good morning, Sister Flannigan. My name is Chase Fulton, and I need to speak with Sister Mary Robicheaux if she's available."

The nun's tone rose at least two octaves. "Oh, Mr. Fulton, you're nearly a saint around here. Of course you can talk to Sister Mary Robicheaux. It's so good of you to call. We all owe you so much. Oh, it's just *so* good to speak with you."

"I don't know what to say, Sister Flannigan. I'm just glad I could help. Thank you."

Her high-pitched excitement continued. "Oh, my goodness. No, no, thank you, Mr. Fulton. Please hold, and I'll have Sister Mary Robicheaux on the line in just a moment."

A couple of years before, I helped convince a pedophile who was stalking children at Saint Francis School to find some other country in which to live. With a little further persuasion, I convinced him to have his family make a sizable donation to the Catholic school. That donation provided the revenue the school needed to continue operating and educating hundreds of children in Saint Augustine. I wasn't a Catholic, but good work is good work regardless of the banner under which it is done, so I was proud to help.

"Hello, Mr. Fulton. How good it is to hear from you."

I couldn't suppress my smile. "Hello, Sister Robicheaux. It's great to hear your voice. I hope things are running smoothly at the school."

"Oh, things couldn't be better, thank God. And you . . . you'll never know how much your efforts mean to all of us here at Saint Francis. But something tells me this isn't a social call."

"You're wise beyond your years, Sister. I wanted to check on you and make sure everything is going well. It's been too long."

"Oh, yes, all is well here, Mr. Fulton. What can we do for you?"

"It's just a small favor, and I hate to ask—"

"There's no favor too big for you. The answer is yes, no matter what the request—of course, subject to the will of God."

"Of course," I said. "My request is simple. I find myself in need of a laboratory for"—I turned to Mongo, and he threw up four fingers—"four hours or so. I've come across some old documents that need a little attention before they'll be of any value to me."

"But, Mr. Fulton. . . . Don't you have access to the FBI's crime lab?"

I wasn't willing to lie to a nun. "This is a personal matter, Sister, so I'd like to keep it in the family, if you know what I mean."

"Of course I do, and I'll make arrangements with the science department for you to have access to a laboratory. When would you like to use it?"

I grimaced. "That's the tricky part. I'd like to get in there as soon as possible. This is a relatively time-sensitive situation."

"I understand. Can I call you back as soon as I can arrange the lab?"

"That would be terrific, Sister. And thank you again for everything."

She huffed. "Oh, stop that. You never have to thank us for anything. We're eternally in your debt."

"Eternity is a long time, Sister."

She chuckled. "It certainly is, and I know there's a special place waiting just for you. We'll talk again soon."

Clark shook his head. "That was your nun, wasn't it?"

Clark had warned me against getting involved in the pedophile case. I didn't listen then, and I wasn't going to listen now.

"I scored a lab for you, Mongo. It'll be a high school chemistry lab, but a lab nonetheless."

The big man smiled. "Anything is better than a teakettle on a catamaran."

I studied him for a moment. "Why haven't you ever mentioned your abilities until now?"

"I've spent my life being the guy who could move heavy stuff, and that's always seemed more valuable than my brain, so I guess I break things when people are watching, and I think when they're not."

"You're the walking example of the old adage, 'Never judge a book by its cover.'"

* * *

Sister Robicheaux called back in no time, and we had Mongo and the contents of the safe inside the lab thirty minutes later.

Our resident chemist asked, "What do you want me to do with the documents when I get them rehydrated?"

I was quick to answer. "When you get them ready, I'll take high-definition photographs of them and then have our favorite analyst run them through her supercomputer and super brain. Something's bound to come up."

He pulled on his gloves. "Sounds good. Now, get out of here and let me work. Give me two hours, and bring your camera."

Without a word, I pulled the door closed and left Doctor Mongo to his work.

Maple Street Biscuit Company was four blocks from Saint Francis School and served the finest biscuits and gravy in Saint Augustine. Eating without Mongo felt wrong somehow, but that didn't slow us down. Five minutes into the meal, Clark's beard looked like he'd been slimed by the gravy fairy. Hunter ate in silence, which told me he was deep in thought.

I washed down a mouthful with a long swallow of black coffee. "What's on your mind, Hunter?"

He looked up with his eyes but didn't raise his head. "I don't like it."

"You don't like the gravy?" I asked.

"No, the gravy's fantastic. I don't like getting handled the way we did by those two old guys last night. I can't get it out of my head. We did everything by the book. It was perfect, and they still outdid us. I don't like it."

Clark leaned in and wiped gravy from his chin. "This isn't the place for this conversation, but you guys got your butts in a sling precisely because your actions were textbook perfect. Those guys were practicing our tradecraft before you were born. We'll get 'em next time. And there *will* be a next time."

* * *

Two hours passed, and we strolled into the chemistry lab with the best camera I owned slung over my shoulder. "How's it going, Mongo?"

He looked up from his work and wiped his brow. "It's slow, but it's a lot better than trying to pull this off on the boat. I wish I hadn't destroyed the first page."

"It's not destroyed," I said. "You did the best with the tools you had. Let's see your latest work."

He motioned toward a series of corkboards lined up on the countertop. "There they are. All nine pages."

I leaned in to examine the restored pages, and he was right. The ones he worked on inside the lab were mostly legible and almost whole.

"Great work, Mongo. Let's get some pictures, and then, I guess, you have some way to preserve the originals?"

"Sure. I'll vacuum-seal them and lock 'em in your safe aboard *Aegis*."

I shot digital images of every page, including close-ups of each. It was impossible not to mentally scan the documents in an effort to piece together their cryptic message, but I stayed focused on taking the best pictures I could so Skipper would have a quality sample to work with.

As I was taking the last few pictures, Clark's phone chirped, and he stuck it to his ear. "That was quick. Let me guess. You came up empty?" He paused as the caller said something that obviously interested him, and then his eyes turned to giant orbs. "Oh, really? That's definitely interesting. How about known associates—especially ones who are long, lean, and bald?" He listened again and finally said, "Okay. Thank you, Brenda. I owe you one."

He hung up and slid the phone back into his pocket. "You're never going to believe what your forked-up fingerprints returned. It's a full thumbprint and two partials—an index and ring finger." He hesitated, apparently for dramatic effect, and we hung on his every word. "The prints come back to a Gary Weathers."

"That sounds like a made-up name," I said.

"It does," he admitted, "but it's apparently real. The only problem is, Mr. Weathers died eleven years ago."

Chapter 18
A Little Help?

Back aboard *Aegis,* I emailed the pictures of the documents to Skipper and followed up with a phone call.

"The pics are downloading now," she said. "I'll dig into them as soon as the download is done."

"I have a more important assignment for you, so put the documents second place behind the name Gary Weathers. The final pictures in the email are a full thumbprint and two partials. First, confirm the ID, and then go to work on aliases and background. I need known and suspected associates, especially any matching the description of a tall, thin, bald Caucasian guy in his mid to late sixties."

Sounds of pencil on paper proceeded. "I'm on it. Is there anything else?"

"There will be more, but for now, just work on Weathers and then the documents."

Skipper cleared her throat. "Um, Chase. There's something you need to know."

"What is it?"

She paused. "I, uh. . . . I talked to Penny."

"Okay." Her hesitance concerned me, but I tried not to let it show. "Okay, that's good. She's up in—"

"Yes, I know! There's no need to say it on an open line."

My desire to hide my concern vanished. "Do you believe she's in some kind of danger?"

"Duh. Why else would you have sent her away?"

"Surely she's safe up in . . ."

"Chase, stop it! You're smarter than that."

"Fine. You're right. So, what were you going to tell me?"

"I kind of spent some of your money."

"Come on, Skipper. Spit it out. We've got work to do."

She huffed. "Fine. I put a couple of guys on her and Earl. She told me a little about what's going on down there in Saint Augustine, and I thought it was worth a few hundred bucks to have somebody looking out for her. If that's not okay, I'll pay for it."

It was my turn to hesitate. "I should've thought about that. That's definitely money well spent."

"I thought so, too," she said. "But there's just one more thing. I didn't tell her I was doing it, and I don't love how I feel about that. It feels a little like I'm lying to her, and that's not cool."

"You're protecting her, and there's nothing nobler than that. I'll talk with her tonight, and if you want, I'll tell her it was my idea."

She sighed. "Thank you, Chase. I never want her to think I'm checking up on her or that I think she can't take care of herself, but we get tangled up with some nasty dudes sometimes. I'd never be able to live with myself if she got hurt and I didn't do everything I could to stop it."

A broad smile overtook my face. "Thank you, Skipper. I'll take care of it. You're the best. Now, get to work on Gary Weathers and his freaky-looking friend."

"I'm on it. Bye!"

I briefed the rest of the team on Skipper's tasking and about the security detail on Penny and Earl.

Clark said, "You've got to tell her, man. She's likely to shoot those guys if she sees them watching her."

Hunter and Mongo nodded in blatant agreement.

Penny answered on the second ring. "Hey, you. I didn't expect to hear from you until later tonight. Is everything okay?"

"Hey, sweetheart. Everything's fine. We've made a little progress on the identity of the guys who hit Earl."

"You mean the guys who kicked your ass," she said.

"They didn't kick our asses. They just let us know they weren't going to be pushovers. We could've taken them. We just didn't want to make a scene in the restaurant."

She chuckled. "Okay. Whatever makes you feel better."

"So, as I was saying before you so rudely interrupted, everything is moving slowly but surely. I saw Sister Robicheaux today, and she says hello."

"Aww, that's great. Where did you see her?"

"Mongo borrowed a lab from the school to work on some documents we found in Earl's safe."

Her tone went up an octave. "Oh, you got it open. What was in it? Was it cash? How much was in there? Was it soaking wet? Tell me!"

"Calm down, Road Runner. There was no paper cash. We found some gold coins, a German Luger, and nine sheets of dry-rotted paper with some sort of cryptic writing."

"Sorry," she said. "You know I get excited sometimes. Is that all you found?"

"There was an old compass in there, but it's no good. I've never seen a compass lose its ability to point north, but this one is crazy. It's like it's not even really a compass. When you have time, tell Earl what we found, and see if any of it makes sense to her."

"Okay, I will. How much gold was there?"

"Enough to buy her a new boat . . . a nice new boat."

Penny whistled.

"Yeah, exactly," I said. "I've got everything locked up in our safe for now, and Skipper is working on decoding the documents. She's also looking into the identities of the two guys. Hopefully, we'll have something to go on later today."

"What would you do without Skipper?" she said.

"She's invaluable. Oh, that reminds me. I talked with her, and she's putting a couple of guys on you and Earl, so don't shoot them. They should be invisible, but they'll make sure nobody messes with you. I don't have any reason to think you're in danger, but it never hurts to have an extra set of eyes looking after the woman I love."

"Thank you," she said. "I thought about that, but I was afraid I was just being paranoid. I'm glad you had her hire someone."

I made the conscious decision to let Penny believe the security had been my idea. "I'll check in later. Let me know if any of the stuff from the safe means anything to Earl."

"I will. I love you. Talk soon."

"I love you, too."

Clark ducked his chin and gave me the stink eye. "Nice job taking credit for Skipper's work, there, Honest Abe."

I threw up my hands. "Hey, I didn't lie. She just made an assumption."

"An assumption based on your lie of omission."

I waved him off. "Time to change the subject. I've got an idea. I think we need a consultant on this."

Eyebrows raised in unison, and Clark said, "A consultant?"

"Yeah, a consultant. I think we need Beater's take on all of this."

Hunter and Mongo stared in confusion, but Clark nodded. "That's not a bad idea."

"Who's Beater?" Hunter asked.

I said, "Beater is one of the guys who recruited me into this crazy world with you guys. He's a Cold War interrogation master."

Mongo grinned. "I like him already, and his nickname is awesome."

"You're actually the reason I thought about him, Mongo. He's a lot like you, except he doesn't take up quite as much space."

He chuckled. "Hey, I'm normal-sized. I can't help that you puny little guys stopped growing too early."

"I'm over six-four and two-twenty. I'm not puny in anyone's book . . . except yours."

Mongo shrugged. "Compared to Everest, they're all foothills."

"I suppose you're right, but being able to buy off the rack has its advantages. I think I'll give Beater a call and at least get his advice on all of this, even if we don't bring him in. Are you guys okay with that?"

Hunter reacted first. "You're the boss. What you say goes as far as I'm concerned. I'm always in favor of a little wisdom from guys who've been there and done that."

Everyone shared Hunter's sentiment, so I scrolled through my contacts and pressed send.

On ring number seven, just before I was going to hang up, my old friend said, "Yeah."

"Beater, it's Chase Fulton. Remember me?"

His tone lightened considerably. "Well, if it ain't the boy wonder. How you been, kid?"

"I'm great, Beater, but I've gotten myself into a little jam, and I think you're one of the few people on Earth who can actually help this time."

He chuckled. "Oh, so that's how it is, huh? You never call to wish me happy Bastille Day, but when you need my help, you dial the phone."

"You know how us young operators are. You used to be one."

"What do you mean, used to be? I still am one!"

"Good point," I said. "Forgive me for the slight."

"Forgiven. Now, what can I do to get your butt out of the sling you've landed in?"

I cleared my throat. "Here's the *Reader's Digest* version. My friend, Earline, used to be an Air America mechanic. Her husband, Boomer, was a driver. He may have skimmed off a little management fee from some other pilots to help tuck their money away back in the seventies."

Beater cut in. "Did you say Boomer?"

"I did."

"Are we talking about the same Boomer who stuck a C-Forty-Six in the jungle in Nicaragua?"

I couldn't tell if I was happy or terrified to hear that Beater may have known Boomer. "It could be the same guy, but I imagine there were a bunch of old bomber pilots nicknamed Boomer back then."

"Maybe," he said, "but there was only one Air America Boomer. He's been dead . . . must be thirty years now. What are you doing getting yourself wrapped up in some Air America pilot's thirty-year-old crap?"

"Like I said. . . . His wife—or widow, I suppose—is a friend of mine, and a few days ago a couple of guys came looking for something on her boat. They roughed her up pretty good, but she put a bullet in one of their legs for the trouble. They also sank the boat she lived on."

The sound of a door closing firmly echoed through the phone. "And just where did this happen?"

"In Saint Augustine Municipal Marina, but they cut the boat loose and sank it about three quarters of a mile downstream in the Matanzas River."

The curiosity rose in his voice. "Is your friend all right?"

"She's going to be all right," I said. "I have her tucked away someplace safe under the watchful eye of a few good men. That's not why I need your help, though."

Sounds of a lighter clicking and the satisfied exhalation of the first draw of fine Cuban tobacco smoke wafted through the phone. "Yeah, I figured as much, but you know me"—he paused and enjoyed another draw—"I'm a real softie. I always want to make sure the innocent ones are safe before I start breaking heads."

I laughed. "Yes, that's you . . . a big teddy bear. So, here's the story. There are these two guys who Earl thinks were also Air America. Two other hitters and I walked up on them in a restaurant last night, and they handed us our asses."

He roared with laughter. "Are you telling me you let two seventy-year-olds kick your ass last night?"

"I don't think they're seventy, yet, and they didn't really kick our asses. They just made sure we knew they could. They were sharp, quick, and confident. I'm sure we could've taken them if it had come to blows, but we would've walked away with some knots on our heads."

"You're leaving something out, kid. What did they come to find?"

I sighed. "I'm still not sure what they came to find, but the part I'm leaving out is a safe that was hidden in the construction of Earl's boat. When I dived on the wreck, I discovered it, and we brought it up."

"Now this story is getting interesting," he said. "Let me guess. Your friend didn't know anything about the safe, and she didn't have the combination."

"You're good at this."

"I've been in the game a long time, kid. I'll be in Saint Augustine by sundown. Where can I find you?"

"I'm aboard *Aegis* in slip number seven."

"*Aegis*?" he almost yelled. "I thought your little Russian girlfriend sank *Aegis*."

"She wasn't my girlfriend, and this is the new *Aegis*. She's a fifty-foot sailing cat, and she's hard to miss. The gate code is—"

The phone clicked, and I was left talking into dead air. Every eye stared at me.

I said, "He's on his way."

Chapter 19
A Little More Help

Beater kept his word, just as I knew he would. We watched the sun sink behind the Old City as he yelled, "Permission to come aboard?"

"Come aboard," I yelled as I descended the ladder to greet my old friend.

Hugging isn't something Beater did, but a round of handshakes and introductions precluded the pouring of the best bottle of scotch I owned and the lighting of five Cuban Cohibas.

Beater surveyed the collection of operators around the table and then examined his cigar. "Cohiba means *tobacco* in Taíno, the native language of Cuba's indigenous Arawak people, before the Spaniards showed up and screwed up the place."

I eyed my cigar. "I didn't know—"

Beater held up one finger. "I wasn't finished." He took another draw and then a swallow of scotch. "It's a simple, beautiful word, *Cohiba*, but it's come to mean a lot more than tobacco. This is the most expensive production cigar in the world. Did you boys know that?"

No one spoke, but everyone shook their head.

"Now, you can buy more expensive cigars, but these are the most expensive factory-produced cigars on Earth." He pointed toward his glass. "And that's a five-hundred-dollar bottle of whiskey. Chase pulled the cork and opened the humidor without a grunt. That means something. I think it means he respects you guys more than he respects the thousand bucks it cost him to have us sit down at his table."

Clark stared at Beater like a mesmerized child while Mongo leaned back in his chair, pretending to be more interested in the cigar than the man.

Beater pointed toward Clark. "You're in charge, but not on this one. Am I right?"

Clark nodded.

Beater continued. "None of you drank until Chase did, so you respect him, too, but not exactly the same way he feels about you. He's clearly in charge, and all of you are clearly okay with that. I like the dynamic here, but you"—he motioned toward Mongo—"I'm most intrigued by you, Marvin."

Mongo grinned. "Nobody on Earth calls me Marvin except my momma and the woman I sleep with. And sometimes she calls me Big Daddy."

Beater narrowed his eyes. "Why would your momma call you Big Daddy?"

Laughter erupted, cutting through the seriousness of the moment, and glasses were raised.

When the frivolity quieted, Beater said, "Seriously, Marvin— unless you'd prefer that I call you Mongo—you're the one I can help. There's no hope for the rest of this ragtag bunch of trigger-pullers."

Mongo leaned in. "A man with your résumé can call me whatever he wants. If you're willing to teach, I'm willing to listen."

Beater rolled his cigar between his lips and watched the plume of white smoke disappear into the night sky. "It's not important what you can *do* to a man. It's important what that man *thinks* you can do to him."

Beater suddenly had everyone's attention. "More importantly than that is what that man *believes* you're willing to do to him. You're a giant. There's no denying that. Your size alone is enough to scare the hell out of most people, but that's not enough. I'll prove it."

He motioned toward Hunter. "You. What are you, five-eight? Maybe five-nine and a buck ninety?"

"Something like that," Hunter said.

Beater pointed toward Mongo with his chin. "Are you afraid of that giant?"

"No, I'm not afraid of him."

"Why not?"

Hunter wrinkled his brow. "Because I know he won't hurt me even though he could."

Beater smiled a huge, toothy grin, snapped his fingers, and pointed directly at Hunter. "Bingo. Even though he could, you know he won't hurt you. That's exactly my point. Intimidation requires belief in sinister intent."

He paused and individually met eyes with everyone at the table. "Don't forget that phrase, *belief in sinister intent.* If your foe doesn't believe that you have the will, ability, and even the desire to do him harm, you are absolutely no threat to him. Back during the Cold War, I used to punch the wall about a dozen times before heading into an interrogation."

He held up his ham-sized fists. "I did it to turn my knuckles into bloody, shredded meat. When I slammed a pair of battered, nasty fists on the table in front of a detainee . . . that's what you call them now, right? Detainees?"

We nodded, and he continued. "We called them red commie bastards, but they're the same animal. When that man believed I was looking forward to pounding his head into his torso—and that I was looking forward to it—it was amazing how quickly he started talking. It's not about reality. It's about the perception of reality, boys. That's how my game works. I can't help you with all of that double-oh-seven crap you do, but I know a thing or two about intimidation. If that's what you brought me down here to do, I'm your man; otherwise, we'll just smoke up Chase's humidor and drink all of his whiskey."

Wisdom and experience are priceless commodities in the covert operations community. My team was sitting at the feet of one of the few remaining masters.

Beater said, "So, what's it going to be?"

It was my turn to be a leader. "I'm not sure we're willing to kill these two guys."

"You don't have to be," he said. "You just have to make them believe you're willing to kill them in some way that's too nasty for their brains to imagine."

I exhaled, my frustration obvious. "If these guys are former Air America, they're cowboys to the core, and they're obviously not afraid of us."

"Are you afraid of them?" he asked.

Mongo spoke up. "We're not particularly *afraid* of them, but it's safe to say we've got a healthy respect for their skill set."

"Same thing," Beater said. "Are they afraid of you?"

Hunter chuckled. "Hell no. They made that clear"—he pointed across the street to the rooftop restaurant—"right up there."

Beater swallowed the last of his scotch. "I thought we covered this already. Just because they didn't *act* scared of you doesn't mean they weren't. We're back to that perception thing again. They didn't appear to be afraid of you. My guess is, these guys are nervous as . . . something that's really nervous . . . but they didn't let you see that. They showed you what they wanted you to believe, and it worked. You're scared, and you think they aren't. Look who's already on top in this little game."

His words rang true and pierced the facades we thought we'd put up.

Beater stood with his empty glass in his hand. "Think about this while I'm refilling this dead soldier. Other than Marvin, who's the scariest member of your little team?"

He obviously expected us to discuss it and reveal our answer when he returned, but the unified answer rose as a chorus. "Anya."

He froze in place. "Ah, your little Russian girlfriend."

Surprising Beater wasn't easy, but Mongo did it. "Actually, she's *my* little American girlfriend who *used* to be a Russian."

Beater looked at me and then at Mongo. "This sounds like a story I've got to hear."

He refilled his glass and topped ours off before reclaiming his seat. I spent the next twenty minutes explaining how Anya had ended up on Mongo's arm and Penny Thomas had ended up with my last name.

His eyes were filled with questions, but the one he chose to voice made everything about his lesson in intimidation rise to the surface. "So, why isn't she here?"

The answer made me sound like anything but a warrior. "Penny's afraid I may not be over her, even though she's waking up with our giant every morning."

He held up the empty ring finger of his left hand. "That's precisely why operators die alone. Sometimes it happens in a gunfight ten thousand miles from home. Other times, it happens in a nice comfortable bed with only one side of the covers disturbed. There's never been a Mrs. Beater, and your mentor, Rocket Richter, never loved anybody except Anya's mother. And we all know that bastard, Dmitri Barkov, cut out her heart so Richter couldn't have it. We all make choices about how we spend the only fortune we'll ever have—our lives. I gave mine to the fight for freedom against tyranny. What you do with yours is up to you, but dragging somebody else into a world like ours is just about the cruelest thing any of us could do to somebody we claim to love."

His words felt like a dagger plunging into my chest. The decisions I'd made, and especially the ones that had been made for me, left me strung up between two worlds, suspended between what I believed and what I desired, and knowing the two could never breathe the same air.

Clark, the man who knew me better than anyone on the planet, motioned for me to follow him. We walked toward the bow, and he pointed to the main boom overhead. "Remember when I taught you about the importance of balance in a fight?"

"I'll never forget that lesson. Right up there on that boom. Falling hurt."

"It always does," he said, "but making the decision to lean into a punch instead of ducking away from it hurts, too. That's what makes this so tough for you. If the guys who hit Earl's boat aren't intimidated by us, we only have two choices. We can either hit them hard and fast so they know we're not playing, or you can scare the hell out of them with a weapon they'd never see coming."

"I don't like it." I said, "but I know you're right. You're always right. We need a little more help."

He landed a hand on my shoulder. "Everybody wants to be captain 'til it's time to do captain stuff."

Clark returned to the table and left me standing alone beside *Aegis's* telephone-pole-sized main mast, staring into the night sky.

As if she could sense what was stirring inside my soul, Penny's name flashed on the caller ID screen as I pulled my chirping phone from my pocket.

"Hey, Chase. I've been thinking about you, and I'm worried. I know you don't need the stress of me nagging you, but I just want to hear your voice."

Comfort comes in countless forms. Having someone care for me the way Penny did was worth more than any paycheck I'd ever earn, but comfort isn't the only emotion carried on a thousand wings. Agony often drifts close behind, and that's the sword I felt in my belly when I said, "I'm bringing Anya to Saint Augustine. We need her for the op."

I could almost hear her heart breaking two thousand miles away.

"I knew you would. She's the one thing you just can't seem to get by without."

For the second time in one day, I found myself talking into a phone full of dead air.

Chapter 20
Stormy Weather

"Yes, Chase. I will come, but not for money. I will come because you asked me."

Hearing Anya's voice somehow made the fog I'd been living under even denser. I found myself in a world of extremes, a world of polar opposites in every way. I was being torn apart by unseen forces pulling at my every edge in all directions. The woman I loved, and who loved me more purely than I could ever deserve, was two thousand miles away and crying herself to sleep every night because I couldn't turn my back on what may have been my destiny, or perhaps my undoing.

Beater, a dinosaur of the Cold War, sat before me, preaching the psychology of fear based in perceived threats, while Mongo, the most compassionate person I knew, drank in every word.

Earl, the brilliant, hardworking diesel mechanic who lived in near squalor aboard a thirty-year-old boat and never hurt a soul, was in hiding from a pair of men determined to take something from her she never knew she had.

And Anya, the lying, manipulative, former Russian assassin who'd devoted the first twenty years of her life to learning the craft of tearing men's souls from their bodies, was the person to whom I turned when five of the world's most lethal operators couldn't defeat a pair of men over twice our age.

My life had become an exercise in dichotomy, and I was powerless to stop any of it. I was left to tug against unyielding forces and surrender to others in a desperate attempt to do what I believed was right. Perhaps Earl was an innocent victim of circumstance and forces beyond her knowledge and control, but the possibility remained that she was complicit in Boomer's scheme to embezzle fortunes from his fellow pilots in the jungles of Central America.

Light without darkness is nothing. Good without evil cannot exist. Would the extremes ever release me, or was I condemned to wage war within myself as long as I drew a breath? Only time and my decisions would pour out an answer—if an answer could be found.

Hunter pulled me from my stupor. "Is she coming?"

"Huh?"

He snapped his fingers inches in front of my face. "Hey, Chase. Where'd you go, man? Are you okay?"

I pawed at my eyes with the heels of my hands and gathered my wits. "Yeah, I'm okay. I've just got a lot on my mind."

"I know you do, but we need you. Whatever else is going on in there has to wait. You asked for our help, and we're here. Now, pull your head out and call a pitch, catcher."

When I'd squatted in the sand and clay behind home plate, I was in command of the whole world. I'd watched every player on the field, and I could read a baserunner's intentions before he knew them himself. It was easy back then. If I made the wrong call, losing the game would be the worst thing that would happen. That is the epitome of opposing worlds. When winning and losing is defined by the numbers on a scoreboard, the whole world is one big game, but when losing meant flags draped over caskets and three-volley rifle salutes, the weight of the universe rested on my falling shoulders.

I slapped my partner on the back, directing him toward the table. "Let's have a chat."

He offered part of a smile and a quick nod.

"Here's the plan," I began. "We find out where these guys are sleeping and what they're doing when they're awake. Clark and Hunter, that's your job. Mongo, you're on the documents. Get with Skipper and find out where we stand on the reconstruction and translations. Beater, you're with me. Skipper will have a dossier on Gary Weathers soon. I need your memory and contacts to find out exactly who and what we're up against."

The eyes that had been full of questions morphed into confidence and faith in me. Seeing my team reenergized and focused gave me the confidence I needed to see the fight through to the end.

"Oh, one more thing. Anya will be here tomorrow. These old spooks may know all of our tricks, but they've never seen most of hers. Hopefully, she won't have to 'gut them like pig,' but just like Beater said, she doesn't have to do it. She just has to make them *believe* she can and will."

Skipper emailed the abbreviated dossier on Weathers, and Beater tore into it as if he were cramming for a final exam. Mongo stuck the phone to his ear and buried himself in the documents with Skipper via a long-distance call. Clark and Hunter hit the streets in search of our prey.

I called my wife, and to my surprise, she answered. "Hey, I'm sorry I hung up on you earlier. It's just that all of this is a little overwhelming for me. I'm not mad. I promise."

"It's overwhelming for me, too, and I'm sorry for dragging you into my chaos."

The laughter I loved so much returned to her voice. "You didn't drag me. I jumped with both feet. I had no idea what I was getting into, but I still jumped."

"We've both done our share of jumping over the past few years, and I don't know if that'll ever change, but I can't think of anyone I'd rather take leaps of faith with than you."

"That's sweet, but I feel like more of an anchor than a parachute. I don't like bringing you down."

"There will be plenty of time to talk about that and work it out when all of this is over, but right now, I really need to talk to Earl."

"Sure. She's right here."

"Hey, Stud Muffin. How's it going down there?"

"We're making some progress, momma, but I have a couple of questions, and I need you to tell me the absolute truth. Don't leave anything out, and don't sugarcoat anything, okay?"

"When have you ever heard me sugarcoat anything?"

I cleared my throat. "First, was Boomer skimming money from the other Air America pilots in Central and South America?"

She didn't hesitate. "Probably, but I didn't know the details. He was always a planner, in spite of his crazy life. He always had a scheme of some kind in the works. After a while, I didn't think anything of it. He was just always working on a plan to retire young, if you know what I mean."

"That's a good start. Now, I need to know if you think you've ever seen either of the guys who attacked you before. I need you to think hard. This one is important."

"I know I've never seen the tall bald guy. I would've remembered him, but the smaller guy with the scar, I keep thinking I've seen him somewhere."

"Does the name Gary Weathers ring any bells?"

She clicked her tongue against her teeth. "Yeah, I think maybe it does, but I can't quite nail it down."

"Keep working on it," I said. "If anything, and I mean anything, comes to mind, you ring my phone. You got it?"

"Sure, Baby Boy, you got it. But hey . . ." I could hear her moving around as if she were scanning the room. "This girl of yours ain't doin' so good. I think she may've stolen more chain than she can swim with. You know what I mean?"

"Stole more chain than she can swim with? No, Earl, I have no idea what you mean."

Her voice lowered. "Yeah, I ain't so sure she knew what she was getting into when she jumped in bed with you. Your life ain't exactly nine-to-five and white picket fences."

"Yeah, I know. In fact, that's part of the reason we were in Saint Augustine. We were headed to the Pacific to take some time off together."

She sighed. "Chase. You mean you stopped that to help me?"

"You're our friend, Earl. That's what friends do."

"No, Chase, it ain't what friends do. I can't have you—"

"Listen to me, Earl. We're going to get to the bottom of all of this, and then we'll continue our trip. It's not up for debate."

"I ain't never gonna forget this, Baby Boy."

I chuckled. "Ah, sure you will. You're old and senile. You probably won't remember your name in another year or two."

Her tone lightened. "You better watch it. Who's gonna take care of them motors you're so hard on?"

"Call me if you think of anything, especially anything about Gary Weathers."

"I will. You wanna talk to that girl again?"

"Her name is Penny, Earl, and yes, I'd like to talk with her again if she's around."

"I know her name," she said. "I just don't like giving my competition any credit. You know how it is. Hang on. Here comes what's-her-name."

Penny chuckled. "What was that all about?"

"Oh, it was nothing," I said. "Earl's just cutting up. I just wanted to hear your voice again before I hang up, and I want you to know I love you."

I never remembered a time when Penny hadn't immediately returned my words of affection, but instead of saying she also loved me, she asked, "Is Anya there yet?"

I'd never learn.

"No, not yet, but she'll be here tomorrow."

She was quiet for a long moment. "Okay, just be careful. The most dangerous animals in the woods aren't always the ones that growl. I love you, too, and I trust you."

The line went dead, and I tried to digest what she'd said.

"Hey, kid. I think I've got something."

I turned to see Beater with his bear-claw hands juggling a dozen pages of the Weathers dossier. "What is it?"

He spread the pages across the table and pointed out several dates. "I'm getting old, and the gears don't always turn like they used to, but there's a few things an old fighter never forgets. One of those is the first time he gets knocked out. January of nineteen sixty-three was mine."

"That was forty years ago," I said. "What could you getting knocked out have to do with any of this?"

"Yeah, it was forty years ago, but it wasn't just a knock-out. I was part of the U.S. advisory team in South Vietnam in the winter of sixty-two and sixty-three. I was in Ap Bac, a rat-hole village in the Mekong Delta about seventy clicks southwest of Saigon. We were so-called unarmed advisors to the South Vietnamese military. Anyway, in January, we got hit hard by some little ragtag gang of Viet Cong. We had them outnumbered at least four to one, but they kicked our teeth in. That's when I knew a war was coming like nothing we'd ever seen. Korea sucked, but it was going to be a backyard brawl compared to what was coming in 'Nam."

"What does that have to do with this?"

"Keep your shirt on, kid. I'm getting there. When the fight was over—by the way, I wasn't unarmed for long, and I fought back—those North Vietnamese commies took no prisoners. They killed everybody they could find. Me and a kid named Broadway made it across the river and about twelve clicks to a place called Ben Tre. Broadway was a commo troop of some kind. We 'procured' a radio, and he started making calls all over the world. Kennedy was still alive, and he wasn't afraid of a fight like Johnson was. He sent in a handful of guys to clean up the mess and pick up the few of us who'd survived. When me and Broadway finally got picked up, the two guys doing the flying were insane. They put Broadway and me on the door guns and ordered us to plow the ground with fifty-cal when we flew over what was left of Ap Bac. The whole time, those guys were yelling, 'Stormy Weather's a-comin'."

I was mesmerized. "That's a great story, Beater, but I still don't have a clue what you're talking about."

"Stormy Weather, kid. The two pilots who flew me and Broadway out of there were Stormy Sanderson and Gary Weathers. You put those two maniacs in the same cockpit, and there was no way to know what was going to happen next. Everybody from Brunei to Burma knew about Stormy Weather before the war was over."

Chapter 21
Little Sparrow

I locked eyes with my old friend. "Are you telling me the two guys who hit Earl are Stormy Sanderson and Gary Weathers?"

"No, I ain't tellin' you that. I'm telling you a story about two idiots I knew in 'Nam."

Instead of the puzzle coming together, he kept adding random pieces, and nothing seemed to fit.

Beater closed one eye and peered skyward. "I was born in July of nineteen twenty-six, so that would've made me thirty-six in January of sixty-three. As I remember it, Stormy and Weathers had to be at least my age, and maybe even a little older. What year is it now? Two thousand three?"

I nodded as he worked through the math.

He pursed his lips. "That means I'm seventy-seven. And you think your adversaries are at least ten years younger than me, right?"

"None of this is making sense," I whispered to myself, apparently loud enough for Beater to hear.

"Sure it does, kid. You just have to think like a spook. What time is your Russian girlfriend getting here?"

I leaned in. "You've got to quit calling her that. She and Mongo are together now, and I'm married to Penny. Anya is just a *sometimes* member of our team when we need her particular skill set."

His smile was laced with condescension. "I thought you were smarter than that, kid."

I frowned. "What are you talking about?"

"Tell me the one thing you know for sure about that girl."

"She's dangerous."

He waved a huge hand and scoffed. "Ah, the whole world knows that. All women are dangerous. Especially the beautiful ones. Tell me the one thing you know about her that perhaps no one else knows perfectly well."

I tore through my memory of Anya from the moment I first saw her until the mission on the Pan America oil rig where she slaughtered men as if they were nothing. All the lies, the emotion, the passion—sincere from my end, but performance art from hers.

Before I could piece together what Beater wanted to hear me say, he leaned toward me. "The one thing you know better than anyone on Earth about the Russian is that she will make any sacrifice, take any life, feign any emotion, and become absolutely anyone to get close to you. That's what she's programmed to do, kid."

I stared at the deck for what felt like hours. "Are you saying . . ."

His paw landed on my knee. "I'm not going to be the one to tell that Goliath of yours that she's using him to stay next to you, but somewhere down there, where your heart is supposed to be, you know that's the truth. You can trust her if you want, but you can stretch a roll of barbed wire fence as tight as you can pull it for fifty years, but when you cut it loose, it'll tear your leg off trying to curl back up into that original roll."

Why do old guys have to speak in riddles?

He continued. "We are what we're born to be, no matter how hard we pull against it. That's exactly what's wrong with your marriage. You're a warrior and a patriot, no matter how much you think you want to be a family man. That girl is a Russian spy, a red sparrow, no matter how much you think she wants to be red, white, and blue."

"You've not seen the things she's done to prove she's one of us," I argued.

He sighed. "No, I haven't, but I've seen a hundred others just like her—a goddess on the outside and a roiling den of snakes on the inside. Maybe I'm wrong about yours, but in my experience, those Russian girls are the best in the world at becoming whatever they believe you want so they can get exactly what they want. That one of yours was designed, built, and programmed from the assembly line for one job. . . ." He pointed his sausage finger at my chest. "You."

I leaned back in my chair and stared into the heavens. A billion stars filled the sky, but no matter how real they appeared, most, if not all of them, had burned themselves out millions of years ago. All that remained were the streaks of light they'd once emitted, racing through the cosmos for eons, making it easy to believe the source of the light still existed. I saw what I wanted to see and what was easy to believe, and I closed my eyes.

When I finally opened my eyes, Beater was stacking Weathers's dossier and lighting another Cohiba.

"So, what should I do?" I asked.

He ignored me and continued toasting the end of his cigar. A long draw was followed by a satisfied exhalation. "You keep doing what you were built to do, kid. I remember a day not too long ago as the calendar goes, but measured by what really matters, it was a thousand lifetimes ago. Me and Rocket and Ace and Tuner sat around an old wrought-iron table at the Jekyll Island

Club with a confused, arrogant kid on the other side, who didn't even know how to light a cigar. Remember that day?"

I swallowed the lump in my throat. "Yes."

He blew a smoke ring into the still night air. "If you could go back and relive that day, would you make a different decision?"

To my surprise, I didn't hesitate. "No. I'd do it all over again, even though I know how much it hurts."

He winked. "Me, too, kid. Me, too."

* * *

When I awoke the following morning, coffee was already brewing. I poured a cup, wondering who beat me out of bed. I unlocked the sliding door to the cockpit from the main salon and stretched as I took in my first breath of salty morning air. The rigid hull inflatable boat was in place on her davits at *Aegis's* stern, right where she belonged, but beyond the RHIB sat something entirely out of place on the Saint Augustine Municipal Marina floating dock.

"What are you doing sitting out there?" I asked.

Anastasia Robertovna Burinkova brushed her long, golden hair across her shoulder and looked up with the rising sun beaming down on her flawless face. "Am waiting for permission to come onto boat."

I glanced down at my mug filled with coffee that was a little stronger than I preferred. "Did you make this coffee?"

She smiled and stood from her perch on the deck box. "Is good to see you. I would like to come onto boat please."

"Permission to come aboard," I said.

Her smile broadened. "Is what I meant, but I cannot remember exactly phrase every time."

"Come aboard," I said. "It's good to see you, too."

She slid off her shoes and stepped aboard. "I can give to you hug, yes?"

Although my head was screaming no, I sat my mug on the table and took her in my arms. "Thank you for coming. We really need your help on this one."

"I will always come when you ask," she said, barely above a whisper.

I stared down at her, consumed by Beater's warning from the previous night.

"I can go inside, yes?"

"Of course," I said. "Make yourself at home. Mongo is camped out in the workshop. Clark and Hunter are on the pull-outs, and my old friend, Beater, is in the guest cabin."

She froze and looked up at me. "And Penny?"

"She's not here. It's not particularly safe for her right now, so I sent her someplace where she could sleep with both eyes closed."

Without a word, she smiled, turned, and slipped into the interior of my boat.

I finished my first cup of coffee and headed back into the starboard hull for a shower and a toothbrush. When I believed I smelled more like a human, I pulled open the hatch to my cabin and froze. A display of long blonde hair lay across my pillow, and a tall thin form was outlined beneath the sheet.

My first instinct was to drag Anya from my bed by her four-toed foot and banish her from the boat, but the compassionate side of me chose to let her sleep. She'd probably driven all night and needed the rest. Why she was in my bed, though, instead of curled up with Mongo, made Beater's admonishment even more powerful.

I slipped into a pair of cargo pants and a T-shirt and carried my boots back upstairs. Hunter was pouring coffee in the main salon, and Clark was still sawing logs.

Hunter groaned, "Good morning. Want a cup?"

"No, thanks. I had mine already, but that's a bit stronger than usual. You might want to cut it a little."

He took a tentative sip and shrugged. "It's all right."

An hour later, everyone was awake and on the upper deck. A guy with two enormous bags yelled up from the dock. "Ahoy, *Aegis*! Delivery from Maple Street."

I leaned over the rail. "Come on up!"

The man expertly climbed the ladder with his bags in tow. "Good morning. I'm Antonio, and this is the breakfast you ordered."

"Nice job on the ladder," I said. "You must spend some time on the water."

"You might say that," he said as he placed the plastic carry-out containers on the table. "I live on that old Hunter Thirty-Six anchored just north of the bridge."

I peered northward beneath the Bridge of Lions. "Nice. There's nothing like living on a boat, is there?"

"I wouldn't have it any other way. Well, enjoy your breakfast. I've got more deliveries to make."

I stuck a pair of folded bills into his palm. "Thanks for breakfast."

He shot a glance at the tip and smiled. "Thank you. And this is a great boat. I'd love to have a cat someday."

Antonio disappeared as quickly as he'd arrived, and we dug into the feast. Maple Street Biscuit Company made the best breakfast in town. Half of their name was a lie, but the other half couldn't be more honest. They weren't located on Maple Street, but they had mastered the biscuit business.

When almost every plate was empty, Anya said, "Thank you for breakfast, Chase, but I have question."

"Let's hear it."

"You have Clark, Okhotnik, and Marvin. Why do you need me for this job?"

Beater grimaced. "Okhotnik?"

Hunter chuckled. "That's *Hunter* in whatever screwed-up language she speaks."

Beater said, "Ah. I thought she was calling me a dinosaur."

Anya grinned. "Dinosaur is almost same word in English and Russian, but I think you already know this, Bilo."

Beater lowered his chin. "*Da, vorobey.*"

Anya scowled at being called a *sparrow*, the term used to describe Russian agents trained in the art of seduction for the purpose of espionage.

I broke the tension. "You're here because the people we're up against know every trick in our book. They probably helped write the book. You're going to scare the hell out of them to let them know we're serious. We need to know what they were looking for on Earl's boat, and we need to know who sent them."

We spent the next ten minutes detailing the events of the previous days, and Anya listened intently. When we'd outlined what happened on the deck at the restaurant, she turned to Mongo. "This person who put pepper into your eyes. What did he look like?"

Mongo blinked, remembering the experience. "I didn't get a look. I don't even know if it was a man or a woman. I was watching Chase and Hunter, and *bam*, I got sprayed out of nowhere."

"This means at least three of them, and probably more, are working together," Beater said.

"Earl only saw two men," I said, "and the cab driver told the same story."

Beater said, "These men are very smart. Do we know where they're staying?"

"We do now," Clark said. "Hunter and I found them in a house about three-quarters of a mile north of here. The house is on an unpaved sand road that backs up to a fence to the north and another row of houses to the south. To the left and right are

houses about thirty feet apart. It's tight back there. The only way
out for a vehicle is the road, but the fences, front and back, are
easy enough to climb."

Anya looked to Hunter. "Guards?"

"Not that we saw, but there are lights with motion sensors on
the corners of the house."

"How many people inside house?"

"At least three, maybe four," Clark said. "And there's a black
Range Rover backed into the parking spot. No garage."

Anya said, "Is good. Now, you must tell me rules of
engagement."

"Don't kill them yet," I said, "unless they're going to kill you. I
want you to make them understand that you're capable and willing to turn them inside out if they don't give us what we want."

Anya smiled. "This I can do. You will take me to house, and I
will make men beg to tell you everything."

Beater stared at the Russian. "I don't trust you, but I like your
style, little sparrow."

Chapter 22
Very Bad Mood

"Show to me house on map."

Anya's English still needed some work, but she had no trouble getting her point across.

Hunter pulled a street map from his bag and spread it out on the table. "Here's Cincinnati Avenue. Follow that to First Street, and turn right. The road is sand and a little rough. It makes a ninety-degree turn to the left, and the house is three hundred meters on the left."

"We go there now, yes?"

Hunter looked up at me, and I shrugged. "I don't see why not. I'll call Jesus for a ride."

Anya shook her head. "No, I have car. I have American driving license. You want to see?"

I held up my hand. "No, I don't want to see your license. I've never met anyone prouder of having a license than you."

"You give for me Florida driving license. You remember, yes?"

"Yes, I remember," I said. "But I didn't *give* it to you. It was sort of a welcome-to-America gift from some friends."

She produced the small plastic card in spite of my assurance that I didn't want to see it. "Is now Georgia driving license, but I still have first Florida one. This I will keep forever."

The deadliest human I'd ever know was sitting at my table, aboard my boat, displaying her driver's license like a teenager just back from the DMV. In twelve hours, she'd likely be tearing someone's spleen out through his left eyeball. Would the study in opposites ever end for me?

I pulled on my cap and sunglasses. "Let's go. It looks like Anya's driving."

Hunter, Clark, Mongo, and I followed Anya up the walkway toward Avenida Menendez. When we hit the sidewalk, she said, "Look. Someone left for me message."

She leaned across the hood of the black Chevy Suburban and pulled the parking ticket from beneath the wiper blade. She studied the slip closely, then pressed the key fob, unlocking the doors.

Inside the SUV, I said, "Parking tickets aren't good messages."

"Is okay. I have many of them. I am waiting for check to come."

Mongo put his hand on my shoulder and whispered, "Don't ask. You'll regret it."

But I couldn't resist. "What check?"

She held up the ticket. "Each parking message says is fine for twenty-five dollars. I think when I have enough of them, parking people will send to me check for all of fine parking I do."

I trembled in an effort to hold back my laughter.

"See?" Mongo said. "I told you. I just pay the tickets and move on. It's more fun than explaining it to her."

She flashed her smile in the mirror. "I like being fine parker."

We drove the three-quarters of a mile north on Menendez and made the left turn onto Cincinnati. At the intersection with First Street, she continued without turning.

Hunter said, "That was your turn."

"Yes, I know, but map shows other end is also First Street. I wish to see from other end."

We turned right at the second First Street sign and bounced down the puddled, sandy drive. The road was only wide enough for one car, with a tall wooden fence to the north, and each house set directly against the road to the right. Each home had a small parking area, but there were no yards.

Hunter pointed toward a newly remodeled green house. "That's it."

Anya's eyes scanned every detail of the area. There was no doubt she was creating a mental map of every inch of the environment. To my surprise, she stopped the Suburban and hopped from the driver's seat. Seconds later, she was standing on the small wooden porch and ringing the doorbell.

Everyone in the SUV drew a weapon and stared intently as our Eastern European contingent stood waiting for someone to answer the door. A few moments later, she gave up and returned to the truck. "No one is home. Too bad."

"What were you thinking?" I demanded.

"If they come to door, I ask to see Nicholai. There is no Nicholai, and I am dumb girl at wrong house. If they do not come to door, I now know about lock on door and every room I can see from windows. Is simple plan."

"Is insane plan," I said.

"You ask for me to come to do this thing because you cannot, no?"

I surrendered. "Yes, that's right."

She pulled the Suburban into drive. "Then my plan is better than your plan."

We turned left, back onto Menendez, and immediately left again onto Hope Street. A few houses down, we pulled into the driveway of a two-story house with a detached garage in back.

Anya turned to Clark. "Is your turn."

"My turn for what?" he said.

"Go to house and rent apartment over garage for three nights. Is house of widow, I think, and you have charm with women. Marvin is too big. Chase looks too much like playboy, and Hunter looks too much like mercenary. I am pretty girl. Widow will think I have wild party with men. You have trusty face, so go."

Clark slid from the seat and glared back into the SUV. "I'm pretty sure *trusty* isn't a real word."

He was back five minutes later with a key and a sandwich. "I guess you were right. She must've thought I looked trusty . . . and hungry. She made me a sandwich. The apartment is mine for three days, but how did you know she was a widow and that the apartment was for rent?"

"Is simple," she said. "There are many bird feeders in yard, but only low ones have seeds in them. Flowers are in windows, but door is broken. Is for man to fix door and for woman to care for flowers. Apartment has new rail and yellow paint on steps. Is for safety of guests, not for owner."

Clark shot a look through the vehicle. "I hope you guys are taking notes. This is good stuff." He took another bite of his sandwich. "And so is this."

* * *

By the time the sun went down, the rented apartment had been converted into an observation post offering a direct line of sight to the lair of our prey, and Anya was picking the lock.

We'd positioned a body camera on her chest, and everyone wore a set of whisper-comms. Beater took up a position on Cincinnati and notified us every time someone turned down First Street. It was time to play a game of hurry-up-and-wait.

"I am hiding inside storage closet off kitchen," came Anya's first transmission.

"What if they look inside the closet?" I asked.

"Is locked with bolt of dead."

"I'm sure you mean *dead bolt*," I replied.

"Yes, dead bolt. I think is for only owners of house."

Small talk faded, and we continued waiting.

At five minutes after eleven, Beater's voice filled our headsets. "Black Range Rover approaching from the east."

I pulled back the curtain and peered down the sandy street, where a pair of headlights illuminated the houses and fence line. "That could be our boys."

The Range Rover backed into the drive of what was about to become a slaughterhouse if Anya had her way. I silently prayed she wouldn't kill them all. We needed at least one of them to talk to us.

The headlights hit our window, and we vanished beneath the sill.

I spoke into my mic. "They're home."

"How many?" Anya whispered.

I slowly moved back into position in the window, careful to avoid making a dead man's silhouette. "Four."

"Four is good," came Anya's reply.

The seven-inch LCD screen was still black. Anya's position in the closet left her, and us, completely blind.

She whispered, "I will not talk again until I begin working, but you should tell me when anything changes."

"They're inside," I said, but she didn't reply.

The windows of the kitchen were illuminated, and shadows danced across the wall. Minutes later, the kitchen fell dark, and three bedrooms lit up.

"It looks like they're going to bed."

Anya made a small hissing sound but didn't speak.

Soon, the bedroom lights went out one by one.

"Okay, it's lights out in the playhouse," I said.

The next forty minutes passed like hours as Anya waited for the men to fall asleep.

Rustling rattled in my earpiece, and the unmistakable sounds of a door opening and closing rang in my ears.

The body cam sent its broadcast across the sandy street and onto our monitor. Its night-vision capabilities were limited, but we could make out the shapes of furniture, doorways, and windows in the grainy display.

The open-channel mic Anya was wearing gave us crisp, clear audio of every sound inside the house. The air conditioner whispered its breathy tone. The ticking of the oversized clock on the living room wall kept measured time like a distant metronome. The rhythm of Anya's breathing, slow and deliberate, was the only sound that wasn't mechanical. Missing were the sounds anyone else's feet would have made with every step. She moved as if she were a ghost hovering inches above the hardwood floor. Even the camera couldn't capture any vertical movement in her effortless strides.

Approaching the first bedroom, she pressed her hand against the right side of the door, applying pressure to quiet any squeaking from a neglected hinge. Her left hand silently turned the knob, and she floated through the opening. Her unsuspecting first victim lay on his side, facing away from the door, and curled into a fetal position.

She rounded the foot of the bed and slipped her hand beneath his pillow, then withdrew a midsized Glock pistol. With movement too fast for the camera to capture, she leapt on top of the man, forcing him to his back with her right knee planted solidly on his chin. The man's eyes bolted open, and his mouth gaped as Anya racked the slide of the Glock, ejecting the ammunition into the man's mouth. With the Glock's slide locked to the rear and its magazine empty, she shoved the butt of the pistol into his mouth full of brass and lead. An instant later, she wound a roll of duct tape around his head, forcing the pistol further into place.

He struggled against her, but the more he fought, the more tape she unrolled, until he was bound, ankles and wrist, like a rodeo steer. She rolled the bound, defenseless man over the edge of the bed with his head against the floor and his lower half still on the mattress. The only sounds were the man's terror-filled nose-breathing and the crack of his head hitting the floor.

She leaned close to his ear and whispered, "I am night demon, and you are coming with me to Hell."

After allowing the man time to digest her threat, she struck the back of his neck near the base of his skull, and his rigid body fell limp.

Throughout the ordeal, her breathing rate never increased, and she never made an unnecessary sound.

Back on her feet, she whispered, "I did not kill him. This is what you want, yes?"

I was in awe and incapable of saying anything other than, "Yeah."

She moved, if possible, even more quietly toward the second bedroom and pressed her way through the door. The tall, bald man lay on his back, his body perfectly flat against the mattress, arms crossed over his belly. Anya moved in unhurried determination, lacing two pieces of five-fifty cord beneath the bed and across the man's abdomen and neck. Using a knot I'd never seen, she secured the cord into a single looped end wrapped around her left wrist. As if she were setting the hook on a monster marlin, she yanked the cord until it drew taut, digging into the flesh of the man's wrists, arms, and neck. His eyes widened in terror as his body convulsed, unable to take in a breath.

She moved into his field of vision so close he would never be able to focus on her features. In a bone-chilling tone, she whispered, "Is for you to now die slowly. If you fight, I will make also blood from you."

She adjusted the loop around the man's neck barely loose enough for him to force an occasional gasping breath, but she quickly taped a pillow around his head to stifle any sounds he was likely to produce. Just like her first victim, the duct tape bound his ankles and wrists. Blood trickled from his forearms beneath the five-fifty cord.

With her work in the second bedroom complete, she moved toward the kitchen and approached the third bedroom. As her hand embraced the doorknob, my heart stopped.

"Anya, freeze! The light just came on in the bathroom."

The sound of her breathing stopped, and she froze just as I'd ordered.

I whispered, "He's moving from the bathroom back through the bedroom. He's heading for the door."

She backed up and turned the corner into an alcove between the bedroom door and the kitchen. The door opened, and a man in boxer shorts stepped into the short hallway. She let him pass and then stepped behind him.

We sat in silence, staring into the monitor where our Russian assassin was about to slit the throat of the man who'd likely hit Mongo with pepper spray.

I bit the inside of my cheek, praying she wouldn't kill him, but before I could finish my conversation with God, Anya landed her right heel behind the man's knee, sending him spinning and falling. She caught his weight before he crashed to the floor, then straddled his chest. Before he'd come to rest beneath her, she plunged a needle into his neck and then held the empty syringe up for him to see.

"Is neurotoxin and tranquilizer to stop muscles from working. Breathing will stop in three minutes, maybe less. I have antidote, but I am in very bad mood because you hurt my friend."

She stood and stared down at the man lying motionless and terrified on the kitchen floor.

Anya whispered, "Come now. I will have next man ready to talk when you arrive."

I led the way with Hunter, Clark, and Mongo on my heels. We wouldn't get to see what Anya did to the fourth man, but I looked forward to the conversation I was about to have with him.

Chapter 23
Chaos Theory

We came through the door with pistols drawn and the image of what Anya had done to each of her victims imprinted on our minds. We knew the layout of the house from the tour she'd taken us on for just over six minutes. We knew what to expect with the exception of the final man—the man wearing Gary Weathers's thumbprint. There should have been no surprises awaiting us, but the scene inside the house was one of unimaginable chaos arranged in perfect order.

Anya's first victim, whose mouth was full of bullets and pistol parts, lay on his side on the far right of the living room. Beside him was the tall bald man, still bound and gagged, lying facedown on the floor. The man who'd been drugged in the kitchen was lying in a pool of blood, his entrails strewn about the floor around him.

The fourth man—good ol' Thumbprint himself—sat naked on an upside-down barstool. His hands were taped to two of the legs of the stool, and his feet pointed awkwardly down the two remaining legs, with tape wrapped so tightly around his ankles that his feet had turned a purple that looked almost black. Small strips of duct tape held both of his eyes open wider than any human eye should ever be.

Anya was kneeling between Thumbprint's feet with the tip of her bloody dagger pressed against his throat. Her clothes, hands, and arms were dripping with blood, and her blue-gray eyes rested menacingly in her head without the slightest hint of remorse for what she'd done.

Thumbprint's face flushed with recognition when Hunter and I stepped into the room. I hoped he couldn't see the terror in my eyes as I tried to avoid staring at the remains of the mutilated body in the middle of the living room floor.

I leaned down, hovering over the man. "Remember me, Mr. Weathers? Last time we met, you and your friends were playing tough on the deck at O.C. White's. It would appear the tables have turned."

He hissed. "Fu—," and Anya pressed the dagger against his Adam's apple, drawing a trickle of blood.

"Play nice," I said. "I'm going to ask you some questions, but please, don't feel any pressure to answer. Our deadly little friend here will be more than happy to reunite your soul with your gutted buddy's over there, and we'll move on to Lurch. Something tells me he'll have plenty to say once he's seen your liver. Oh, and it just occurred to me how important your liver really is. I don't think you can live without it . . . thus the name."

The veins in his neck and forehead thrust themselves against his skin as if they were trying to escape his body.

I smiled. "Let's start with something simple, shall we? What is your name?"

His eyelids shuddered as he struggled against the tape. "Gary Weathers."

"Oh, would you look at that? We've gone from cursing to lying."

I looked down at Anya, and in Russian, said, "Remind him how important it is to tell the truth."

She traced the tip of her dagger down his chest and abdomen, leaving a thin trail of barely opened flesh, and her blade came to rest precisely where no man would want anything sharp.

Thumbprint swallowed hard. "Oh, God! Make her stop. My name is Jerald Davis. Special Agent Jerald Davis, DEA."

I placed a hand on Anya's shoulder. "*Podozhdite.*"

Mr. Davis flinched, telling me he didn't know the Russian word for *wait*.

I pulled my Secret Service credential pack from my pocket and let it fall open in front of his face. "Well, then, Special Agent Jerald Davis of the Drug Enforcement Administration, it's your lucky day. I just happen to have the credentials to verify your story. Pardon me while I make a call to Virginia."

The corners of his mouth began to quiver as Anya continued pressing her blade ever more firmly against a part of his body he seemed to value. Before I could finish pretending to dial my phone, he said, "Okay, enough. There's no need to make that call, and for God's sake, please call her off in whatever language she speaks."

I lowered the corners of my mouth in mock disappointment. "Oh, so you're not with the DEA? Or you're not really Jerald Davis? Which one? Or is it both? I'm having trouble remembering the Russian word for *stop.*"

Beads of sweat dripped from his brow and chin. "No, I'm both. I *am* Jerald Davis, and I *was* DEA—a long time ago."

"Now we're getting somewhere," I said.

I let my hand fall across Anya's shoulder again. "*Vy ochen' khoroshi v etom.*"

Without looking up, she said, "*Spasibo*, Chasechka."

I lifted my hand from Anya's shoulder and gave Davis a crisp slap, just to remind him of his position in the pecking order of the room. "I was just telling my friend that she is very good at this. I'm sure you'd agree."

He dared a glance downward at the blood-covered assassin between his knees.

I chuckled as a thought rushed through my head. This guy would've fantasized about Anya in exactly that position if he'd seen her on the street, but having her kneeling in front of his naked body at that moment was the stuff of night terrors, not fantasies.

I continued my little game of tit-for-tat with my new friend. "I'm going to take you at your word that you're Jerald Davis, formerly of the DEA. I'm going to ask you about your fingerprints later, so go ahead and work on an answer to that question while we cover a few other housekeeping issues."

He wore the look of a surrendering man; a man who'd reached the limit of both his will and ability to resist. "Will you please take the tape off my eyelids?"

"It's not my tape," I said. "It would be rude of me to remove someone else's tape." I motioned down toward Anya. "Ask her. I'm sure she'd be more than happy to rip it off for you if you asked nicely . . . and in Russian, of course."

He sighed. "I clearly underestimated you and your team, and you've made me regret it. Can't we do this like civilized men? You get her away from me, and get me off this perch, and I'll tell you what you want to know."

I growled. "Civilized men? You mean like the way you treated my friend when you beat the hell out of her and sank her boat? You mean the way you were behaving when she put that bullet hole in your thigh?"

I shoved my index finger into the still messy wound six inches above his knee, and he winced from the pain. "Is that what you mean by behaving like civilized men?"

I motioned toward Anya. "Oh, and in case you haven't noticed, *she's* not a man, and civility isn't one of her strong suits."

"Okay, okay. You've made your point. What do you want from me?"

I leaned in to within an inch of his face. "What I want is for you to give me one tiny little reason to end this night with two bodies to dispose of instead of just one, Jerald. So, lie to me one more time . . . please. Refuse to answer me just one more time . . . please. Ask me for one more favor . . . please."

The whites of his eyes turned blood-red, and his body started shaking.

Hunter spoke up for the first time. "He's having a stroke, or maybe a heart attack. You've got to cut him loose."

In Russian, Anya said, "No! He is faking. Is old interrogation trick from Cold War. Watch." Then she drove the tip of her blade beneath the nail of his big toe.

He roared a string of obscenities ending in, ". . . get that crazy bitch away from me!"

"Jerald, Jerald, Jerald. I thought we covered this. You were going to cooperate, and I was going to let you live."

Anya said, "*Mogu li ya ubit' yego seychas?*"

"No, you may not kill him yet," I said, thankful she was playing along.

I took Davis's face in my hand and forced him to look directly into my eyes. "This is your last warning. If you do anything— and I do mean absolutely anything—other than cooperate fully, you'll beg God to take you quickly while she slowly slices your worthless soul from its pitiful little mortal shell."

I walked away and opened the refrigerator, took out a bottle of water, and made a show of drinking it slowly. When I'd finished, I crushed the bottle and dropped it at his feet.

"I'm all out of patience, and I'm missing my beauty sleep, so let's get down to business, shall we? She's going to introduce that plastic bottle to a part of your body that was designed to be an exit only if you don't immediately answer every question."

I gave him no time to respond.

"What were you looking for on that boat?"

"What boat?" he asked.

I threw a right cross to his left temple, sending him and the stool sprawling across the floor, blood pouring from his eye. "Kill him now!"

Anya leapt to her feet, and Davis yelled, "A safe! We were looking for a safe!"

"What was inside the safe?" I demanded.

He whimpered, "Money. Probably two million dollars or more."

"Why did you sink the boat?"

"To make it look like the woman died in an accident."

I grinned. "Surprise, asshole. She didn't die. And she just happens to be our friend. All of that adds up to attempted murder during the commission of a felony, and piracy since you did it on a vessel on a navigable waterway. I bet you're starting to hope I do kill you tonight."

He grunted but didn't speak.

I lifted him back to a vertical position on the stool that felt like part of his body.

Lurch grunted as if he were trying to speak, so I surrendered the floor to him by yanking the gag from his mouth. "Let's hear it," I ordered.

He gasped for several jerky breaths and finally found his voice. "We were DEA agents in Central America, tracking drug cartel shipments flown by former Air America pilots."

I turned back to Davis. "See? Your partner understands the concept of cooperation. You're quickly losing any value you had to me."

"Listen to me. I'll tell you everything," Davis said, his breath coming in raspy howls.

I was caught inside a confession crossfire. Both men obviously wanted to be the one to give me the gold nugget I wanted. Both must've believed I'd spare the one who gave it up first. That hadn't been part of my plan, as if I had a plan, but I wasn't going to look a gift horse in the mouth.

"So, what's your name, Lurch? And don't tell me it's Stormy Sanderson. He's old enough to be your dear old daddy."

He closed his eyes as if praying for absolution. "My name is Eustis Carmichael, or at least it used to be."

"Well, Eustis, are you going to make me ask the questions, or are you going to spill the beans?"

"We got busted for taking bribes from the cartel, but we were onto Boomer and his money-grabbing scheme. We did a little over a dime in federal prison for it. I didn't do it, but I wasn't going to rat out my partner, so we both went down."

He licked his lips in an effort to fight off the cottonmouth, so I pulled another bottle of water from the fridge and poured a third of it in the direction of his mouth. He lapped up the cold water like a sponge.

With his thirst quenched, he said, "Boomer was raking in the cash and having a boat built in Cartagena. He was selling some kind of crazy investment scheme. A 'retirement fund for the pilots and crews' is what he liked to call it, but the only retirement he was funding was his own."

I'd been taught to never interrupt when a prisoner started talking, so I stood, taking in every word.

He continued. "We got wise to his scheme, and I'm ashamed to say we wanted a piece of it, so we finagled our way aboard a C-Forty-Six he was flying. It was just him, some stupid little native co-pilot, and the two of us. We confronted him in the air, and he knew there was no way he'd get off the plane alive if he didn't cut us in."

Davis picked up the story. "Yeah, that's right. That's when he told us he'd cut us a ten-percent share. We negotiated a little better rate than that by the time it was over, but Boomer said he had to go to the bathroom. We let him out of the cockpit to hit the head. When he came out, he was wearing a parachute, and he ran straight for the door and disappeared into the clouds."

I was mesmerized by their story.

"Neither one of us knew how to fly, so we made the other guy circle back around. There was a whole storage box full of parachutes, so we strapped up and stepped out the door. We figured the only way to make Boomer keep his end of the bargain was to catch him in the jungle."

Lurch wrapped up the story. "We never found him, but we got busted less than two months later and swore a blood oath that we'd find the money before we died, no matter what it took. The trail went cold for over fifteen years until we learned both the boat he built in Cartagena and his old lady were still alive and kicking. That's how we ended up here."

Chapter 24
Resurrection

I glanced down at Anya's body cam and then back at my guest of honor. "So, Jerald Davis and Eustis Carmichael. Those are your real names, right?"

Both men nodded in submission.

"I need you to answer me out loud."

They mumbled, "Yeah, those are our real names."

"That's good. Now, you are the two men who unlawfully boarded the boat moored at Saint Augustine Municipal Marina last Friday night, assaulted the female occupant of the vessel, and then sank the vessel approximately three-quarters of a mile south of the marina in the Matanzas River. Is that correct?"

Neither man flinched, so I pointed toward the bloody heap on the floor behind Anya.

Both men swallowed hard.

"Yes, we did all of that," Davis said.

I motioned toward the unconscious man with his mouth still full of pistol. "And what's his name and affiliation with you and your criminal activity?"

Davis said, "He's Lyle Canton, an ex-con we did time with. He wasn't involved."

"And the other guy? Who *was* he?"

Davis bit his lip and whispered, "He was my little brother. He was the driver."

I said, "This concludes the confession of Jerald Davis and Eustis Carmichael. I am Supervisory Special Agent Chase D. Fulton. Time now, zero-zero-one-six."

I reached down and pressed the small black button on the body cam, shutting down the device.

Without ceremony, I untaped Davis's eyes and ankles and motioned toward Hunter. "Get some clothes on him, flex-cuff him, and put him on the couch."

My partner led the man toward a bedroom.

I motioned for Mongo. "Wake him up and get that gun out of his mouth. Cuff him and get him comfortable on the couch."

Mongo did as I ordered, and Clark moved without any instructions from me. He went to work gift-wrapping Carmichael.

Anya was on her feet, and I pointed toward the bloody heap on the floor. "You made that mess, so clean it up."

She dragged Davis's younger brother across the floor and gathered the fish entrails she'd used to decorate the scene. The fish went down the sink and through the garbage disposal. She delivered a second injection to counteract the tranquilizer she'd used to give the man that nice cozy dead look.

Hunter returned with Davis slung over his shoulder, his wrists and ankles bound securely with flex-cuffs. He let the man fall from his shoulder onto the couch beside the three other victims of our little exercise. Seeing his brother clean, uninjured, and slowly regaining consciousness sent Davis's head shaking in disbelief.

Anya emerged from the bathroom wearing a clean black T-shirt and her hair in a tight ponytail. "Is miracle. Brother is alive again, and I learn English."

Davis closed his eyes and let his head slump in realization of the humiliation he'd endured.

Clark came back into the house with our seven-inch monitor in hand. After three minutes of cutting, splicing, and editing, I emailed audio of Davis's and Carmichael's confessions to the Saint Augustine Police Department and dialed an old friend.

"Officer O'Malley. Who's calling?"

"Sorry to call so late, O'Malley, but this is Chase Fulton. Remember me?"

"Of course. Special Agent Fulton who doesn't want to be a special agent when he's on vacation. How are ya?"

"I'm great," I said. "I've got a little gift for you. In fifteen minutes, you'll want to be at number seven First Street. You'll find four guys who've conveniently flex-cuffed themselves together. I'm quite sure they'll leave the door open for you, so you won't need to break anything. Your chief of detectives received an email with an audiotaped confession from two of the guys."

O'Malley chuckled. "I should've known it was going to be something crazy from you, Fulton. Just what did these guys confess to doing?"

"Remember the lady who got roughed up and lost her boat at the marina last Friday night?"

"Yeah, sure I do. It was Earl at the End. Are you tellin' me these are the guys who did that?"

"That's exactly what I'm telling you, O'Malley, and they've got a nice red bow tied on top of them. Do you think you can make it here in exactly fifteen minutes?"

I could almost hear him rolling his eyes through the phone. "I suppose you plan to be out of there in fourteen minutes and thirty seconds. Am I right?"

"I'll put it this way, my friend. There will be no representation from the Secret Service on scene when you arrive, but your prisoners will be waiting patiently on the couch in the living room."

"You know, Fulton . . . If you ever want a job on the Saint Augustine PD, it ain't gonna be waitin' for ya."

I laughed. "Oh, don't I know it? I'm not police department material, O'Malley, but it's nice to have friends in low places."

I set my watch to count down fourteen minutes and approached Davis. "Cheer up, Jerald. Look at it this way. You got your brother back from the dead, so, in return, how about you telling me about those fingerprints of yours?"

He shot a look at his hands. "It's not so hard when you know the system inside and out to change a name in a database, especially when you've got friends like mine in little dark rooms in buildings without names or addresses."

"Well, your days of masquerading as Gary Weathers are over, and the same is true for your freaky-looking buddy. Stormy Sanderson gets to rest in peace while the two of you get to rest in prison for what's left of your miserable lives."

Anya hit all four men with a small dose of her magic sleeping potion just as my watch alarmed.

I pressed the button. "We've got sixty seconds to turn into the wind."

We filed out the door and down the steps to find Beater behind the wheel of Anya's Suburban parked in the sandy lane. Blue lights reflected from the Spanish moss dripping from the centuries-old oaks as we turned left onto Cincinnati and disappeared into the late-night mayhem of Old Town, Saint Augustine.

* * *

Back aboard *Aegis*, we briefed Beater on the events of the evening, and he couldn't stop laughing.

He kept repeating, "She did that?"

A round of cocktails and Cubans followed the debrief.

Clark tapped on his glass with his lighter. "First, here's to Anya for pulling off the best con-job I've ever seen."

"Here, here!"

Glasses rose, drinks followed, and Anya took a bow. "I was afraid fish parts would not look like real person's insides, but in darkness, I think it was good enough, yes?"

"Absolutely," I said. "But where did you get the fish guts?"

"From fishermen. I say to them I am voodoo witch, and they give to me everything I want."

Clark pounded on the table. "I'm not finished. Second, what's your plan now, College Boy? You caught the bad guys, but you've still got a bunch of documents nobody can read, a pile of gold, and a broken compass."

"That's not up to me," I said. "That's up to Earl. All of that stuff is hers."

My phone chirped before I could continue.

"Chase here."

"Chase, it's O'Malley. I thought you might like to know that we made an arrest in the marina case tonight."

"You don't say."

He chuckled. "I gotta go. Enjoy wherever you are, and look me up if you ever get back down this way. We'll have a pint and talk about the good ol' days."

"You've got it, O'Malley. Congrats on the collar. Good night."

I stuffed my phone back into my pocket and rejoined the party.

We laughed and talked until the adrenaline wore off and the energy waned. One by one, we made our way inside and found soft spots to sleep off the long night. Anya turned left in the main salon instead of following me into the starboard hull, but brief flashes of the past poured through my head as I climbed into my bed . . . alone.

* * *

It wasn't the sun that roused me from my slumber. It was the ringing of my phone.

"Yeah, this is Chase."

Skipper shouted, "I figured it out!"

"Woah. Calm down. What did you figure out?"

She said, "What do you mean, calm down? Chase, I figured out the documents. It's a simple code based on the Maya glyphs."

"Slow down, Skipper. I'm just waking up, and I don't understand anything you're saying."

"It's simple," she demanded. "The ancient Maya wrote in glyphs that are kind of like Egyptian hieroglyphs. In fact, when archeologists first discovered the Maya glyphs in the eighteen hundreds, they called them *hieroglyphs* because they thought they were similar to the ones found in Egypt, but they were wrong. They're not the same at all. The glyphs in Mesoamerica are more closely related to—"

"Stop!" I said. "I don't want an ancient history lesson. Just tell me what the documents say."

She didn't slow down. "It's fascinating, Chase. It really is."

"That's great. You can tell me all about it later, and I promise to listen, but I really need you to tell me what they say."

"It's an accounting ledger. Well, most of it anyway. One page is different than the others, and I'm still working on that one, but I just had to tell you about deciphering the glyphs."

"You're a genius, Skipper. Email me the translations as soon as you have them cleaned up, and stay on that remaining page. Something tells me that's the important one."

"Okay, I'm on it. I'll send these down later this morning. Oh, I almost forgot. How are things going down there?"

I briefed her on the previous night's action, and she was almost as giddy over the arrests as she was over the glyphs.

My watch reported ten minutes after eight. I didn't like missing the sunrise, but my body needed the rest. I loved the feeling after a good, solid night's sleep, but there was one thing I didn't like about my situation. The other side of my bed was cold and undisturbed.

Penny answered after five rings. "Hello?"

"I love your sexy morning voice."

"Oh, hey," she said, still groggy. "Is everything okay?"

"Yes, everything's great. The guys who attacked Earl are in jail, and Skipper deciphered most of the documents."

"That's great news. Is everybody okay?"

"We're all fine," I said. "I'll tell you all about it when you get home. It's perfectly safe to bring Earl back to Saint Augustine whenever you'd like."

"That is good news, and I'm glad you're okay. You know I worry about you. Was it Anya?"

"Was *what* Anya?" I asked.

"Did she catch the bad guys?"

I laughed. "It was a team effort. Even Beater pitched in. They're going away for a long time. I got a full confession on tape."

"I'm proud of you, Chase. I'll call the charter guys, and we'll be back in Florida later today, okay?"

I grinned. "Of course that's okay. I'll see you soon. I love you."

"I love you, too."

After a quick shower, I met the rest of the team on the upper deck. Well, most of the team.

Chapter 25
The Meaning of Life

"Where's Anya?" I asked.

Mongo looked up. "You asked her to come here to help, so she said her work was done, and she went home."

"I wasn't expecting that, but what she did last night was remarkable."

Clark kicked a chair toward me. "So, what do we do now, boss?"

I settled into the chair and sat my coffee mug on the table. "For now, we're in a holding pattern, but I do have some good news. Skipper deciphered all of the pages but one."

Mongo's eyes lit up, and he leaned in. "I can't wait to hear this."

"I thought you might be interested," I said. "It turns out the gibberish isn't gibberish at all. It's something called Maya glyphs. Apparently, it's like hieroglyphics from Egypt."

Mongo said, "Actually, Maya glyphs aren't like Egyptian hieroglyphics at all. They're—"

I held up a hand. "Oh, I know. Skipper made that clear. But I'm not smart enough to care, so I didn't let her finish the history lesson, either. The important part is the writing on the documents is a cipher *based* on Maya glyphs, not the glyphs themselves. She says the pages are an accounting ledger of some kind. She'll have the translated documents to us in a couple of hours."

Mongo's disappointment was obvious on his face. "Just because you're not smart enough to care doesn't mean the same is true for the rest of us."

In unison, Hunter, Clark, and Beater said, "Yes, it does."

"Thanks for the support," I said. "The rest of the news is that Penny and Earl will be back later today. I think it's safe for them to come back now that we have our adversaries off the street. Don't you?"

Everyone nodded . . . except for Beater.

He said, "How do you know those four are the only bad guys in town?"

I narrowed my eyes. "That's a good point. I guess I don't know if they're the limit of the team that hit Earl. Do you think there are more?"

The old warrior shrugged. "I don't have anything to suggest there's more, but I've stayed alive nearly three times as long as any of you by never underestimating the enemy."

Mongo grinned. "It's hard to argue with that. You *are* old."

Beater lowered his chin and eyed the mountain of a man. "Keep it up, youngster, and you may find yourself on the receiving end of an old-man ass-whoopin'."

Watching the two bruisers exchange playful verbal stabs was entertaining, but what followed was the knockout.

Mongo stuck out his hand. "I'm sorry. I didn't mean to hurt your feelings, but I'm surprised you can still hear well enough to catch what I said."

Beater grasped the island-sized hand that Mongo offered, twisted his wrist through a hundred eighty degrees, and dragged the giant from his chair. Mongo landed on his knees on the deck, grabbing at his wrist.

Beater grinned. "What's that you were saying, sonny?"

Mongo groaned. "I was just saying how much I respect your experience."

Beater released the vise-like grip on Mongo's hand. "That's what I thought."

That received a well-deserved round of laughter, and something told me no one would let Mongo forget the experience anytime soon.

Beater said, "Has anybody checked the weather forecast for today?"

"I always check the weather," I said. "It's supposed to be in the high seventies, no chance of rain, and wind out of the east at ten to fifteen knots offshore and five to ten inside."

"That sounds like a perfect day to do a little sailing while we're waiting for the girls to get home."

Hunter laughed. "Beater, I'm not sure it's politically correct to call full-grown women *girls* anymore."

"I'm seventy-seven years old. Any woman under sixty is a girl to me."

I joined Hunter in laughing. "I'm not sure Earl makes it into that age bracket of sub-sixty, Beater, but I definitely agree that it's a perfect day to go sailing."

I warmed up the diesels while Hunter and Clark cast off the lines. *Aegis* quivered beneath my feet with anticipation of spreading her wings. We motored beneath the Bridge of Lions, out the Saint Augustine Inlet, and into the blue North Atlantic.

"This was your idea, Beater. Where do you want to go?"

He shielded his eyes from the bright morning sun and scanned the horizon from south to north. "How far is it up to Mayport?"

"About thirty miles," I said. "In this wind, we can make that in less than three hours."

He held up his watch. "Perfect. That'll put us there just in time for lunch at the O-Club. I'm buying."

With the bow still in the wind, I called for the main, and Hunter went to work sending the wing aloft. As the mainsail luffed over the centerline of the boat, I let *Aegis* fall off to port as I unfurled the genoa. Two minutes later, the diesels were silent, and we were making twelve knots on a beam reach, heading 350 degrees magnetic, parallel to one of the longest beaches in the country.

Beater asked, "Is it safe to go up top while we're underway?"

"Absolutely," I said. "In fact, I'll go with you."

I set the autopilot and took the handheld remote with us as we climbed the ladder. Hunter, Mongo, and Clark made their nests on the trampoline up front and left the upper deck to us.

Beater and I sat in silence for half an hour watching the world go by. Sitting in silent reverence is often the best way to take in the wonder of the ocean since our feeble minds aren't capable of grasping the magnitude of the Earth's waters. Respecting and admiring the ocean is far better than understanding it, so that's what we did.

"What's your biggest fear, kid?"

I turned to my old friend and didn't hesitate. "Getting Penny hurt or killed because of what I do for a living."

He pursed his lips and slowly nodded his head in time with the passing waves. "And just what is it that you do 'for a living'?"

Confusion overtook my face, and he noticed. I said, "You know what I do."

"Oh, yes, I know quite well what you do. But do you do it for a living?"

I continued staring into the face of wisdom until he said, "How old are you, kid?"

"I'll be thirty in January . . . if I live that long."

He laughed. "Ha! Thirty, indeed. At thirty, I was making fifteen dollars a day. That's four hundred and fifty dollars a month. Back then, that was all the money in the world. I couldn't spend it all even if I tried. I was rich and getting richer every time I pulled another month off the calendar."

I didn't know where the conversation was going, but he had my attention. I made no effort to interrupt, and I sat patiently waiting for him to continue.

He finally did. "I'm no math whiz, but if you're thirty years old, that means you've been alive somewhere around ten thousand days. I guess it's a little more than ten thousand, but that makes the math easy enough for even me. Best I can figure, I guess you're worth something north of ten million dollars."

He poked his finger into the air as if he were working out a math problem on an invisible blackboard. "Unless I've forgotten how to divide, that means, on average, you've made a thousand bucks a day, every day, since the doctor spanked your ass and you drew your first breath."

His guess at my net worth was a little low, but I was anxious to hear the point he was making.

"From where I sit—remembering my fifteen-dollar-a-day life fifty years ago—you've made your living. What you do from here on out is making your *life*."

"Are you saying I should quit?"

He smiled. "Quit? Quit what? Living? No. Based on what you said you're afraid of, I'm saying I think you should *start*."

Silence followed, and soon, the Saint Johns River came into view off the port bow.

I motioned toward the inlet. "There's Mayport Naval Station. I guess I should get back to the helm, unless you want to keep going to Norfolk."

He looked over his shoulder. "No, the grouper basket is better here. Go on back down there and play captain."

Disengaging the autopilot, I let *Aegis* roll downwind and headed into the mouth of the river. I've never loved downwind sailing, but my boat was as good at it as any I'd ever been aboard.

She settled into a peaceful, rolling rhythm and carried us past the breakers as if she knew where we were going. The truth is, she knew as well as I did. That was my first trip into the Saint Johns. Unsure what to do next, I fired up the diesels and came about into the wind. My crew came to life and went to work bringing down the mainsail while I furled the genoa.

With *Aegis* rigged for steaming, I called up the ladder. "Where are we going, Beater?"

He descended the ladder as if he were twenty years old and on a WWII aircraft carrier. When his feet hit the deck, he pointed to the southwest. "Head into the naval basin."

"They'll rake our decks with fifty-cal if we even think about poking our bow in there," I said.

He closed one eye. "We'll sink every ship in the harbor if they do. Damn the torpedoes. Full speed ahead, kid."

I'd walked through a lot of doors that led to places I didn't belong, but the naval ship basin at Mayport topped the list. I had more firepower on my boat than most of the ships in the basin, and the MPs—or whatever the Navy equivalent of an MP is— would hang me from a yardarm if they boarded and searched us.

I shot a look of uncertainty toward Beater. "Are you sure you know what you're doing? If not, this is a terrible plan."

"Have I ever led you astray, kid?"

I rolled my eyes. "You recruited me into a world where somebody new tries to kill me every few weeks, so I'd say yes, you have led me astray."

"You've got a point there, but trust me on this one. Stay to the left, and turn into the tug basin short of *The Wasp*."

"I don't know what any of that means."

He grunted. "Head for that big ship, and turn left before you hit it. Is that simple enough for you, civilian?"

I followed his instructions and laid *Aegis* alongside a rugged-looking dock among half a dozen Navy tugboats.

A pair of seamen in navy blue coveralls tossed up three lines, and we made them fast on the bow, stern, and amidships.

A uniformed man who looked too old to be in the Navy stepped from a van and approached *Aegis* with a confident stride. His khaki uniform looked stiff enough to support itself without him being inside of it. I was more nervous with every step, and the two seamen seemed to be as nervous as me. They snapped to attention and whipped out a pair of crisp salutes as the khaki-clad officer continued his approach. He returned the salutes and dismissed the seamen.

Beater leaned over the lifeline. "Bart? Is that you, you salty old cuss?"

The officer blocked the sun with his palm and stared up at us. "Welcome aboard Mayport, you old dinosaur. It's good to see you. Who'd you bring with you?"

We stepped to the dock, and Beater shook the officer's hand. "Bart, this is Chase, Hunter, Clark, and Marvin, but these guys call him Mongo. Guys, this is Admiral Bartholomew Whitehead."

The admiral shook our hands in turn. "Just call me Bart," he said. "Any friends of that old man's are friends of mine. Let's go get some lunch. What do you say?"

I was still in awe of the whole experience, and the admiral picked up on my discomfort. "What's wrong, Chase? You look like Alice in Wonderland. You haven't slipped through the looking glass. This is just a Navy base."

I motioned toward my boat. "Are you sure it's okay for me to dock here?"

Admiral Bart and Beater roared with laughter. "Son, if anybody messes with your boat while we're gone, those two sailors will show us their corpses when we get back. Don't you worry about a thing. You'd have to sail five hundred miles to find anybody who outranks me, so a parking pass from me is as good as a get out of jail free card."

"Whatever you say, Admiral."

We piled into his van, and the driver delivered us to the officer's club where we demolished the seafood buffet and listened as Bart and Beater told sea stories.

Dessert came in the form of hot fudge cakes all around.

The admiral said, "So, I hear you're the boys with the Mark V up around Kings Bay."

I couldn't tell if it was a statement or a question. "When we're not out gallivanting around," I said, "I've got a little place on the Saint Marys River near the submarine base."

He folded his arms across his chest. "I see. Well, I guess that means you don't know why you're here."

I looked from the admiral to Beater and back. "What are you talking about, Admiral?"

Beater stood from his seat. "Why don't you boys go for a walk with me while Bart and Chase have a little talk? I'll tell you about that LHD."

Hunter and Clark stood without hesitation, but Mongo stayed in his seat long enough to demolish his cake. He wiped his mouth, stared at me, and flashed the diver's okay signal.

I gave him a quick nod and returned the signal. With that, he stood and followed Beater and the others toward the door.

I turned back to my host. "What's this all about, Admiral?"

He wiped his mouth and let the napkin fall to his plate. "Your men follow you as if you were General MacArthur. What's your secret?"

I tossed my napkin onto my plate, matching his. "I don't think I'm here to discuss leadership styles, so let's quit talking about how to build a clock, and just tell me what time it is."

He snapped his fingers. "That must be it. You don't pussyfoot around. You get right to the point and get things done. I've heard that about you, and that's part of the reason you're here, young man."

He paused, apparently awaiting a reaction, but he got none.

"Well, then, let's get to it. The Navy has all sorts of needs, Chase. We need ships and airplanes and people to operate those machines. Those assets are easy to come by these days. The economy is good, and the country's behind our military, especially after nine eleven, but there's one more thing the Navy and this country need. You're familiar with the Naval Special Warfare Command out in Coronado, right?"

I gave him a curt nod. "I'm familiar with the SEALs."

"Of course you are. We'll get back to the SEALs in a minute, but first, tell me what you're good at."

"This is starting to sound like a job interview, Admiral, and I'm not interested in becoming a SEAL or whatever you have in mind."

He leaned back in his chair and let out a hearty laugh. "What are you, Chase? Six-foot-four or five and two thirty?"

I shrugged.

"We don't need any SEALs your size or with your pedigree," he said. "What we need is a way to get inside a man's head and find out if he has the nuts and bolts to become a SEAL. Hell, everybody thinks BUDS is about physical strength and endurance. I can teach a gorilla to run, swim, and do push-ups. Basic Underwater Demolition SEAL school is about finding out if a man has the psychological capacity to endure extreme prolonged discomfort and continue to fight." He took a long drink of his tea. "We've been working on a protocol to screen for whatever it is in the human brain that gives a man that capacity. We've got some top-notch scientists in the Navy, and we've got the best warfighters on the planet, but what we don't have is a warfighter without military influence in his training and education who is also a trained psychologist."

The pieces were falling into place for me, but I wasn't sure I liked the picture the puzzle was forming. "I'm not a PhD. I've just got a simple little bachelor's degree in psychology from UGA. I've never been to a military school in my life, and I've never served a day in uniform." I paused, remembering the U.S.S. Tennessee. "Well, I was in a Navy uniform once on a submarine in the Med, but. . . ."

He shot me with a thumb and finger pistol. "Exactly. And while you were on that boat, you uncovered one of the biggest infiltration operations by a foreign government in the history of the submarine service. You have an eye for looking into a man's head without cutting him open. Hell, kid, we've got more PhDs than we could drown in that ship basin out there. We need somebody with your brain and experience in the field to help us come up with a way to screen SEAL applicants so we don't have to waste so much money and time weeding out the quitters before we can start turning them into warriors."

"I don't know, Admiral. This is a lot to take in and a lot to consider. I can't give you an answer right now. I've got too many other irons in too many other fires to just jump into your boat today."

He frowned. "Is it about money, son? If it is, we can write a nice contract, get you some research grant money, and hell, we can probably even throw in a car and house in San Diego."

Beater's pitch on the upper deck was beginning to make sense. "No, Admiral, it's not about money. I can afford all the houses and cars I want anywhere in the world, and I definitely don't want a government grant that'll allow me to poke around in SEALs' heads. I'm not qualified for the job you're offering, and—"

He slammed his hand onto the table—the act of a man who is entirely unaccustomed to having people tell him no. "There's nobody on Earth more qualified to do what I'm asking you to do, Chase. You know how the brain works, and you know how it feels to return fire when the nearest help is half a world away. You're not afraid of the Kremlin, and you love the salt water.

Think about the project. That's all I'm asking. Talk it over with Miss Penny, and we'll talk again soon."

He slid an embossed business card across the table. "All of my numbers are on there. Call me anytime."

I gave the card a look, memorized its contents, and slid it back across the table. "My wife is due back in Saint Augustine this evening, and I want to be there when she arrives. She's bringing a friend of mine with her who's gotten herself into a little bit of a jam. I'm helping her out, and I want to make sure she knows she has my full attention when she decides what to do next. Thank you for lunch, and thank you for not raking my decks with fifty-cal when I sailed into your basin."

Chapter 26
Carnival Rides

The southbound leg of our sailing trip was far quieter than the northbound portion. I had a lot to think about, not the least of which was the fact that Beater had set me up without any warning. I wasn't altogether comfortable with that scenario.

The sailor in me wanted to hand-steer *Aegis* back to Saint Augustine, but the rolling waves from the east, pushed by three thousand miles of wind across the Atlantic, made the task far more tolerable in the capable hands of the autopilot. The downside of not steering was that my mind had plenty of time to wander and wonder.

Working for the Navy would take me out of the field, and likely, out of harm's way for the most part. I would still be serving my country by implementing a unique set of skills and knowledge I possessed to produce warriors, but it would be an academic service and not one of boots-on-the-ground. That would ease Penny's mind and give me the solace of coming home every night without bullet holes in my body.

One of my greatest concerns was disappointing Clark. I'd made a commitment to an organization that invested a fortune in time and money to turn me into the weapon I'd become. Clark had spent years by my side honing that weapon and building a confidence in me that can't be bought. If I walked away from the organization, I'd be robbing Clark of one of the tools in his chest. He knew what I could and couldn't do. He knew my work ethic and my limits. Perhaps it was arrogant of me to believe he needed me, but I had become one of the tools he kept within easy reach near the top of the box. There was likely no one on Earth who knew me better than Clark Johnson, and the thought of letting him down sickened me.

So much of me wanted to believe the mystery of Earl's attack was over. I hoped she'd take the gold from Boomer's safe, buy herself a new boat, or maybe even a home solidly affixed to terra-firma. The gold wasn't enough to live on for the rest of her life, but it certainly wasn't a bad start.

The ledgers written in coded glyphs intrigued me, but the more I thought about them, the more I came to believe they were names and accounts of people who were long dead, and that finding the accounts would be nearly impossible. I couldn't think of anything Skipper could discover on the final page that would interest me enough to devote much more time to the project. I wanted to make sure Earl was made whole to the greatest extent possible, even if I had to come out of pocket to make that happen. Beyond that, the job was over as far as I was concerned. It was time to welcome my wife back, send everyone else home, and continue our journey to Vanuatu on the far side of the world.

It took just over three hours from the moment we cast off the lines at Mayport until I shut down the diesels in the slip at the Saint Augustine Municipal Marina. Other than commands to hoist, dowse, haul, or ease a sail, I don't remember saying a word to another living soul.

With *Aegis* secured in her temporary home, I called Hunter and Mongo to the main salon. "I need you two to break down the observation point in the garage apartment on Hope Street and make it look like we were never there."

Hunter checked his six and leaned in. "Are you okay? You haven't been yourself since we left Mayport."

"Yeah, I'm okay. I've just got a lot on my mind after talking with the admiral. I'll tell you all about it when you get back."

"I knew there was something going on," he said. "Have you talked to Penny? Do you know when they'll be back?"

I checked my watch. "I suspect they're in the air, but I'll give her a call. We'll all have a nice dinner tonight to celebrate."

He lowered an eyebrow. "You don't seem to be in the celebrating mood, but we'll see."

I slapped him on the shoulder. "Get to work, you slacker. I'll see you in an hour."

I found Clark sitting in a dock chair talking on his phone. He covered the mouthpiece and looked up. "Are you okay, man?"

I gave him the okay signal and finished my walk-around, making sure *Aegis* still had all the big pieces attached.

When I finally made my way to the upper deck, Beater was sitting at the table with a pair of Cohibas and two tumblers. He scratched at the side of his nose. "You gonna forgive me for that one or stay mad all night?"

I sat down, lifted one of the Cubans, and toasted the end. "I'm not mad, but I really wish you hadn't blindsided me like that. It would've been nice to have a little heads-up."

He poured three fingers of bourbon into each tumbler and recorked the decanter. "I've been in this business a long time, and I've learned one thing for sure about operators like you. They don't like other people creating their options for them. When you're in a gunfight . . . You *have* been in a gunfight, right?"

In homage to Padre, the old man from Charleston who told me more about my father than anyone else on Earth, I dunked the butt of my cigar into my whiskey and gave it a stir. "Yeah, I've been in a few."

He stared at my bizarre use of eighty dollars' worth of cigar to stir my drink and grunted. "Well, when you're in a firefight, guys like you and me like to shoot their own way out and not have some white knight on a steed make an egress route for us."

I lifted the cigar back to my lips and savored the sweet taste of the tobacco with the earthy bite of the bourbon. "I don't know about that. I've been in a few situations where I would've been happy to see a white knight come galloping in."

"Nevertheless," he said, "I think you get my point. We don't like folks meddling in our affairs, but I know a pickle when I see one, and you're in a pickle. You love that woman of yours, and you want to make her happy, but you're starting to doubt you can hang on to what you believe is your calling and hang on to her at the same time. Even if you don't take Bart up on his offer to work for the Navy, I wanted you to know you've got some options."

I sat, contemplating his insight. "I didn't like how you did it, but I appreciate the gesture."

He waved me off. "Maybe I'm just jealous of what you have with that pretty girl of yours. I never had that and never will. I'm not complaining, mind you. I'm just laying it out the way it is. You screw up a lot, kid, but the difference in you and the other kids who screw up is that you find a way to survive and learn from every train wreck you cause. You get a little better every day, and that's what makes you one of the best covert operatives in the business."

Taking a compliment was never a strong suit of mine, so I dismissed it with a waggle of my head.

"I mean it, kid. Look around you. You've got three of the hottest shots in the world with ribbons and medals hanging off every corner of their uniforms, and they're falling all over themselves to do whatever you tell them. The way I hear it, you've got a sniper back up north who's just as good at what he does as these guys are. I heard the story about you splitting the money from that thing you did on the oil rig, and I don't agree with what you did, but that's not the point. If you were trying to buy their loyalty, you wasted your money 'cause loyalty from men like them ain't for sale. They'd follow you into the pits of Hell if you asked them to, and that ain't got a damned thing to do with dollar bills. They trust you." He pointed his cigar directly at my face. "And don't you ever take that trust for granted, kid. Once you lose it, it's gone forever."

I let his words rattle around inside my skull for a long moment. "I love what I do, Beater."

"I know you do, kid, and it shows. You've got a lot of decisions to make, and you've got a lot of hurdles to jump. I think the biggest hurdle you have is the one you refuse to acknowledge."

I cocked my head, intrigued by what was coming next.

Again, he pointed with his cigar. "It's that little Russian girlfriend of yours. She's still twirling around in your head, and she knows it. You watch her walk away every time she goes, and you shut up and listen every time she talks. I may be old, but don't you think for one minute that I don't know what a woman like that can do to men like us. Answer me this. Have you ever gone to bed with that wife of yours and thought you might wake up with a dagger in your chest?"

"No, I've never once thought Penny would hurt me."

He gave me a wink. "Now, have you ever gone to bed with the Russian when you didn't think you might wake up with a dagger in your chest?" He leaned back in his chair, picked up his tumbler, and watched a tugboat pushing a construction barge beneath the drawbridge.

When the show was over, he said, "There's a lot to be said for a rollercoaster. It gets your heart rate up and makes you feel alive, but that nice, gentle, safe Ferris wheel sure gives you a lot more time to enjoy the scenery and eat your ice cream cone."

We finished our cigars and bourbon, and Clark joined us.

"Is everything good in Miami?" I asked as I poured him a drink.

He took the glass from my hand. "Somedays, I think she'd never be able to make it without me, and other times, it's like she doesn't need me at all."

"And what kind of day is today?" I asked.

"She's got the tiger by the horns today."

Beater looked at Clark as if he'd lost his mind, and I couldn't control my laughter.

"You gotta love those horned tigers," I said.

"Ah, you know what I mean," Clark growled.

"Actually, I have no idea what you mean, but I can't get the picture of Maebelle and a tiger with horns out of my head."

He swallowed half of his bourbon. "Today's one of the days she definitely doesn't need me. The restaurant is on autopilot, and the customers can't get enough. She and that crazy dog of yours have it all under control."

"Charlie isn't my dog anymore. He's Maebelle's, and I can't believe the health department in Miami lets you keep a black lab in a restaurant."

He took another drink. "He stays outside, as far as the health department knows."

I watched Jesus's van pull to a stop on Avenida Menendez, and Penny and Earl climbed out. Earl was still moving gingerly, but definitely better than when she left. They came through the gate and stopped as Earl looked over the marina. I could almost feel her heart breaking when she didn't see her home tied up at the end.

I descended the ladder and met them on the stern. Penny leapt into my arms as if we hadn't seen each other in weeks. She was wearing cutoff blue jean shorts, a T-shirt tied up in a knot, and my UGA baseball cap with a ponytail sticking out the back. I'd never seen her look more beautiful.

"Oh, it's good to be home," she said. "Where is everybody? What happened with the bad guys? Did anybody get hurt? Have you eaten? Is Anya still here?"

I'm rarely the smartest kid in the room, but I was smart enough to know which question to answer first. "Anya left this morning."

Penny grinned. "Good. I'm hungry. Do you have reservations yet?"

I held her in my arms. "No, my dear. I don't have any reservations at all."

Chapter 27
Something Manly

Hunter and Mongo returned from their cleaning mission only minutes after Earl and Penny arrived.

"How does it look?" I asked.

Hunter said, "It looks like we never turned the knob."

"I knew it would. Thanks for taking care of it. Hopefully, we won't get pulled back into this thing, but I don't want to involve the widow, even if we do have to testify."

There was no discussion of where we'd have dinner. The Columbia is always the choice.

Earl pulled me aside and whispered, "I can't afford to eat at that place. If it's okay with you, I'll stay here on your boat and just have a sandwich. I'm pretty tired anyway."

I threw my arm around the best diesel mechanic I knew. "Nonsense. Dinner's on us. It's the least we can do. You gave us this grand adventure, so we've got to pay you back somehow."

"Piffle. Grand adventure, my ass. You guys saved my bacon. I'm the one who's indebted to you."

"Wait here," I said. "I'll be back in just a minute."

Leaving Earl in the main salon, I rounded everyone else up in the cockpit. "You guys go ahead and get us a table at the Columbia. Earl and I will be five minutes behind you."

No one protested, and I headed back to have a moment with Earl. "Follow me. I've got something to show you."

I led the way down the stairs into the starboard hull. Earl grunted her way, still a little sore from her ordeal. "If you're going to show me a motor, I already know where that's at, and if you're trying to trick me into your bed, you'd never survive it, Stud Muffin. I'm way too much woman for you."

"Don't I know it, Old Girl. I think you'll like where we're headed even better than either of those two options."

I opened the locker and the hidden hatch revealing my onboard safe, and pulled out the stack of sealed documents, the broken compass, and the collection of small gold bars. The array of seemingly unconnected items looked like pieces of a psychedelic puzzle lying on my desk.

"This is what was inside your safe."

Earl pulled the documents toward her and slid her glasses onto her face. Her fingertips traced every line beneath the protective sheets, and I thought she was going to cry.

"Are you okay?"

She carefully examined every page. After several minutes of poring over the documents, she looked up and pulled her glasses from her nose. "Boomer and me used to hunt for these things in the caves and ruins in Central America. They never meant nothing to me, but Boomer loved 'em, and I loved seeing his eyes light up every time we'd find a new one. They're some kind of ancient writing from the Mayans. He'd go on and on about them, but like I said, they were never that interesting to me. It feels a little weird to see them again after all these years without him."

Part of me hated to yank her out of her memories, but she deserved to know what was going on. "Can you read any of that?"

"No, it's just scratching to me, but Boomer sure loved it."

"I sent pictures of these to Skipper, and she deciphered them. Eight of the nine pages are an accounting ledger of some kind. She's still working on the ninth page, but she thinks it's something entirely different."

Earl made a face, half apologetic and half ashamed. "I wish I'd have paid more attention, but I was just a girl chasing a boy through the jungle back then. I spent more time watching his cute little butt in them shorts he used to wear. You know, Chase, I didn't realize how much I missed that man until right now. Thank you for showing this stuff to me."

"I'm glad it brings back some good memories for you. Maybe we'll have some answers about what that ninth page says soon. Skipper's pretty good at what she does."

"Ha! 'Pretty good' don't cover it," she huffed. "She's as good with them computers as I am on them diesels back there. Don't you sell that girl short. You've got a good one in her."

"I know I do," I said. "I'm thankful for everyone on the team."

"You're lucky to have them guys, but I gotta ask you something kind of personal."

She leaned in close and waggled a finger. "You ain't still dibblin' in that Russian girl, are you?"

"No, Earl. No dibblin'"

"All right, then. I didn't think you was, but I needed you to look me in the eye and say it. You've got a good one in that wife of yours, and I'd sure hate to see you mess that up by doing your thinking at the wrong end."

"Penny's been through enough without me adding that to the list," I said. "Sometimes, I feel like I dragged her into the deep end before she knew how to swim. She's the only link I have to normalcy. I'm afraid if I let her go, I'll never have anything close to a normal life again. Sometimes I don't know if I'm holding on to her to keep from falling, or if she's doing the holding."

Earl cocked her head. "I don't know nothing about nothing except motors, but it sure looks to me like you two are taking turns holding on and pushing away. Maybe if you both set your heads to holding, things would work out a little better. But I ain't no marriage counselor, Baby Boy. I'm just Earl at the End. Well, I guess I'm just Earl now since my home at the end of the dock is on the bottom."

While I pondered her wisdom, she picked up the broken compass and turned it over in her hands.

I watched her examine the worthless relic. "Do you know why Boomer would've kept a broken compass in the safe?"

For the first time during the conversation, she smiled, and then she started bouncing the compass in her palm. "It's just like you."

She was probably right. I knew I had a purpose in life. The Earth's North Pole pulls on magnets and tells every one of them which way to turn. Perhaps we humans have a needle inside our minds that is supposed to point toward that North Pole, but mine seemed do a lot of spinning as if it had lost its sense of direction.

I scoffed. "Maybe you're right. Maybe I'm broken, just like that old compass."

She put her hand on mine. "You're not broken, Baby Boy, and neither is this compass. You know which way is up, but you live your life in places most people never go. So, the way you see the world is a lot different from them folks who go to work every day and fret over a house payment and a grouchy mother-in-law. When you go off and do them things you do, you trust your gut and that head of yours to tell you what's right." She pressed the compass into my palm. "If you put this compass in the right place, it'll tell you exactly where to go when every other compass on Earth would be losing its pointed little mind."

I stared down at the battered old hunk of metal and glass. "What are you talking about?"

She grinned and lifted the compass from my hand. "It wasn't just like this one, but Boomer had a compass that wasn't good for nothin' until we got close to them Mayan ruins, or in one of them caves he loved so much. That thing pointed right toward the center of every one of them places. It never made sense to me, but there's something special about them old places. They ain't like the rest of the world. I know all that sounds like hocus-pocus witchcraft, but it ain't. I've seen it with these two eyes, a long time before I needed glasses."

"That's fascinating, but the real reason I brought you down here was to give you these." I pushed the stack of gold bars toward her. "There's about three hundred fifty ounces of gold there. That's more than enough money to replace your boat and get you started again."

She ran her fingers across the gold bars and then looked up at me. "So, am I just supposed to take it to a pawn shop? Do you think I could get twenty-five or thirty thousand out of it, maybe?"

I took her worn, weathered hand in mine. "No, you don't take it to a pawn shop. You take it to an investment gold broker. I don't know what the price of gold is today, but the last number I heard was around four hundred dollars an ounce."

Her eyes turned to saucers. "Four hundred dollars? And how many ounces did you say was here?"

"If it's stamped correctly, there's three hundred fifty-five ounces."

Her eyes shot to the ceiling, and I could see the gears turning. When the arithmetic was done, she smiled again. "I guess I was wrong. I *can* afford dinner at the Columbia."

I locked everything back into the safe, and we walked arm in arm up the dock. "Do you feel like walking, or should I get a cab?"

She laughed. "Who's walking, Stud Muffin? I'm floating. We don't need no cab."

The hostess led us up the stairs and motioned toward the table where Penny, Beater, Mongo, Hunter, and Clark were already captivated by Elizabeth's tableside performance.

Earl and I joined the crowd, and my favorite waitress tossed a sugarcane stick at me. "Where have you been?"

"I've been cheating on you, I'm afraid. There's a waitress at the Waffle House who is so much better at making mojitos than you are."

Elizabeth put her hands on her hips, and her white shirt stretched tightly across the hint of a swollen belly. "Well, then, you can just go right on back to your Waffle House girl, and I'll take care of these good people."

I poked at the stressed buttons on her shirt with the tip of my sugarcane stick. "What's going on here?"

She rubbed her tummy. "I guess you'll find out in about six and a half months. And no, it's not yours. But don't you wish?"

A raucous explosion of congratulations came from the table, but Elizabeth blew us off and poured drinks.

When everyone's glass was full, she glared down at me. "Do you still trust me, or should I call that Waffle House girl to find out what to feed you?"

"I trust you, but *you're* the one who wishes the baby was mine."

She disappeared, and Beater stared over his menu with a look of anger, hunger, and confusion. "Is she coming back to take our order?"

Penny came to my rescue and pulled the menu from Beater's paws. "There's no need to order. Elizabeth is the best waitress on Earth. She'll bring us exactly what we want without us saying a word. Just wait and see."

"Well, good, because I couldn't decide anyway. Everything sounds amazing."

"Everything *is* amazing," Penny said. "You'll love it."

Fifteen minutes later, Elizabeth returned with help. Two other waiters each carried a pair of enormous trays over their heads. Plates and bowls landed in front of us, and everything looked and smelled heavenly.

Elizabeth inspected her work and poured another round of drinks. "Okay, guys, enjoy your appetizers. The main course will be out shortly."

We laughed and dug into the Spanish feast. Elizabeth put one hand on my shoulder and the other on her belly. "And remember, this ain't Waffle House, and you're tipping for two now."

We ate for hours. The drinks kept flowing, and even Mongo ate his fill. Dessert arrived with coffee and the chirping of my phone. I pulled it from my pocket and checked the screen. "It's Skipper. Excuse me for just a minute. I'll be back."

I stood from the table and found a quiet alcove. "Hey, Skipper. I hope you've got good news about the ninth page."

The phone was quiet for a long moment, and then she said, "Are you at the Columbia without me?"

"How did you know?"

"I think I hear Elizabeth making mojitos."

"Stop it," I said. "You're tracking my phone."

"I'm always tracking your phone. You should know that by now. I hope the food is great, as always."

"It is," I said. "What have you learned?"

"I deciphered the final page, but it's a little confusing."

"Can you email me what you have? Maybe Earl can help figure it out."

"It's already in your email inbox. There are references to a guy named Cash Malone. That's probably not his real name. *Cash* is a little too conspicuous with the rest of the document being a ledger, but I've run it a dozen times. The computer keeps spitting out the name Cash."

"I'll talk to Earl and see if that name means anything. What else did you find?"

"The other thing is even weirder. It's a latitude and longitude way back in the mountains of East Tennessee. I mean, it's way remote, like out there where there's nothing but bears and millions of miles of trees."

I let the location roll around in my head for a minute. "Have you turned the lat-long around and put it in the southern hemisphere?"

"Yeah, of course. That puts it eight hundred miles west of Santiago, Chile, out in the Pacific Ocean. I also tried the two other options in the eastern hemisphere. Those would put it halfway between Australia and South Africa in the middle of the Indian Ocean, or north of the equator in the mountains of Northern Tibet."

I put my geography skills to work and tried to picture the four locations. "I guess none of those is any weirder than the others, but we'll start with the original spot in Tennessee. The coordinates are in the email, right?"

"Give me a little credit, would you? It's all included in the email. Now, go enjoy your dinner . . . without me."

"I'll make it up to you, I promise. Oh, and call off the security in Colorado for Penny and Earl, please."

She said, "It's already done, spy boy. I'll call you if I come up with anything else. In the meantime, let me know if Cash Malone is a real guy. I can't find any record of anybody with that name."

"Thanks for everything, Skipper. Get some sleep. You've earned it."

I hung up and returned to the table. "Hey, Mongo. Why do you have two empty plates in front of you and my plate is mysteriously missing?"

He wiped his mouth. "I don't know, boss. Elizabeth said something about you having dessert at Waffle House. I can't explain it."

Elizabeth appeared at my shoulder and handed me the bill. "If you don't show up a little more often, you're going to find yourself scattered, smothered, covered, and chunked. Pay up and get out. I need to turn this table so I can get some respectful customers."

I slipped a stack of bills into the black plastic folder and pointed to Elizabeth's stomach. "You're naming him Chase, right?"

She rolled her eyes. "No. If it's a boy, I plan to name him something manly."

I briefly considered shortening her tip, but I deserved the jab.

As we approached Avenida Menendez, Beater took my elbow in his hand and led me toward the Plaza de la Constitución and one of the old cannons still aimed seaward in memory and honor of its life spent in defense of America's oldest city.

"It's time for me to go, Chase. I've said and done everything I came to do. Thank you for reminding an old man that just like this cannon"—he rubbed his palm against the smooth surface of the aged gun—"there comes a time when an old warrior's battles are over and he's left as a reminder to the young that there's still something worth defending. I hope this doesn't sound condescending, but I'm proud of who and what you've become."

He stared out over the river for a moment, and then rested against the cannon. "Your day will come sooner than you realize, and you'll be standing in front of some young, scared kid, and you'll have to pass the torch. It'll be scary as hell. It was for me, but I picked the right scared kid, and I know you will, too."

Before I could muster anything worth saying, he was gone, and I was left alone, leaning against the cannon. I could swear I almost felt the old gun humming as if it had just fired a nine-pounder into the broadside of a man-o'-war under full sail.

I don't know how long I stood there, but I remember hoping Ace, Tuner, and especially Dr. Robert "Rocket" Richter felt they had placed the torch in worthy hands when I accepted it from them, never knowing what my life would become.

Chapter 28
Mongo of Troy

Back aboard *Aegis*, I printed several copies of the email from Skipper and passed them around. It didn't surprise me when Mongo was the first to ask a question.

"Have you plotted thirty-five degrees, fifteen point one-six minutes north by eighty-four degrees, thirty-one point one-four minutes west? That has to be five hundred miles north of here, doesn't it?"

"I haven't plotted it," I said, "but Skipper said it's in the middle of nowhere in the East Tennessee mountains."

Earl looked up. "East Tennessee? That's where Boomer's from."

Hunter got that look in his eye. "Things are coming together."

That itching feeling to solve a mystery was coming back. "Let's slow down a little before we get too excited. First, what could we possibly find on the top of some mountain in Tennessee that has anything to do with what happened here in Saint Augustine?"

Earl was reading the email again, but everyone else was looking at me. Hunter raised his hand as if he were in third grade again. "I say we plot it just to see how remote it is before we decide we're not going mountain climbing."

I retrieved the laptop from the main salon and brought up a map of the southern Appalachian Mountains. I typed in the coordinates, and a red pin appeared in the Cherokee National Forest about fifty miles northeast of Chattanooga.

Everyone leaned in to see the position, but Earl shouldered her way to the front. She poked a finger toward the screen just southeast of the pin. "That's where Boomer was from. It's a little place called Reliance. It's not much more than a crossroads, really. I've only been there once, but it was beautiful."

I looked at Clark. "Those are your old stomping grounds. What's the terrain like up there?"

He said, "It's rugged off the trails, but there are hiking trails all through that part of the National Forest. You'll have to find a map from the park service to know for sure, but that looks like Gee Creek in the Lost Corral section of the forest. It's mostly hardwoods, and it's pretty steep, but it's passable."

I turned to Earl. "Have you ever heard Boomer mention Gee Creek?"

"No, I don't think so, but I do remember him saying something about Lost Corral. And this guy. . . ." She pointed toward the email. "Cash Malone. I remember that name. He was a friend of Boomer's—a real character, as he told it. Apparently, he was a bootlegger and all-around troublemaker. That's the kind of folks Boomer liked. He called them 'his people.'"

I was getting sucked back in, and my will to resist vanished. "Skipper said she can't find any record of anybody named Cash Malone."

"That don't surprise me. According to Boomer, people in them mountains was born at home back then. Sometimes there was a midwife, and sometimes there was just a preacher's wife. Cash may not have ever had a birth certificate or a driver's license."

I said, "Okay, so if we go on this wild goose chase into the mountains, what are we looking for?"

Everyone was silent.

Earl finally wiped her nose. "Likely, the money."

"What money?" I said.

She held up her hands as if surrendering. "I don't know, but you said those guys who sunk my boat were looking for money they say Boomer stole. You also said Skipper thinks most of them pages are accounting ledgers of some kind, right?"

"Yes, ma'am."

"Well, I'm not the smart one here, but it looks to me like we may have found where Boomer hid that money, if there is any."

Clark spoke up. "It sounds to me like you guys are going on a hike."

"What do you mean, you guys?" I said.

"I know what those mountains look like, and there's no way my back can handle that country. You and Hunter can do it, but depending on how much money is hidden up there, you may need some help carrying it out."

My eyes fell back on Earl. "You keep saying you don't know anything about the money Boomer allegedly schemed from the other pilots in Central America, but if you know *anything* you're not telling us, now's the time to come clean. Was he investing money for the other pilots?"

"I swear to you, Chase. I don't know. It sounds like something he'd do, but he never discussed it with me."

"How about skimming? Does that sound like Boomer?"

She bowed her head. "Maybe, but I just don't know."

"It's okay, Earl. Obviously, we're going up into those mountains, and we're going to find it if it's there, but I'd like to know what to expect when I get there."

"I'm sorry. I just don't know. It sure seems like he went to a lot of trouble, so I'd think it must be a lot of money."

"What's a lot, Earl? I was still wetting my diapers when all of this happened, so I need some perspective. Was it a million bucks?"

She grimaced. "I wish I knew, Chase, but I'm in the dark just as much as you."

"Let's assume it's a million bucks," I said. "If it's in hundred-dollar bills, that weighs around twenty-five pounds and fits in a big gym bag. If it's in fifties, it's twice that, and twenties would make five times that size and weight."

Hunter said, "The weight isn't a problem, but it'll get bulky. And what if it's more than a million?"

Earl raised a finger as if she were going to ask permission to go to the bathroom. "What if it's gold?"

Mongo spoke up. "What was the price of gold in nineteen seventy-four?"

I did a web search. "Gold closed in nineteen seventy-four at a hundred eighty-three dollars an ounce."

Mongo closed one eye as he did the math. "That's over five thousand ounces of gold."

I pulled up the calculator on my phone. "Five thousand divided by sixteen ounces per pound. . . ."

Mongo interrupted. "That's not how it works. Gold is measured in troy ounces, not avoirdupois ounces. A troy ounce is about one point zero-nine-seven avoirdupois ounces."

I scratched my head. "How do you know this kind of stuff?"

Mongo grinned. "I thought everybody knew that. You can put your calculator away. That would be around three hundred and fifty pounds of gold . . . real American pounds."

Clark chuckled. "Yeah, College Boy. We thought everybody knew that. What did they teach you at that fancy school anyway if it wasn't avoid-ah-orope-oy ounces or whatever he said?"

I wadded up my copy of the email and hurled it at Clark's head. "You sit over there and hush. The grown-ups are talking. If you behave, I'll get you some ice cream later."

He took the paper wad to the face like a champ. "I like ice cream."

Mongo grinned. "It sounds like you're going to need me to do the heavy lifting on this one."

Earl waved her arms as if she were trying to stop a train. "Whoa! Hold on a minute. Are you guys really planning to hike into some place you've never been to find a bunch of money that might not even be there?"

Hunter, Mongo, and I nodded.

Earl squinted in disbelief. "Why?"

The three of us exchanged glances, and Hunter said, "Because it sounds like fun."

Penny sat through the whole discussion without saying a word, and that surprised me.

I took her hand. "What do you think about all of this?"

She forced a smile and whispered, "We need to talk."

Nothing strikes fear into a man's heart like those four words. I'd rather wrestle an alligator than hear that phrase, but it was too late to find an alligator.

"Excuse us," I said. "We'll be right back."

Penny followed me into the main salon, and I settled onto the settee. She remained standing, and that frightened me even more.

She said, "I think we should go downstairs for this conversation."

Maybe I could find an alligator if I tried really hard.

I followed her to our cabin, and she crawled on the bed. I panicked as she nestled against the pillow where Anya had taken a nap the morning she arrived.

Maybe I can find an alligator who's willing to eat me.

Penny bit her bottom lip and curled her long legs beneath her. "I don't really know how to tell you this, Chase, but . . ."

She paused, and my heart stopped. I sat on the end of the bed and waited for the worst.

She took a long, slow breath. "I got a phone call while you were printing out Skipper's email." Another dramatic pause. "It was Graham Lightner."

I stared blankly at my wife. "I don't know who that is."

She chuckled. "Yes, you do. He's the agent from Nashville whose granddaughter you saved from the kidnappers."

My desire to find an alligator faded. "Oh, *that* Graham Lightner. Your agent."

"Yeah, my agent. It's so weird to think that I have a real agent. Anyway, he did it."

"He did what?" I asked.

"He sold my screenplay. They're holding a casting call."

I lowered my chin. "That's great news . . . right?"

"Yeah, it's the best news, but it means I need to be in Los Angeles. The producer and director want me there for the casting call."

I leapt to her side and took her in my arms. "Penny, that's amazing. Why do you seem unhappy about it?"

She cast her eyes to the pillow she'd subconsciously squeezed against her body, then pulled a long blonde hair from the pillowcase and tossed it aside. "My hair gets everywhere. I'm like a shedding dog or something."

I let out the breath I'd been holding.

"It's just that I really want to go," she said.

"Of course you want to go. Why wouldn't you?"

She wiped her eye. "Our trip to the Pacific. You put everything on hold so you could come with me to Vanuatu, and now I have this amazing opportunity in L.A."

I brushed her hair back across her ear. "Penny, listen to me. You've dreamed of this day for years. This is yours, just like the missions are mine. I love you, and I absolutely want you to go to L.A. You have to go. The Pacific isn't going anywhere. We can go see your parents anytime."

"Thank you for understanding. I was so scared to tell you."

"Don't ever be afraid to tell me anything. I'm your husband, and I love you. It's not like I'm an alligator waiting to snap at you."

"That's a weird thing to say, but okay. Go back up there and plan your little hiking trip. At least I don't have to worry about anybody shooting at you in Tennessee."

I rejoined Hunter, Mongo, and Earl, but Clark was missing.

Hunter looked up. "Is everything okay?"

"Oh, yeah. Everything's great. Penny's agent sold her screenplay, and they're making a movie. They want her in L.A. for the casting call. She was nervous about telling me for some reason."

"That's fantastic. Her agent is the guy from the kidnapping thing in Nashville, right?"

"Yep, that's him," I said. "Thanks to you, Mongo, and Singer, that little girl is alive, and my girl's screenplay is headed for the theaters."

Hunter turned to Mongo. "How about doing some of that fancy math in your head and figuring out what our cut of the movie royalties will be?"

Clark rejoined us before I could crush their dreams of cashing in on Penny's screenplay. He said, "I just got off the phone with Skipper. She's looking for a backcountry guide for you three. It'll probably be tomorrow before she can find anyone, but I told her to coordinate with you."

"Why me?" I asked.

He looked at his watch. "I'm going back to Miami Beach, where I belong."

"Where you belong?" I scoffed.

"Yeah, where I belong. I'll still shoot when I have to, but now I can call you when the world needs saving. Go find that pot of gold in them there hills. I'm going back to my own pot of gold on South Beach. She may not technically need me there, but I miss Maebelle, and I know for sure that I need her."

Chapter 29
Heathen Agreement

Dawn came as it has for eons, but for me, that particular rising of the sun brought a new light to the world as I perceived it. Jesus took Penny to the airport, while Hunter, Mongo, and I made ready for our sail out of Saint Augustine to Bonaventure Plantation. No one waited in some distant, godforsaken corner of the world for my team and me to pull them out of the temporary hell into which they'd fallen. No one from the Kremlin lay in wait for me around the next corner. Penny wasn't left behind in tears, wondering if I'd return in a coffin. My wife was on a journey she'd dreamed of taking since she was a child, and I was on a mission to find a little money that had been tucked away nearly three decades before . . . maybe.

As I sat in the cockpit, Earl stared down the dock to where her boat used to rest, tied securely at the end. She caught a tear before it could fall from her cheek. "You know, I don't get choked up about much."

"It's perfectly understandable," I said. "That boat was your home for a lot of years. Losing her is enough to get anybody a little emotional."

She laid her hand on my knee. "Yeah, I'll miss my old boat, but that's not what makes me feel like crying this morning. It's the fact that all of you did all of this for me. You came down here, and you risked your lives for *me*. I don't deserve none of it, Baby Boy. I'm just a worn-out old woman. Why would you do such a thing for somebody like me?"

I covered her hand with mine. "Because we love you, Earl. You're our friend, practically family, and you needed our help. There are no limits in times like those. We have a collection of skills that most people never dream of amassing. Sometimes we're called on to use those skills to do unthinkable things in places nobody can spell or even find on a map. But sometimes we get to put those skills to use doing something good to help somebody we love. That alone makes everything we've sacrificed to earn those skills worth the trouble. You're never alone, Earl, and you're definitely not old nor worn-out. You've got a lot of good years of wrench-turning left in those hands."

She looked up at me with her eyes glistening behind the tears she wouldn't let fall. "If Boomer had been more like you. . . ."

I squeezed her hand. "If Boomer had been more like me, he'd never have been good enough for you. Now, let's deal with that gold of yours. I have to get going to those mountains in Tennessee, but I'd like to buy your gold from you before I go."

"You don't never have to buy nothing from me, Baby Boy. If you want or need that gold, it's yours."

"No, it's not that. You can take it to a gold broker. I'm sure there's one around somewhere. Or I can pay you whatever today's value is for it. I don't own any gold, and I've always thought I should, so it's a win for both of us. You turn your gold into cash, and I get to keep a little precious metal in my safe for a rainy day."

I brought up the laptop and checked the most recent gold price. "It's your lucky day, Earl. Gold is worth four hundred twenty-one dollars today. I'm not as good at math as Mongo, so I'll use the calculator. Three hundred fifty-five ounces at four hundred twenty-one dollars per ounce is one hundred forty-nine thousand, four hundred fifty-five dollars."

I pulled fifteen banded stacks of one-hundred-dollar bills from the safe and slid them into an inconspicuous locking bag. "If you'd like, I'd be happy to walk you to the bank so you don't have to carry this money around."

She lifted the bag, apparently surprised at how light it felt. "How about you just sell me a pistol since mine's still on the bottom of the river?"

I laughed. "I won't sell you one, but I'm happy to lend you one."

I pulled a thirty-eight revolver from the safe, made sure it was loaded, and passed it over. "That should fit the bill."

Earl took the pistol from my hand, pulled it from its holster, and inspected the cylinder and frame. "Yep, I'd say that'll do just fine." She wrapped her arms around me as if she were trying to split me in half.

I returned the hug with slightly less exuberance. "I'll be in touch as soon as we find whatever we're looking for in Tennessee."

"I reckon I'll have a new boat by then, thanks to you." She bounced the bag in her hand. "Thank you for everything, Baby Boy. I love you, you rascal."

"I love you, too, Old Girl. Now get off my boat. I've got hiking to do."

We motored out of the slip with Mongo at the helm. If he was smart enough to convert troy ounces to whatever a normal ounce is called, he was smart enough to drive a boat.

The drawbridge came up, and we motored northward and out the Saint Augustine Inlet. Fifteen knots of wind out of the southeast blew us toward the North Pole, according to my compass that worked. If the conditions held, we'd make Saint Marys inlet in just under six hours.

Sailing didn't come as easily as mathematics to our resident mental and physical heavyweight, but with a little tutelage, he soon had the hang of it.

Mayport Naval Station passed off our port beam.

Hunter said, "Are you ever going to tell us what that admiral wanted the other day?"

"It was a job offer," I said without hesitation.

"A job offer?" he asked. "What kind of job offer?"

"I don't know. He said something about being a psychologist in the recruiting program for the SEALs. I didn't pay enough attention to get the details. He did offer to buy me a car, though."

Hunter laughed so hard he had to take a seat. "A car, huh? Wow, the Navy is a big spender."

I laughed along with my partner. "I'm sure he had a nice car in mind."

He caught his breath. "It better be a fleet of Maseratis. You did tell him you weren't interested, right?"

I stared at the silhouettes of the massive warships in the distance. "I told him I'd let him know."

Hunter lowered his chin and glared up at me. "You're not cut out to be a desk jockey."

"I think you're right. I'm probably doing exactly what I'm supposed to do."

He winked. "What's that? Treasure hunting in Tennessee?"

"Maybe."

* * *

The conditions didn't hold; they improved, and we made our turn into the Saint Marys inlet just over five hours after setting the sails. The tide was running in, so I couldn't resist having a little fun with our newly minted helmsman.

I stood beside Mongo at the wheel. "Now it's time to make some decisions. Which way is the wind blowing and the tide running?"

He looked around as if searching for the answer in the clouds. "The wind is at our back, but I don't know what the tide's doing."

I pointed toward a channel marker. "Look at the water around the base of that buoy, and imagine the buoy being a boat leaving a wake. Which way would it be moving if it were creating the wake behind it?"

He studied the buoy and its wake. "It'd be moving to sea if it were moving because the wake is on the back side, but of course, it's sitting still."

"That's right. So, since the wake is on the inland side of the buoy, the tide is running inward. Think about what that'll do to our boat—especially our rudders."

"It'll increase our boat speed over the ground but decrease our speed through the water, also decreasing our rudder effectiveness."

I patted him on the back. "Look at you, all smart and stuff. One evening, I came upon a nuclear submarine with her bow run aground, in almost exactly these conditions, right over there. It was the biggest mess I'd ever seen, so we turned south and spent the night tucked in behind Amelia Island."

I could see Mongo trying to picture the catastrophic scene. "I'll bet that U-boat's skipper spent the rest of his career on a tug."

"I wouldn't doubt it," I said. "The safest way to negotiate these conditions is to start both engines and use the throttles as differential steering. That'll have more effectiveness than the rudders."

"How about the sails?"

"We can leave them up for now. There's plenty of room inside to turn into the wind and bring them down once we get on the leeward side of Cumberland Island."

He maneuvered the boat into the channel as if he'd done it a thousand times. He didn't look as good as Penny when she did it, but no one could compete with her. I also had no interest in seeing Mongo in cut-off blue-jean shorts and a knotted T-shirt.

The sails came down, and under Mongo's command, the starboard hull kissed the floating dock at Bonaventure as gently as a leaf falling to the ground.

"Nice job, big man. We may turn you into a sailor after all."

He shut down the engines and grinned. "In our business, it never hurts to add a new feather to your cap."

Singer, our Southern Baptist sniper, met us on the dock and helped us tie up. "Welcome home, guys. How'd it go down there?"

I gave him the Cliff's Notes version of the story, and he listened intently.

"That sounds like fun. I hate I missed it. So, what's next?"

"We're headed to Tennessee for a little treasure hunting. Interested?"

Singer raised his eyebrows. "Interested? Absolutely. I'm in. When do we leave?"

"That's what I love about you, Singer. You're always up for an adventure. You don't even know what we're hunting yet."

"It doesn't really matter," he said. "If it's up there, we'll find it . . . whatever it is."

"What's been happening here since I've been gone?"

"The police chief came by a couple of times to brief us on the case with the shooters."

"What case?" I said. "You sent them to meet their maker."

"As it turns out, it was a whole coordinated effort. There were two more shooters in the bell tower of the church, and they intended to take a few shots at folks running away from downtown. I guess we scared them off, but the third guy from the roof rolled over and spilled his guts. The cops rounded up the whole gang."

I stopped in my tracks. "I'm disappointed you didn't spot the shooters in the bell tower."

He held up a hand. "Wait a minute. I wasn't the one with the periscope."

"Point taken," I said. "Let's get some grub. I'm starving."

"There's a new seafood joint on the left at the bottom of the hill. A couple of folks from church said it was good."

"Lead the way," I said. "If the Baptists declare it good, I'm sold."

We ate shrimp and crab until even Mongo couldn't hold another bite.

Hunter wiped his mouth and tossed the napkin into the center of his plate. "Singer, you can tell your church buddies that this place is approved by heathens like me, too."

Singer laughed. "Aww, you aren't a heathen, Hunter. You're just a wayward sheep. We'll haul you back into the flock. Just you wait and see."

Back at Bonaventure, I checked my phone and discovered I'd missed a call from Skipper. She answered before the first ring. "Hey, I found you a guide in Tennessee."

"Good work, Skipper. What's his name?"

"Well, actually, I found you a guide company. It's called Bigfoot Outfitters in Benton. They do all sorts of adventure sports like kayaking, whitewater rafting, canoeing, and hiking, and I think the guy said they have a hang-gliding instructor on staff. They're a one-stop shop for however you want to kill yourself in the mountains."

"Sounds like my kind of place. Let them know we'll be there late tomorrow morning. We'll fly into the Cleveland Airport. It looks like the closest airport to Benton."

"I'll let them know," she said. "Are you going to rent a car, or should I have them pick you up?"

"If they'll pick us up, that'd be great. Let them know there will be four and a half of us."

"Four and a half?"

"Yeah. Mongo's going with us, and he's at least one and a half full-grown men."

She giggled. "You're terrible, but I'll let them know to bring a livestock trailer. Is there anything else you need from me?"

"I think that's everything. I'll let you know when we take off in the morning."

* * *

A good airplane in competent hands is a thing of beauty. Hunter did the flying from the left seat of the Caravan, and he made it look easy. He greased the landing at Cleveland and taxied to the parking apron like an airline captain.

I pulled off my headset as he shut down the engine. "Not bad for a knuckle-dragger like you. We'll do some water landings on the way back home if you want, and you'll be ready for a check ride."

"Sounds good to me," he said. "But let's do a little backcountry hiking first. Whaddya say?"

Chapter 30
Be Cool

"So, you're the only Cessna Caravan on floats, and you have a Sasquatch-looking behemoth with you. You must be my hikers."

I wasn't sure how the man could see any of us through the ten thousand scratches cut into the lenses of his Costas, but his tattered Bigfoot Outfitters T-shirt and hemp sandals were enough to convince me he was our guy.

I stuck out my hand. "I'm Chase, and this is Hunter, Singer, and Mongo."

The man ignored my outstretched hand and shoved his glasses onto his forehead. "Chase, Hunter, Singer, Mongo. I dig it. I'm Jerry. I'll take you guys back up to the shop, and we'll get you hooked up with your guide. He'll think you dudes are far out."

I took a look at my team. "All right. We can deal with 'far out.' Do you want us to hump our gear out to your truck, or will they let you pull out here on the ramp?"

Jerry spun on one heel and motioned toward the FBO. "The gas guy is my brother-in-law, so he'll let me come out here and get your gear. You'll be carrying it far enough when you get in the woods. You might as well take it easy for now."

I strolled into the FBO and slid my credit card across the counter to the young lady who seemed to be losing a battle with a fingernail. "I'm in the Caravan. If you wouldn't mind, I'd love to find a spot in a hangar for a few days."

"Hang on just a minute. These dang nails won't stay on for nothin'. I got 'em done up in Sweetwater, and I knew they wasn't gonna last no time. I ain't never going to trust nobody except my girl ever again. This is just plain ridiculous."

I watched as she gave the nail one final yank and won the battle. The girl leapt from her chair and hopped around on one foot as if she were doing some sort of ceremonial rain dance. "Dang it. I knew that was gonna hurt."

"I'd love to help if I could, but manicures aren't my bailiwick."

"Baili-what? I don't know what that means, mister. How long did you say you'd be staying with us?"

"I'd like a hangar if you have one. We'll probably be here a week or so, maybe a little longer."

"We ain't got no hangars big enough for that thing. It sits up too high. Them guys at the rescue school down at the end are the only ones with a big hangar, but they keep that helicopter in it. You might could talk to them, but otherwise, you'll have to take a tie-down. It's twenty dollars a night, unless you buy gas, then it don't cost you nothing."

"I'll definitely be buying gas. If you could have Jerry's brother-in-law top it off with Jet-A and put it on that card, I'd appreciate it."

She slid a sheet of paper across the counter. "Sure thing. Just fill this out and sign it at the bottom where it says *signature*." She leaned over the counter and pointed to the signature line with her nailless finger. "Right there."

"Yes, I see it. Thank you. I don't know if I could've found it without you."

"Yeah, I know. A lot of people miss it. That's why I point it out every time."

I filled out her form and motioned down the ramp. "Did you say the rescue school is at that end?"

She stood on her tiptoes and motioned out the window. "Yeah, just go all the way down there to the end. You'll see the big hangar. You'll know which one it is on account of it's so much bigger than the other ones. That one beside it with the rusted doors? That one used to belong to Hugh Farmer. You know that slutty Pam Farmer? It was her daddy's, and he took every waitress in town into that hangar, but he's dead now. He's still got two or three airplanes in there if you know anybody who's looking for one. His widow, Peggy . . . She'll make 'em a real bargain on one of 'em or all of 'em after what that man put her through. You don't even wanna know."

I made my escape and headed to the south end of the parking ramp. Fingernail girl was right. Hugh Farmer's old hangar doors were rusted so badly I could almost see inside. Two men in flight suits were hooking a third man to a cable suspended from a swing set frame as I walked up.

"Good morning," I said, loud enough to get their attention.

Both flight suits turned in unison, and their victim was left dangling from the cable. "Hey, good morning. Can we help you with something?"

I stuck out my hand, and unlike Jerry, both men accepted a shake. They seemed to have forgotten about their dangling friend. "I'm Chase Fulton." I turned, pointing toward my airplane. "And that's my Caravan back there."

What I saw left me more confused than my experience with the young lady inside. A forty-year-old yellow school bus with at least six whitewater rafts strapped to the top was parked beside my Caravan.

The younger of the two men in flight suits said, "Oh, you must be going rafting. That's Trevor's outfit, isn't it?"

"I don't know," I admitted. "They sent a guy named Jerry to pick us up, but I wasn't expecting a bus."

Flight suit chuckled. "Yeah, those rafting guys are a mess. You'll have a lot of fun, though. Are you doing the whole river, or just the middle?"

"Actually, we're here to do some hiking, and the guys at Bigfoot Outfitters are providing a guide for us."

The other man snapped his fingers. "Yep, that's it . . . Bigfoot Outfitters. That's Trevor's place. He and Jerry do a good job up there. Real first-class all the way. A lot of those guys running those river trips are a little shoddy, but you picked a good one. Do the whole river. That upper section is a lot of fun, but make sure you get a wetsuit. You'll freeze to death without it."

"Thanks for the tip," I said, "but I came down here to talk to you about your hangar."

They looked up at the biggest building at the airport. "What about it?"

"As I said, that's my Caravan, and I'd like to get it out of the weather for a few days. The lady at the FBO said you might be willing to rent me some floor space for a week or so."

The first man pulled off his cap and scratched his head. "Yeah, I guess we could do that. Come on in here and take a look."

I followed the two men toward the hangar. "What about that guy you left hanging back there?"

The older man said, "Ah, he'll be all right. He's learning the ropes, so to speak."

We walked through a single door and into the massive space of the hangar. The floor was spotless and polished to a shine that made it look like a mirror. A gray Bell H-1 Huey helicopter rested on a cart in the center of the space.

"Nice Huey," I said as I admired the chopper.

"Thanks. We use it to teach backcountry search and rescue, mostly basket and hoist operations. And we just had the winches rebuilt. It's got a pair of custom-built five-thousand-pounders. There's not much we can't snatch off the mountain with those things."

"That's impressive," I said. "I didn't know anyone taught that sort of thing around here."

"We're the only ones east of the Mississippi right now. There was an operation over in Asheville, but they dumped their Four-Twelve into a ravine over on Walnut Mountain. The crew got out, but they lost the helicopter. There was some drama with an insurance policy or something. I don't think they're going to re-open."

"I'm glad the crew is okay," I said.

"Yeah, I think it was an insurance job. If you want my opinion, they dumped her on purpose."

"I guess that's okay with you guys, huh?"

The older man said, "I don't like to see anybody lose an airplane, but they weren't the best-run company around. We're glad to pick up the slack. So, anyway, we may have to pull your airplane in and out to get the Huey out, but I think we can fit it in here."

"I'd really appreciate that. How much do you charge for use of the hangar?"

Both men shrugged. "I don't know. Just whatever you think it's worth is fine with us."

I pulled two hundred dollars from my wallet and held it out for the older man. He threw up his hands. "Oh, no. Give that to him. He's the money man. I'm just the pilot. I don't have the brains to handle the cash."

"Thanks again," I said. "And again, my name is Chase Fulton. Here's my card with my cell phone number and an emergency contact. Her name is Elizabeth, but she likes to be called Skipper."

The younger man took my money and card and handed back a card of his own. "I'm Danny, and he's my much older brother,

Doug. That number on there rings here at the school, but if nobody answers, it'll forward the call to one of our cell phones. If we're out flying, we'll call you back."

"It's nice to meet you both, and don't forget about your guy hanging out there in the harness."

Doug slapped his forehead. "Oh, yeah. He's probably ready to go flying."

I walked back toward my airplane flanked by the school bus and still couldn't believe the sight.

Mongo was closing the rear door just as I walked up, and he motioned toward the bus. "This is Skipper's work. She told them to bring the biggest vehicle they could find because I wouldn't fit in anything smaller."

I looked him up and down. "Well, she wasn't wrong."

He took a giant stride toward me and threw out his arms. "Come here. You're getting a bear hug."

I danced backward. "Oh, no, you don't. You're not crushing my spine."

We loaded up on the bus, and Jerry tossed his tattered cap onto the front seat, exchanging it for a shiny brimmed driver's cap. He took a little bow. "I'll be your chauffeur."

We fell into our seats, and Jerry pulled away from the Caravan. He shot a look up into the oversized mirror and waggled his finger. "No smoking, fighting, or sticking gum under the seats. Got it?"

Hunter pounded the seat in front of him. "Dang it! Those are my three favorite things to do on a bus."

Jerry squinted and focused on Hunter. "Don't make me report you to the principal, young man. You know he's got that paddle with the holes in it, and he's not afraid to use it."

As we wound our way through the countryside, Jerry pointed out a few meaningless landmarks. "Oh, I almost forgot. There's one strip club and seven churches between the airport and the river. If you're not careful, you'll wander into the wrong one and stumble out broke, scared, and wondering why you ever went in. And the other one has two-for-one lap dances on Thursday nights."

Everyone laughed except Singer. In retaliation, he said, "What do you get when you cross a pig with a bus-driving whitewater rafting guide?"

Jerry shrugged. "I don't know. What?"

Singer grinned from ear to ear. "Nothing. There's some things a pig just won't do."

"Yes, sir. You win. But I'm adding that one to my repertoire."

After three hundred curves on a road barely big enough for a mule cart, Jerry turned the bus into a gravel drive and headed up the side of a mountain. Nestled into the tree line was a quaint little cabin-style shop with a ten-foot statue of Bigfoot guarding the door.

We filed off the bus and headed inside. A mid-thirties guy dressed a lot like Jerry was shooting basketball and smoking something hand-rolled. As soon as I was in range, he launched a chest-pass and hit me squarely in the hands. I took the shot, and out of pure luck, sank the thirty-foot jumper.

A chorus of oohs and aahs rose from my team. I thumped my chest. "D-one collegiate athlete and College World Series MVP right here, boys. Don't you ever forget it."

Mongo clapped his hands once and ordered, "Gimme the ball." He took four running strides and made a one-handed dunk that would've made Michael Jordan proud. He scooped up the ball and threw it to me with more force than necessary. "Let's see you do *that*, baseball boy."

I gently laid the ball on the ground. "You must be Trevor. I'm Robin Hood, and this is my merry band of fools."

The man rolled the ball toward himself with his foot and kicked it into the air. He dribbled twice, launched his five-foot-ten-inch frame into the air, crushed a two-handed dunk, and remained hanging from the goal like Tarzan. With a flamboyant dismount, he landed at Mongo's feet and tossed the ball up to him. "Your turn."

Mongo stuck out a hand. "Point taken. I'm Marvin, but everybody calls me Mongo. You already met Chase. He's the boss, and those two non-ballers are Hunter and Singer."

"It's nice to meet you guys. Welcome to Bigfoot Outfitters. Come on inside, and we'll see if we can wake up your guide."

We followed Trevor into the shop, where we saw a guy who looked like he just walked off the set of Kung-Fu. His head was shaved clean, but his white goatee was braided with tie-died-colored beads woven sporadically into the strand. He was sitting cross-legged on top of the mini refrigerator, chanting some sort of mantra in a language I'd never heard.

Trevor placed his finger over his lips and shushed us. He whispered, "Don't interrupt him. He gets weird if you do. Just lean in close and listen. It's the coolest thing you've ever heard."

He gets weird? He's already weird.

Mesmerized by the chanting, we all leaned in closer but didn't say a word. I was beginning to believe we'd been sucked into an episode of *The Twilight Zone*, when the chanter leapt from his crouch as if he'd been shot from a cannon, then yelled like a wounded beast as he flew through the air.

Mongo took one enormous stride forward, caught the little man by one arm and one leg, pinned him against the wall, and froze in position. Hunter and Singer drew their pistols to the low-ready, and the little guy's eyes looked like balloons. "Whoa, dudes! I'm Animal. I was just messing with you. Be cool. Be cool."

Chapter 31
My Nemesis

Mongo lowered Animal to the ground and dusted him off. To see the two of them side by side was one more addition to my world of polar opposites. Animal was the size of one of Mongo's legs, but his sense of humor and willingness to take a joke all the way to its end was larger than life.

Animal shook off the shock. "That sure didn't turn out like I planned, but since you didn't shoot me, it's pretty funny, right?"

Hunter holstered his pistol. "We weren't going to shoot *you*. We were going to shoot Mongo if he tried to kill you. There's no other way to stop him."

Animal looked up. "Well, I guess I should thank you for that. Anyway, Trevor says you need a guide into the Lost Corral section of the National Forest."

I said, "That's right. We're looking for a cave."

"A cave?" he said. "You won't have any trouble finding those. That part of the mountain is full of caves."

"We're looking for one particular hole in the ground," I said. "I have the lat/long, but I hear it's pretty rugged back there."

Animal jerked his head. "Come on back here, and we'll look at a map."

I gave him the numbers, and he plotted the spot on an enormous map covering most of one wall. "Ooh, man. That *is* deep. Why would you want to find one particular cave that far back in the National Forest?"

"Let's just say we've got a friend who may have left something in there for us."

Animal shrugged. "Suits me. I'll take you back there, but I hope you've done some rough-country work before. It's not exactly a Sunday afternoon stroll."

"You might say we've done a little mountaineering," I said. "I think we can keep up."

Animal squinted and studied my team. "You guys aren't going to tell me, are you?"

"Tell you what?" I said.

"What you really are and what you're really doing up here."

We all smiled as if we'd practiced our response.

"We're just a bunch of guys looking for a little backcountry adventure. That's all."

Our guide threw up his hands. "Hey, dudes. It's all the same to me. I don't ask questions, but you have to know I've got a wife and kid. You can't be putting a bullet in my skull back in those mountains. First of all, you'll never find your way out without me, and second, I'll haunt you as long as you live . . . maybe longer."

I put on a reassuring smile. "All we want is for someone to get us to that cave and back out. That's all. We're the good guys, and that's all you need to know."

"Cool, man. I'm down with it. I'm two-fifty a day, and if you fall, get stuck, or get hurt, and I have to rescue you, I expect a nice tip. You cool with that?"

"We're more than cool with that, and we're not the type who need rescuing very often, but if you put us on the cave we're looking for, you can expect the best tip of your life."

His toothy grin said he was all in. "When do you dudes want to leave?"

I checked my watch. "There's no time like the present."

"I meant two-fifty a day, or any *part* of a day. You dig?"

I pulled a thousand bucks from my pocket. "Yeah, we dig."

Animal hesitantly took the cash from my hand and motioned for someone near the door. Trevor sidestepped into the room, and Animal shoved the money toward him. "I'm taking these dudes up Gee Creek for three or four days. This is their deposit. If, you know, something happens or whatever, take it up to my place and give it to my wife, would you?"

Mongo laid his hand on Animal's shoulder. "Nothing's going to happen to you. I can promise you that much. Besides, I owe you one after slamming you into the wall."

Animal looked up. "Yeah, all the same. I'll be leaving the cash here."

Trevor slid our deposit into his pocket. "Do you guys need a receipt?"

I shook my head. "No, we're all handshake-and-cash guys, and I get the feeling you're the same way."

He gave me a fist bump. "Have fun up there, and don't let him run off and leave you. They don't call him Animal for nothing."

Our kung fu guide motioned for the door. "Go double-check your gear. If there's anything you don't have, we've probably got it here at the store. Don't worry about humping a bunch of water. There's plenty in that valley."

We followed his instructions and rechecked each of our packs. Everything was in order, including four oversized bags with shoulder straps in case we came off the mountain with a few hundred extra pounds of cash.

Animal showed up with a day pack slung over his shoulder. "Everything good?"

"Yep. We're good to go," I said. "Where's your gear?"

He shot his chin toward the pack on his shoulder. "This is all I'll need. Come on. My truck's over here. It'll be a tight squeeze, but it's not far up to the horse barn."

I froze. "Horse barn? We're not taking horses, are we?"

Animal chuckled. "Well, yeah, *I* am. You got something against horses?"

"I've got everything against horses. I hate them, and they hate me. You might say it's a mutual understanding."

He waved a hand. "These horses are as gentle as baby lambs. We've even got a draft horse for Mongo. Come on. We need to get to the first campsite before dark."

The five of us piled into Animal's four-wheel-drive Bronco with our gear stowed in the cage on top. Instead of heading down the gravel drive back to what qualified as a road in Polk County, Tennessee, Animal turned up the hill. We ran out of gravel after a thousand yards and hit a dirt trail through aged oaks and walnut trees that must've been there when Washington was president. For twenty minutes, we bounced and slid across the mountain trail and crossed three paved roads on the way.

I braced against the door and center console. "Do you have some special distrust of pavement?"

No answer. Just another Animal grin.

Ten minutes later, we pulled into a clearing with a stacked-log barn and small corral. Animal slung open his door. "Here we are. Let's go make some friends."

No horse would ever be my friend.

As we approached the barn, a young woman of perhaps twenty-five ambled out the door wearing boots, filthy jeans, a flannel shirt, and a University of Georgia Bulldogs hat.

Animal threw an arm around her. "This is Becky. She's the farrier, groomer, closest thing we've got to a vet, and all-around horse whisperer."

"Hey, guys," Becky said. "Come on in. We'll get you paired up. I'm quite the matchmaker."

"Nice hat," I said. "Are you from Georgia?"

She pulled the hat from her head and gave it a quick look. "Oh, this? No, I'm from North Carolina. I just wear this to piss my brother off. He went to Georgia Tech."

"Too bad he couldn't get into a good school," I said.

She shook her hat at me. "I'm going to like you. What's your name?"

"I'm Chase, and I'm an old Bulldog."

"No kidding? When were you there?"

"Ninety-two to ninety-six."

"Nice. We were there at the same time. I was a biology major. I bet you were in engineering, right?"

"No, nothing that useful, I'm afraid. I'm a psych major."

"I've got just the horse for you," she said. "Follow me."

Becky opened a stall and led out a massive mare, bigger than any of the horses at Bonaventure. "This is Ugga. She's got a little bit of an attitude at times, and check this out." She pulled Ugga's mane out of her face, revealing a patch of white hair that looked as if it had been printed on her head to look like a white English bulldog.

"I guess it's fate," I said as I took the lead rope from Becky's hand.

She paired each of us up with a horse of our own, then went to Mongo. "I've got a special girl just for you. Meet Velvet. She's a Belgian and as sure-footed as a mountain goat. She doesn't get in a hurry, but I've never seen her stumble."

Mongo laid his arm across the horse's neck. "Hello, Velvet. I think we're going to spend some quality time together."

Fifteen minutes later, we were saddled, packed, and headed northeast. Animal led the way. I was in the middle of the pack, terrified at every step, and Mongo brought up the rear with a pair of pack mules in tow.

The ride was beautiful. Hints of the autumn colors still hung in the trees, but most of the hardwood foliage had already turned brown and started falling. After half a mile or so, I started to believe Ugga and I could get along.

The trail we seemed to be following was mostly covered by leaves with a few rocky outcroppings. The horses appeared to know the trail as well as Animal, and they lumbered along at a slow, comfortable pace.

Just as I relaxed in the saddle and let the reins rest on the horn, Ugga turned into a five-ticket carnival ride. She reared upward onto her hind legs, cracking me in the forehead with the back of her head. Determined to stay in the saddle, I clamped my left hand around the saddle horn and dug my heels into her sides. She bucked and leapt sideways off the trail, landing on her haunches. I was still in the saddle, but Ugga and I were in a slide for our lives down the steep embankment.

Neither of us was going to stop until we reached the bottom. Staying in the saddle was my best chance at not ending up underneath the horse, but that was going to be no easy task. As we slid, she dug at the earth with her hooves, trying to find purchase. Her digging made my task of staying aboard like trying to wrestle a Tasmanian devil. I'd been thrown by every horse I'd ever ridden, but I was going to ride Ugga until every inch of her stopped moving.

At some point in our descent, we found ourselves with Ugga's head pointed up the slope and her hind legs on something firm. Suddenly, our motion slowed, but the momentum of our combined two thousand pounds sent her front legs towering into the air. We were going over backward, and there was nothing I could do. It was at least another hundred feet to the bottom of the slope behind us, and I was about to make the descent with Ugga solidly on top of me.

I looked up, hoping for a tree limb or an angel from Heaven. Neither appeared, but something just as good flashed in my peripheral vision. A lasso fell across my head and shoulders. The loop was enormous and fell down my body until it landed across the front of the horn and beneath the back of the saddle. When the rope came taut, my legs were caught between the rope and the falling horse. My eyes followed the rope up the hill where Animal sat on his horse, backing up around a giant oak. The rope cut into the bark of the mighty tree, and Ugga froze with her front hooves six feet off the ground. We were locked in position with Animal's rope holding us perfectly motionless.

Finally, we overcame gravity, and Ugga got all four hooves back on the ground. Animal tied the rope to his and Hunter's saddle horns and slowly backed their horses until Ugga and I clawed our way to the trail.

Animal shook the lasso loose, and I slid from Ugga's saddle.

"Well, that was exciting," I said.

Animal dismounted and ran toward me. "Are you all right?"

"Yeah, I'm okay. Just a little shaken."

He reached up and took Ugga's bridle in his hands. "I was talking to the horse."

Laughter cut the tension of the moment until Mongo stepped down from the rock outcropping where my joyride had begun. In his hand was a huge timber rattler. The snake was as thick as Mongo's wrist, and his mouth was splayed wide open with razor-sharp fangs protruding into the air. Ugga bucked and pulled away from Animal. I caught one of her reins and kept her from bolting back toward the barn.

Animal moved toward the snake with bizarre curiosity in his eye. "Ah, man. That thing is huge. I think that's the biggest one

I've ever seen. It's a little late in the year for them to be active, but now we've got something to eat."

Using his knife, Mongo turned the rattlesnake into two distinct pieces as everyone except me remounted.

Animal took the lead again. "There's a clearing just up ahead. We'll camp there, cook up the snake, and get an early start tomorrow."

Ugga and I walked side by side on the trail until we reached the clearing. She and I had been through enough, and neither of us needed the burden of the other at that moment.

We pulled our gear from the pair of pack mules, and Animal patted his horse on the rump. "Take 'em home, girl. I'll see you in a few days."

His horse gently turned and ambled back down the trail with the four other horses and two mules following in step.

I couldn't believe what I was seeing. "You're just sending them off by themselves?"

He laughed. "Yeah, they got up here by themselves. We were just passengers. They know the way home. Besides, it's too rugged for the horses the rest of the way in. We're on our own now."

Chapter 32
Communion

I learned that timber rattlers taste like chicken when grilled over an open fire, and I wish Ugga could've been there to watch the snake meet its end. I think she would've appreciated the revenge.

With the exception of nights spent aboard *Aegis*, the eight hours of sleep I got under the stars in the Tennessee mountains were some of the best of my life. As the sun came up, we became our own pack mules and headed farther into the mountains.

Animal led the way with his ten-pound pack while we followed with at least five times as much gear as him. "We'll stay on the ridgeline as long as we can. It's rocky down there along the creek. We'll have to turn down for some water later, but we'll make better time up high."

His plan was sound, and we made good time. Our pace was slower than on horseback, but every step took us one stride closer to Boomer's mysterious coordinates.

The sun reached its zenith in the sky, and Animal took a seat on a fallen walnut tree. With a tattered map rolled out on his knees, he pointed toward a break in the contour lines. "Here we are, and the coordinates you gave me are about a half mile up that creek you hear running below us. It's four or five hundred feet down to the water, but that's where we're going to find your cave—if it's there."

I pulled my handheld GPS from my pack, and to no one's surprise, Animal was spot-on. We were exactly where he said, and the coordinates I'd entered put the cave three thousand feet to the east.

I examined the steep slope leading down to the creek and then turned to my team. "When Boomer plotted these coordinates, no one had ever heard of GPS, so he could've been way off."

Hunter scratched his chin. "I don't know. That guy had a ton of experience in jungles all over the world. If anybody could plot a position on a map, I'd put my money on him."

We started down the slope, making switchbacks every fifty feet. The descent was anything but easy. It was, likely, the most dangerous portion of our trek, and everyone knew it. A broken ankle—or worse—this deep in the woods would be a mission-killer. We couldn't afford risking an injury by hurrying.

When we reached the bottom, the scene was breathtaking. A mountain stream ten feet wide ran across smooth limestone rocks that had endured the flow for millions of years. The sound of the ocean soothed my soul and healed my wounds, but the sounds of that mountain stream took me someplace I'd never been. It was like a siren song beckoning me to never leave.

I drank from a pool and splashed the cold water over my face. "All water should taste this good."

Animal sat on a flat rock and pulled off his boots and socks. The idea must've appealed to my team. Soon we were all bare-foot and sliding toward the water. Animal took the ritual a step further, though. Before we knew it, he was completely naked and sitting on the bottom of the pool. His braided goatee floated on the water like a twig, twisting and turning in the current.

Our guide wore the same expression as when we'd met him sitting on top of the refrigerator in the outfitter's shop. He was completely at peace. We watched in disbelief until he finally opened his eyes and let out a long, satisfied sigh. "Dudes, you gotta commune with it. Water is life. Our spirits have to return to it, or we dry out. You can't let your spirit dry out, man. That's not cool at all."

Hunter was the first to give in, but soon, there were five naked dudes sitting in a pool of freezing water. October in Tennessee isn't the best time to commune with it, but after the shivering stopped, it was a moment I'll never forget.

We dried in the sun, pulled our clothes back on, and headed up Gee Creek. I'd been up a lot of creeks in my life, but I hoped this one wasn't a matter of national security.

Animal, his spirit fully rehydrated, motioned toward the steep terrain left and right of the creek. "Keep an eye out up both banks. Most of the caves are fifty to a hundred feet above the creek, and some of them are pretty hard to spot."

We trekked up the rocky terrain, and I was thankful Animal had brought us most of the way on the ridgeline. Hiking the creek was more like crawling than walking.

Singer, who'd barely said a word the whole trip, pointed up and to the right. "There's one."

We stopped crawling and followed his finger into the sky. About seventy-five feet above our heads was a dark patch in the leaf-covered slope.

"I wish I had the eyes of a sniper," I said.

"I wish I could dunk a basketball," Singer said. "We've all got our gifts."

Animal dropped his pack. "I'll check it out."

He scampered up the rocky slope like a squirrel until he reached the dark spot, then used a broken limb to scratch the leaves and debris away from the opening. He looked down at us. "It's a cave, all right, but the mouth is barely big enough for me to fit through. Do you want me to check it out?"

I shook my head. "No. If it's that small, I don't think that's the one we want. Something tells me the one we're looking for is a lot bigger."

"Suit yourself," he said as he slid back down the slope.

We continued up the creek until we reached a waterfall ten feet tall. It looked like something out of National Geographic. The foaming whitewater at the crest turned to glass as it fell, creating a wall of transparent water.

I stood in awe of the site, absolutely oblivious to anything happening around me. Human hands would never create anything that approached the beauty of nature.

Singer laid his hand on my shoulder, "God's pretty good at making stuff, isn't He?"

We shared a silent moment, taking in the majesty of the world around us.

Mongo interrupted our moment. "Hey, are you guys hungry, or are you just going to stare at the waterfall all day?"

I turned to see Mongo and Hunter unpacking our rations. We drank water from the stream and ate MREs. It felt like we were a million miles from civilization, and something about it just felt right.

I made it to my favorite part of any MRE—the peanut butter and crackers. As always, I had to knead the tube of peanut butter to turn it back into something edible, but it was almost as good as a chili dog at a Braves game.

Hunter watched our guide as he stared into the sky. "You really love it out here, don't you, Animal?"

He grinned. "I'm at home out here, man. Everybody should experience this. You dudes are obviously comfortable in the woods, too. So, come on. Spill it, man. What are you guys, like military dudes? Special Forces or something?"

It was my turn to control the conversation. "We used to be something like that, but now we're just treasure hunters, you might say."

"I knew it," Animal said. "You cats are like the A-Team or whatever. Look, man. I'm just a simple little dude who spends his life in the woods and on the water. I got nobody to tell, so I'm not going to dime you out. You can tell me what's up."

I shot a glance at my team, and Hunter shrugged.

I said, "Let's start with you, Animal. What's your story?"

"I don't have a story. I already told you. I live my life right here where the world is simple and beautiful. That's it, man."

"How about your real name, then? Surely your mother didn't really name you Animal."

He took a bite of a granola bar. "No, but she would have if she could've looked into the future. My name's Shawn Malone. I picked up the name Animal from some dudes on the river 'cause I'm not afraid of anything. Other dudes will sit on a rock in their kayaks and try to build up the guts to run a rapid. Meanwhile, I'm hitting that thing in my canoe like I'm part of the river. That's kind of how I see it. I'm part of all of this out here, and it's all part of me, you know?"

"Did you say your name is Shawn Malone?" I asked in disbelief.

"Yeah, man. Shawn 'Animal' Malone. That's me."

I couldn't believe the coincidence. "By chance, you're not related to a guy named Cash Malone, are you?"

Animal narrowed his eyes. "Dude, that ain't cool. Who are you for real, and how do you know my dad's name?"

He let his hand fall to the knife on his belt.

"Relax," I said. "We're no threat, and we don't know your father. We're just following some thirty-year-old notes about this place, and the name Cash Malone came up in some of the old papers."

He didn't remove his hand from his knife, but the muscles in his shoulders relaxed slightly. "What kind of notes? This is all getting a little too out there for me. You've got to come clean, man."

Singer silently slid behind our guide, who was focused on me.

I kept my eyes locked on Animal's and held up two hands. "It's nothing sinister. You've got nothing to worry about. We're looking for a cave that's mentioned in code on some old documents we found. A guy named Boomer—"

At the mention of Boomer's name, Animal shuddered, and Singer yanked the knife from beneath the guide's hand. Realizing he'd been disarmed, Animal sprang to a crouch. "That's it, man. You dudes are freaking me out. I'm out of here. You can follow this creek and it'll get you out, but whatever this is, it's too messed up for me."

"Wait," I said with both hands up in surrender. "Don't go. You obviously know who Boomer is. I saw it in your eyes."

I motioned toward Singer. "Give him back his knife."

Singer spun the weapon around in his hand and offered it to Animal, handle-first.

The guide took his knife and slid it back into its sheath. "Yeah, I remember Boomer. He was like an uncle when I was little. He and my dad were tight, but he's been dead a long time, man."

"Yes, we know. We know Boomer's widow. She's a dear friend, and that's why we're here. He may have hidden something in the cave, and if we find it, we could make her life much better. That's why we're here. Nothing more."

Animal finally relaxed from his crouch and let his knees rest on the ground. "Why didn't you tell me that yesterday, man? You don't have to be so mysterious, and you sure don't have to be so scary. I've been through some shit in my life, too. You dudes aren't the only ones. I can look at you and tell you're soldiers.

Anybody can see that. But just because I've never worn a uniform doesn't mean I can't understand what it's like to. . . ." He swallowed hard and snapped the strap across his knife. "Come on, man. I know where your cave is."

Chapter 33
Grate Expectations

We packed up our gear and followed Animal farther into the mountains. We moved without a word, and he found a narrow trail above the creek that made our hike feel a lot like a walk in the park.

We'd walked for half an hour when our guide stopped, looked toward the sky, and turned to face us. "Okay, man, here's my story. My grandfather made moonshine back during the Depression and on into the forties. When I was a kid, maybe nine or ten, my dad brought my brother and me back here and showed us the still site in the mouth of a cave. Of course, the still was long gone, but dude, I'll never forget how my dad's eyes lit up when he told us about how he helped his dad carry corn and sugar for miles through the woods. It was his best memory, I guess. Ultimately, my grandfather wound up going to prison, and my dad was never able to keep a job. He spent his whole life back here in these woods trying to relive his childhood."

My team and I stood in silence as Animal's story continued.

"I took to the woods just like my dad. I've always loved it, just like he did, but my brother was different. He went off to school up in Knoxville and got a job on Wall Street. I guess we really couldn't have been much different—polar opposites, you might say."

There it was again.

Animal chewed on what was left of the nail on his little finger. "So, anyway, I went to see him in New York one time. He said he was living his dream in the Big Apple. I didn't like it, but he felt just as much at home in Manhattan as I do right here. He took me out to some place in Hell's Kitchen. We had some drinks and met some girls. At the end of the night, we were walking home with the girls, and these four dudes came out of nowhere. A couple of them had knives, and one had a gun. My brother told me to just give them our wallets and everything would be fine, but I couldn't do it. Of course, I didn't have a knife or a gun because I'd flown to New York, but I wasn't afraid of anything."

He paused and studied the lines on his palms. "I ended the night with about a hundred stitches, the girls got away, and my brother never got up off that sidewalk." He swallowed the lump in his throat. "If I could've just been like my brother and handed over my wallet, he'd still be alive."

The psychologist in me wanted to tell him about coping mechanisms and the slow, predictable course of grief after the loss of a loved one, but Singer stepped up. He put his arm around Animal and told him the story of his own brother who'd become trapped inside himself, unable to function in anyone's world, and spending his life in silence under the watchful eye of a group of monks who'll never know the horror his brother has to endure every day of his life. Then, he prayed.

When the prayer was over, I was at a loss for words, so in my typical awkward style, I said, "How much farther is it to the cave?"

Animal's grin returned, and he pointed across the creek. "There it is, man."

Overgrown with vines and tree roots stood a metal grate across the mouth of a cave. It looked like an old-timey jail cell from the movies. I pulled out my GPS.

Animal said, "You can put that away. That's your cave. There's no question about it."

I tucked the device back into my pack and headed for the creek. We crossed the water and climbed the other side. The grate was welded to metal plates that had been pinned to the rock with some sort of metal anchors. I gave it a shake. It rattled, but it didn't offer to surrender.

"Who did this, and why?" I asked.

"The National Park Service did it. A couple of kids got lost in there and died a few years ago. They were going to seal it off with concrete, but an environmentalist group discovered some rare bats that live in the cave. They decided to just gate it off so the bats could still come and go, and this is what they came up with."

A cutting torch or even a good hacksaw could get us in, but we had neither. I didn't want to make the hike back out just to bring a saw, so I turned to the next best thing, and Mongo cracked his knuckles.

"Move back. I'll see what I can do," he said as he leaned into the grate.

The metal groaned and creaked beneath Mongo's efforts but didn't give. After ten minutes of an unstoppable force meeting an immovable object, Mongo wiped his brow. "Do you still have that rope you used to lasso Chase yesterday?"

Animal pulled the rope from a nylon bag hanging beneath his pack. "Here you go, but it's only rated for five thousand pounds."

Mongo took the rope and looped it through the grate and around an oak tree ten feet down the bank. He continued looping the rope until he'd reached its end, then he tied the ends with bowlines and began scrounging through the underbrush around the cave.

"What are you looking for?" I asked, completely lost.

"A lever," he said. "Surely you remember studying simple machines in physics. You know, the lever, the screw, the incline plane."

"Apparently, you and I went to very different schools."

He finally came up with a log about six feet long and six inches in diameter. "This'll do. Give me a hand, guys."

Halfway between the grate and the tree, we hefted the log between the loops of rope.

"Now, all we have to do is turn this lever and wind up the rope. It should put enough tension on the grate to warp it or maybe even pull a couple of the anchors out. We'll see."

We spun the log perpendicular to the strands of rope, winding it up like the rubber band on a toy airplane. When the rope came taut, the grate recreated the sounds from earlier under Mongo's influence, but this time, the sounds got louder and higher pitched.

"Keep pushing," Mongo grunted as we fought the log's insistence on spinning free.

With all five of us pushing and pulling on the log, the grate finally surrendered and snapped from its anchors on the right side. Vines and tree roots still held it in place on the left, but even Mongo could squeeze through the opening we'd created.

I threw a high five to our giant. "What would we do without you, big man?"

"Hike back out and bring in a blow torch, I guess."

"I'll buy you a new rope," I said, "but we need to destroy this one."

"It's yours, man," Animal said. "I wouldn't trust my life to it after the stress we just put it under anyway."

I untied the bowlines and cut the sealed ends off the mountaineering rope. Inside the sheath, or *mantle* as climbers call it, the interior of the rope is a series of thin cords called *kern*. The hundred feet of rope Animal brought had thousands of feet of kern inside, which would make perfect breadcrumbs.

We pulled headlamps from our packs and filed into the cave one-by-one. I tied one piece of thin cord to the grate and headed into the darkness. We dragged the cord behind us through a dozen twists and turns. I wasn't interested in befalling the fate of the two boys who never found their way out of that cave, so our thin white cord was our yellow brick road back to the entrance.

I slipped the broken compass from Earl's safe out of my pocket and held it flat on my palm. The needle bounced around and quickly came to rest, pointing directly into the bowels of the cave.

Animal shined his light on the compass. "What's that?"

"You wouldn't believe me if I told you," I said.

"Give it a shot. You'd be amazed at what I'll believe."

I handed him the compass. "I found this with the documents I told you about. Apparently, it points to the center of Mayan ruins, and now it's pointing into the heart of this cave."

"Oh, yeah," he said. "I've got one of those. It's not worth a dime at pointing at the North Pole, but it finds lodestone. These old caves are full of that stuff. I didn't know the Mayans used it, but that's cool."

A thousand feet or so into the cave, I pulled a book of matches from my pack and struck one. The flame danced for a few seconds and slowly melted away. "The air's getting thin in here. If anybody starts to feel lightheaded, speak up."

We crept on, careful to breathe deeply and slowly. As we rounded a hard right-hand bend in the cave, my light hit the surface of the wall, but it didn't look like the rest of the cave. It was cracked like a spiderweb and smooth to the touch. The rest of the interior was jagged and rough.

"This is it," I said, pulling my knife from its scabbard.

The rest of the team, including Animal, drew their knives, and we soon had the clay chipped away from the opening. We were winded and dripping with sweat, even in the cool thin air of the cave. Our headlamps fell on two dozen Vietnam-era ammunition cans, each about the size of a large shoebox. My vision was starting to blur, and my head pounded from lack of oxygen, but I was determined to drag at least one of those cans out of the hole.

I leaned into the opening and grasped the handle of the closest can. It felt like it was filled with lead and glued to the floor of the cave. I didn't have the strength to budge it, so I turned to ask Mongo for a hand, but he was wilting like a dying plant.

"We've got to get out of here," I said. "There's not enough oxygen back here."

We dragged ourselves back toward the entrance until we could finally breathe again.

The next three hours were spent dragging ammo cans in teams of two. The work was exhausting, and my head felt like it was going to explode.

When the last of the twenty-nine cans saw the light of day for the first time in nearly three decades, I sliced the wax seal on the first can and forced it open. It was stacked to the rim with gold bars of every imaginable size. I sat in mesmerized amazement. I'd never seen that much gold, and based on the expressions of my team, I wasn't alone. As if hypnotized by the sight and ordered into action, everyone drew their knives and sliced at the seals of the remaining cans. With every revelation of another opened can, our astonishment grew. Every can was nearly a carbon copy of the first.

I hefted one of the boxes onto my lap. "How much do you think each one of these weighs?"

Hunter lifted a can into the air. "It's got to be fifty pounds, at least."

"I agree," Singer said. "That means there's over fourteen hundred pounds of gold here. Even if we had the mules, we couldn't carry all this out of here in a month."

I dug into the pocket of my cargo pants and came out with a business card marked with the silhouette of a Huey helicopter on the back. I pulled my satellite phone from my pack and dialed the number.

Less than an hour later, Doug and Danny were hovering overhead with a basket dangling beneath their custom-built twin five-thousand-pound winches. We sent the gold up in five lifts of nearly three hundred pounds each. Mongo was load number six, and the rest of us went up in pairs. The twenty-minute flight back to the Cleveland Airport was a lot less exciting than the two-day trek into the Lost Corral section of the Cherokee National Forest.

Chapter 34
Skipper's Rosetta Stone

The first call I made on my sat-phone after the Huey's rotors stopped spinning was to Silver Spring, Maryland. "Hey, Skipper. Guess what I found."

"A thousand pounds of gold," she said.

"No, not even close. It's at least fifteen hundred pounds."

"Are you serious? That's amazing. Is everybody all right?"

"I love how you always ask if we're all right before anything else. You're the best operational analyst on Earth, mostly because you care more about us than three quarters of a ton of gold. Yes, everybody is just fine."

"Good, I'm glad. Now we can get down to business. It finally came to me."

"What came to you?"

"The gibberish on the ninth page," she said. "It's not gibberish at all. It's the Rosetta stone for the whole set of documents. I can't take all the credit. I had it running through a cipher program I wrote for three days before it finally spit out the answer, but I've got every word translated now."

"That's great, Skipper. Can you email it to me?"

"I already did, but you've been off playing in the woods with your buddies."

I laughed. "Yes, that's what I was doing . . . playing in the woods. I'll read the email and call you back."

My cell phone had long since lost its charge, so I plugged it into an outlet inside the hangar where my Caravan sat as if she belonged there. It took a couple of minutes for the phone to come to life, but Skipper's email popped up seconds after it booted up.

The ledgers were names, addresses, and thirty-year-old phone numbers of thirty-eight Air America pilots and their wives. Each entry was followed by a series of dollar amounts. The numbers were staggering, even thirty years later, but the ledger wasn't the most amazing part of the translation. The ninth and most mysterious page was detailed instructions on how to buy gold bars with the money Boomer was sending home to Reliance, Tennessee, every few weeks. The instructions were specifically written for Cash Malone and no one else.

The final line of the page read, "If I die before you, make sure the gold goes to everybody on the list. You're the only person in the world I can trust to do the right thing."

Doug and Danny let us use their showers at the rescue school, and they also let me print out a copy of the email on one of their office printers. I paid them handsomely for their extraction work.

Doug said, "You and your Caravan are welcome here anytime."

Becky showed up in Animal's Bronco to give him a ride back to the outfitters.

Our favorite backcountry guide shook all of our hands in turn and thanked us for the adventure. "I'll never forget this trip with you cats. And what you said really meant a lot, Singer. Thanks, man. Come back in the spring, and we'll do the river. I'll show you why they really call me Animal."

"We wouldn't miss it for the world," I said.

While he was loading his one bag of gear, I slipped a single ammo can into the back of his Bronco with a copy of the ninth page of the translated document rolled up beneath the handle. On the back of the paper, I wrote, "Thank you for doing the right thing."

The weight and balance calculations were a little tricky in the Caravan with our twenty-eight ammo cans on board, but we had Jerry's brother-in-law pump some fuel back out of the wings to offset the load. Needless to say, Hunter didn't get to make any water landings on the flight back to Bonaventure, but I promised to make it up to him.

By the time we made it home, everyone was too tired to care that we had eight million dollars in gold bars in our possession. We hurriedly locked up the gold, and everyone found a bed.

* * *

My phone woke me the following morning before sunrise, and I stuck it to my face. "Yeah?"

"Chase, it's O'Malley from Saint Augustine. Please tell me you've got an alibi for the past twenty-four hours."

I was suddenly wide awake. "Uh, yeah, I was on a hiking trip with four other guys in the Cherokee National Forest for the last two days. Why?"

"Jerald Davis and Eustis Carmichael escaped from the detention center."

I shook off my blurred vision. "And you think I broke them out of jail?"

"No, they broke themselves out. But we found their bodies early this morning. They'd been sliced up like they fell into a food processor. Somebody with some serious knife skills got ahold of them."

"It wasn't me, O'Malley."

"Yeah, I know," he said, "but the detectives will probably want to hear your alibi. I thought I should give you a heads-up."

I slung my feet over the edge of the bed and went in search of Mongo. I found him on the back gallery, lying in the hammock —the only bed big enough for him to stretch out in completely.

"Wake up, big man. I've got something to tell you."

He rubbed the sleep from his eyes and stretched as if he'd just come out of hibernation. "What time is it?"

"I don't know, but I need you awake for this."

He sat up as gracefully as a baby giraffe learning to walk. "Okay, I'm up. What is it?"

"I just got a call from O'Malley in Saint Augustine. He said Lurch and Thumbprint broke out of the city lockup last night."

Mongo yawned. "You woke me up for that?"

"No, that's not why. I woke you up because O'Malley said they found their bodies early this morning and that somebody with serious knife skills had hacked them up pretty good."

His eyes turned from sleepy to dread in an instant. "Anya?"

"That's the first name that popped into my head, but O'Malley didn't say they picked anybody up for it."

He stared at the decking of the gallery. "She wouldn't have gotten caught. I should probably call her."

He found his phone on the gallery rail and dialed Anya's number. Half a minute later, he pressed the end button. "No answer, but the strange thing is it didn't go to voice mail. It just stopped ringing. What does that mean?"

"I don't know, but I'm sure Skipper does."

When she answered, her tone was far from pleasant. "This better be good. After three days of being awake, I was finally sleeping like a log."

"I need you to ping Anya's phone and find out where she is."

She groaned. "You woke me up to find Anya? Are you serious?"

"It's more than serious, Skipper. I need you to find her."

"Okay, okay. Hang on a minute. Let me get to my computer."

Sounds of shuffling and cursing filled the phone just before her rapid-fire strokes on the keyboard.

"Uh, Chase, the last hit on her phone was fifty-four hours ago in Atlanta. Nothing after that."

"That's not good. Stay on it. I need you to find her."

Her fingers were still flying across the keys. "Okay, I'm on it, but the story better be good."

I sighed. "Jerald Davis and Eustis Carmichael escaped from the Saint Augustine jail and got themselves sliced and diced before the sun came up. The cops found their bodies early this morning."

She whispered, "Oh," and hung up without another word.

* * *

While having his morning coffee in the gazebo by the river, Hunter heard the commotion on the gallery, so he climbed the stairs to join us. We briefed him on what we knew.

"So," Hunter said, "I guess I'll be taking Mongo back to Athens if you'll let us use the One-Eighty-Two. And you're probably going to Saint Augustine."

"That's a good plan if you don't mind the flying," I said.

* * *

I flew the Caravan back to Saint Augustine and found Earl aboard her new home at the end of the floating dock, right where she belonged.

"Permission to come aboard," I bellowed from the dock.

Earl leaned over the rail. "You never need permission, Baby Boy. Get yourself up here, but take them nasty shoes off."

I slipped off my shoes and stepped aboard. "This is quite a boat, Earl. How'd you find it so fast?"

She slid her hand along the portside rail. "I do a bunch of work for a broker up above the bridge. He had this one listed up at Hilton Head, and he made me a good deal on it. I went through the motors and had my friend, Sparky, look over the electronics. We didn't find nothin' wrong that shouldn't be wrong, so I bought it."

"Congratulations," I said. "I'm happy for you."

"It's all thanks to you. I'd have been homeless and broke if you hadn't come to my rescue."

"You've never needed anyone to rescue you, Old Girl. You'd have come out smelling like a rose. I just happened to be in the neighborhood."

"Piffle," she huffed. "You know you saved my butt on this one. I reckon I owe you a few oil changes after what I put you through."

"You'll never owe me anything, Earl. We're family, and that's what family does."

"Speaking of family," she said, "Skipper called a while ago and told me about figuring out how to read them letters. She said she had a bunch of names and numbers of people Boomer was helping put money away. She said it was a bunch of money, but she didn't know how much."

I smiled. "It worked out to be a little over eight million dollars in gold."

She almost fainted. "Eight million dollars? But how. . . ."

I filled in the blanks Skipper had left out.

Earl looked bewildered. "All of this is too much to believe. I never dreamed Boomer done nothin' this big."

"It's up to you, of course, but the money belongs to the people on that list. It's only fair that you keep a good chunk of it so you don't ever have to worry about getting grease under your fingernails again. But those families could probably use their share, as well."

"I've already got Skipper on it," she said. "She's doing all the contact work. I'll just write the checks."

I slid a business card into her hand. "Here's the name of a good attorney who'll make sure everything is done nice and legally and without too much involvement from the IRS."

She held my face in her calloused hands and planted a big sloppy kiss on my forehead. "I don't know what I'd do without you. You're as good as they come, and I sure am glad to have you around."

I gave her a long hug. "I'm glad I could be around, Earl."

She sat back down, and her face took on a serious expression. "I need to tell you about something before you go."

"Okay, let's hear it."

She twisted her hands together nervously. "I had a talk with that girl of yours while we was out in Colorado. She's having some trouble learning to swallow the chunk she bit off."

I listened intently as Earl danced around what she was really trying to say.

Finally, she cleared her throat and looked up. "It all comes down to this. She knew you were into some secret stuff, but she didn't know how hard it would be being your wife. I laid it out for her. I told her how it was living with Boomer all them years, never knowing if the tail of his airplane flying off would be the last thing I'd ever see of him. One day it was, and it's broke my heart every day since then. But I told that girl of yours that I'd live through a thousand Hells for just one more day with that crazy old man."

Serious conversations with Earl were rare, but that one was quickly becoming one I'd never forget.

"I told her how lucky she was to have a man like you and how good life would be in the times when you were home and not somewhere killin' bad guys. I told her that kind of life ain't for weak women 'cause weak women can't handle them good times any better than they can handle them bad ones. She ain't no weak woman. She may be one of the strongest I've ever known, and she's gonna swallow that big ol' chunk she bit off if it takes her ten years to do it, and she's gonna be the best wife there's ever been for you or anybody else."

I was lost for words, so I took her weathered hand in mine. "Thank you, Earl. That means—"

My phone chirped, and I glanced down to see Mongo's name on the caller ID. "I need to take this, Earl. Give me just a second."

I answered, and Mongo said, "She's not here, Chase."

"What do you mean she's not there?"

He cleared his throat. "She's gone. Her knives and pistols are gone, and some of her clothes, too."

I took a long breath and tried to come up with something to say. "I don't know, Mongo. Maybe she just—"

Another call beeped in, and I glanced down at the caller ID.

"Mongo, I'm sorry, but Singer's on the other line. Hang on a second."

I pressed the swap-call button. "Hey, Singer, what's up?"

"Chase, I don't know how to tell you this, but you need to come home right now."

"What is it, Singer? I've got a lot to do here in Saint Augustine."

"Chase, your house at Bonaventure . . ." His breath came hard. "It's on fire."

About the Author

Cap Daniels

Cap Daniels is a former sailing charter captain, scuba and sailing instructor, pilot, Air Force combat veteran, and civil servant of the U.S. Department of Defense. Raised far from the ocean in rural East Tennessee, his early infatuation with salt water was sparked by the fascinating, and sometimes true, sea stories told by his father, a retired Navy Chief Petty Officer. Those stories of adventure on the high seas sent Cap in search of adventure of his own, which eventually landed him on Florida's Gulf Coast where he spends as much time as possible on, in, and under the waters of the Emerald Coast.

With a headful of larger-than-life characters and their thrilling exploits, Cap pours his love of adventure and passion for the ocean onto the pages of The Chase Fulton Novels series.

Visit www.CapDaniels.com to join the mailing list to receive newsletter and release updates.

Connect with Cap Daniels
Facebook: www.Facebook.com/WriterCapDaniels
Instagram: https://www.instagram.com/authorcapdaniels/
BookBub: https://www.bookbub.com/profile/cap-daniels

Made in the USA
Coppell, TX
14 March 2024

30115692R00164